The Adventures of Sarkis and Hagop

By

John Vartoukian

DEDICATION

    This book is dedicated to the memory of William Saroyan, that marvelous, magical reprobate whose wonderful stories filled my dream-hungry youth.

    Books come and go. We grow smarter, more prey to sophistication. The age of miracles has passed. God save us, we even measure the talents of angels. Time for another miracle. Let us drop the veil. Return us to the mystery and wonder of the heart. Who will teach us? The fool, the lover, the clown. He who has no home but is home everywhere.

    We miss you, Willie.

    This ode, this paean, this act of reclamation, then, for him

"Take a walk along the New Jersey coast. with two warm and gentle souls, Sarkis and Hagop. It will warm your heart and bring a smile to your face."

-Jerome Komisar, author of "Church of the Hungry: An Alaskan Romance," "The Last Believer," "In the Shadow of Dante: A Contemporary Love Story, Seven Centuries Old,"

"In his gentle, imaginative tale, John Vartoukian reveals both wit and wisdom and leaves us wanting more offerings from him."

-Reverend Martha Bonwit
 Trinity Episcopal Church

"In the person of Sarkis, the author has given us a character with a propensity for upside down logic, and merry-go-rounds that go backwards. Somehow it all makes sense. The book is a charmer."

- Dr. Melvin A. Bernstein

"I've been reading John's fiction for years and this is one of my favorites. Consider it a fable from a simpler time with some grains of metaphysical magic thrown in. It's a road trip, a buddy book and an examination of our own society hiding behind the humor and whimsy contained on the pages. Buy it, read it and love it."

-Scott Sowers, author of "Life and Death at the Dog Park"

ACKNOWLEDGMENTS

To the literary cohorts in my writers group. Many thanks for your support and encouragement.

ONE SUNNY SUNDAY MORNING

One sunny Sunday morning, Sarkis Levonian, a fifty-year-old tailor, stepped out of his apartment and headed toward the newsstand to buy the newspaper, as he had done most every Sunday for the past eighteen years. On his way to the newsstand he made two significant decisions: First, that he would not be buying the Sunday paper today, and second, that he would not be returning directly home to his wife and two children, who were just finishing breakfast and looking forward to their weekly read of news, comics, and sports.

At the newsstand, Sarkis encountered ten-year-old Jack Silveri, a neighborhood friend of the family whose father and Sarkis had known each other since high school. The boy was standing by the candy rack, munching a Milky Way chocolate bar. He was a slim youth with tousled black hair that kept falling over his eyes like a nuisance. When he saw Sarkis pass by without stopping, he called out, "Sarkis, where are you going?"

"I'm going away," said Sarkis, a paunchy, jowly man with a graying walrus mustache.

"Where to?"

"I don't know."

"When are you coming back?"

"Can't say."

"Are you going to have fun like you always do?" said Jack, who hurried to come abreast of his friend.

"Fun would be a great help."

At that moment Jack Silveri made a significant decision of his own. "Can I come, too?"

Sarkis's eyes widened in surprise. "Funny you should ask. Any other day I'd say no, but today, I'm finding out, is not like any other day. There's something in the air, Jack. Can you feel it? Can you sense it?"

"Does that mean yes?"

"That means I'm not going to be much help telling you what you can or can't do."

"You won't make me go home?"

"Not today."

"Good."

"On a trip like this you have to be ready for anything, Jack. Do you feel ready for anything?"

"I'm ready."

"First thing we have to do is take a train somewhere. Trains are an important part of an adventure like this one."

The time was late August 1950; the place, Washington Heights, New York, although the setting could have been most anywhere. The man and the boy were heading toward the 7th Avenue subway station three blocks away. Beyond that they didn't know where they were going. They were setting out for parts unknown, two characters in a story waiting to be written; two heroes in search of a fable.

"Jack," said Sarkis.

"Yes?"

"We're going to have to change your name."

"Why?"

"Jack is no name for a boy. Jack is a name for an older man. Your parents made a mistake."

"I know."

"From now on, we'll call you Hagop."

"Hah-gope? What's that?"

"Hagop is the Armenian name for Jack. It sounds better in Armenian than it does in English, don't you think?"

"What's Armenian?"

"Armenian is what I am, and what you are now, in an honorary sort of way."

At the 7th Avenue subway station, they took the downtown

express to Pennsylvania Station, where crowds of people bustled through the spacious terminal, most of them busy buying tickets and catching trains, others heading toward the street.

"Where do you think we should go?" asked Hagop.

"I don't know. We'll give the ticket man some money and see what he can do for us."

After waiting in line, Sarkis gave the ticket man a twenty dollar bill and asked him how far the money would take himself and the boy. The ticket man gave Sarkis a faintly smarmy look. Nonetheless, he consulted a chart and called off the names of various locales in the New Jersey area:

"Matawan, Manasquan, Long Branch, Asbury Park ..."

"Asbury Park," said Sarkis, without a moment's hesitation.

Hagop was pleased with the choice. "I like parks," he said as they were leaving the line.

"Asbury Park is not really a park," said Sarkis. "It's a beach where people go swimming and spend their vacations. My parents used to take me there when I was a boy."

"Is it nice there?"

"Very nice. Or at least it was when I was a boy."

"How long can we stay?"

"Hard to say, Hagop. All I can promise you is this: When the time comes to go home, we'll know. We probably won't know a minute before then."

Aboard the train, Hagop hurried down the aisle and took the first window seat he could find, the better to press his nose against the glass and watch the world go by. Once the train pulled out of the station tunnel and into the light of day, the boy began watching streets and buildings pass by, then, later, trees and countryside, and much later, barns and farmhouses. Eventually the train began making stops at small depots to allow for passengers boarding and disembarking.

"We're going a long way, aren't we?" said the boy.

"Yes, we are," said Sarkis. He gave the boy a studied look. "Are you still sure you want to come? It's never too late to go back." The boy shook his head. "Your parents will worry about you."

"What do you think I should do?"

"I'm not sure."

"Maybe I can write them a letter when we get to Asbury Park."

"Yes, you could do that."

"But then my parents will know where I am, and they'll come to take me home, won't they?"

"I'm sure they will."

"Would you have to go home, too?"

"Probably so. But don't ever let that stop you from doing what you have to do. Will you promise me that?"

"I promise."

"Good."

From the far end of the coach, the conductor now made his first appearance. He was an elderly gentleman with white hair cropping out from beneath his peaked cap. The cut of his black uniform was perfect, every crease in place and brass buttons shining. As he came down the aisle punching tickets, he looked like a man of true rank and authority.

Sarkis whispered, "Hagop, here comes the conductor."

"He looks very important."

"He is very important."

"I like his uniform."

"So do I."

The conductor arrived at their side. "Tickets, please."

"We're going to Asbury Park," said Hagop.

The conductor pulled out a pocket watch from inside his jacket and gave it a confident glance that signified respect in an honored timepiece. "We should be there in twenty-eight minutes," he said. "We're running five minutes behind schedule, but we'll make up the time as we go."

"We've been admiring your uniform," said Sarkis.

The conductor acknowledged this compliment with a curt nod. "Next month will make twenty-five years in this uniform. God and the railroad willing, I'll be in it for twenty-five more."

"Is being a conductor like being in the Army?" asked Hagop.

"In a way," said the conductor, visibly flattered by the comparison. "A conductor has rules and regulations to follow. He also has to keep his uniform clean."

"When I grow up, I want to be an admiral or a cowboy," said Hagop.

"When I was your age," said the conductor, "I didn't know what I wanted to be. One day it was an airplane pilot, the next day a race car driver, the next … Who knew? And then one Christmas my father gave me a set of electric trains, and I knew in a flash that trains and I were meant for each other. My whole life just seemed to fall into place. Sounds crazy, I guess, but sometimes the most important things in a person's life happen that way—in a flash, when he least expects it."

"You may have something there," said Sarkis, well aware of the unpredictable course his own day was taking.

"I'd be the first to admit I'm a lucky man," said the conductor. "Some people go all their lives and never know what they want to do. They grow old before their time. Heaven knows we grow old fast enough. No point in getting there too soon."

The conductor smiled wryly, in deference to life's mysterious, inexorable passage, then punched the tickets in his hand and inserted them under the metal seams of the coach chair. With a tip of his cap he bade Sarkis and Hagop good day and continued down the aisle.

"I wish I could be more like the conductor," said Sarkis, "but I don't know if I could keep doing the same thing for twenty-five years."

"Why not?"

"Twenty-five years is a long time to be doing anything. I've been a tailor for twenty years, a husband for eighteen, and a father for twelve. That's a long time to be a tailor, husband, and father." Sarkis made one of his inimitable calculations. "Why, that's fifty years, Hagop!"

"Is that why you're going to Asbury Park? To take a vacation?"

"You might say that, although I wasn't thinking of it just that way. You see, Hagop, when I came outside this morning, I had every intention of buying the Sunday paper and going straight home. But something happened when I started up St. Nicholas Avenue and saw Mr. Gilliam rolling down the awning of his drugstore, as he does every Sunday at 9 o'clock, and Mr. Rabunsky opening up the bakery, as he does every Sunday at the same time. And I thought, my goodness! How long have all of us been doing exactly what we're doing at this moment? And then another thought came to me. Suppose everything that was happening this morning wasn't really happening? Suppose it was all a dream and we were all sleepwalkers having the dream? Was it possible I might spend the rest of my life in this dream and never wake up? Well, let me tell you, I started getting a little nervous at that point. And then when I saw you at the newsstand and you asked to come along, well, I knew this day had to be meant for something more important than buying the Sunday paper and going home."

Hagop shook his head in amused befuddlement. "Sarkis, you're cuckoo."

Sarkis turned up the palms of his hands in an uncontested admission of guilt.

The man and boy lapsed into silence now, both lulled by the lickety-split cadence of wheels on track as the train hurried past country landscapes and marshy fields. The boy, pressing his nose to the glass, which had become vaporized by his breath, watched the passing scenery and also how the sun kept racing with the train and dipping behind trees and spilling through the branches in dazzling flashes of light. After a time he turned to Sarkis, who was resting with his eyes closed and his fingers loosely interlaced upon his stomach. "Sarkis, what are you going to do in Asbury Park?"

"Do?" said Sarkis. One eye peeked open. "Haven't thought much about what to do once we got there." Off the top of his head, he added, "Maybe I'll write a book."

"A book? What kind of book?"

Sarkis ruminated further. "How about a book about you and me going to Asbury Park? How does that sound?"

"Then the story will be a real life story, won't it?"

"It probably won't come out that way once I get through with it."

"My favorite stories are animal stories, hunting stories, and sea ship stories."

"Good! That's the kind of book I'll make it then—an animal, hunting, and sea ship story about you and me going to Asbury Park."

"Sarkis, how can the story be about you and me and about animals, hunting, and sea ships, too?"

"Why not? Any book worth reading is about all those things. The book may have no animals, hunting, and sea ships in it, but if the book has been an adventure for you, like any good book should be, then it will be an animal, hunting, and sea ship story—because it will be everything that makes a book good."

"Whew!" Hagop scratched his head in puzzlement. "Sarkis, you *are* cuckoo."

"I'll try to write the best book I can," said Sarkis, resolving at that moment to try his hand at authorship.

The boy eagerly pulled both his legs up under him on the seat. "What else are you going to do in Asbury Park?"

"What would you like to do?"

"Can we go swimming?"

"Of course we can."

"I like the beach."

"I like it, too."

"Are the waves big in Asbury Park?"

"The waves at Jones Beach are bigger, but the waves in Asbury Park will be big enough."

"What else?"

"Oh, we should have plenty to do. We'll have to find a place to live, and then, I suppose, I'll need to find a job to pay for a place to live."

"A job? Would you still be a tailor?"

"No. I don't think so," said Sarkis. He squinted in thought. "Trouble is I don't know what else I'm fit to do." As Sarkis contemplated his future, his face began to soften. A distant, dreamy look came into his eyes as if he'd been transported to another time and place. "Maybe there is something else I can do. One summer when I was a boy, I worked on a merry-go-round at Rye Beach. To tell the truth, I wouldn't mind working on a merry-go-round again." Sarkis nodded to himself, confirming his choice of occupation. "Yes, that's what we'll do. We'll find a place to live and then I'll get a job on the merry-go-round. You can ride on it free of charge all day if you like."

Hagop's smile took wings. "Asbury Park sounds like the best place in the world."

"Now that you mention it, Hagop, it just may be."

Presently the conductor made his second appearance in the coach, this time to call out the names of upcoming stations. Holding sway with the rocking train, he moved up the aisle and made his announcements: "Asbury Park, Ocean Grove, Belmar."

"We're almost there," said Sarkis, "and knowing the conductor, I'll bet not a minute late."

The conductor tipped his cap as he passed by. Continuing the length of the passenger aisle, he repeated the station names in a clear, confident voice. Even after he disappeared into the adjoining car, his voice could still be heard above the percussive clatter of wheels on tracks. "He sure sounds like somebody who knows his business," concluded Hagop.

"Yes, he does. No doubt about that."

Within minutes, the train pulled into the outdoor depot at Asbury Park.

The iron wheels squealed against the rails and gave off sparks as the locomotive gradually slowed to a stop. Sarkis and Hagop disembarked among a smattering of other passengers and sauntered toward the center of town. Along the way they stopped at a snack stand and bought two salted pretzels. Later they paused outside a volunteer firehouse to watch a hook and ladder truck being hosed down by a T-shirted fireman in knee-high rubber boots. Once reaching the central district, they strolled down Main Street, which had the drowsy look of a homey, Midwestern town. A clock in a barber shop window showed noon. It being Sunday, few people were about. Many were still in church or already at the beach. The skies were sunny, and a light ocean breeze sifted through the air like a hum.

"I'd sure like to go swimming," said Hagop.

"So would I."

"Can we go now?"

"Why not?"

"You said we had to find a place to live first."

"We just changed our minds."

"We need bathing suits."

"And towels," added Sarkis. He pointed across the street. "Look over there—a menswear shop, and it looks like it's just dying for our business. Let's go."

A CANDIDATE FOR THE BEST MENSWEAR SHOP
IN THE WORLD

In the menswear shop, the salesman who greeted Sarkis and Hagop was himself a model of impeccable grooming. He wore a natty, custom-tailored three-button suit and sported a freshly cut red carnation in his lapel. He moved with a suave, graceful air and gave the distinct impression of being not just a salesman, but a connoisseur of fashion, a man who would never be caught less than elegantly attired. "Good afternoon," he said to his customers, "and how may I help you today?"

"We'd like two bathing suits," said Sarkis.

"Of course. Boxer or tights?"

"What's boxerortights?" asked Hagop.

"Styles," said the salesman. "The loose, rugged fit or the snug, shapely look."

"Which would you suggest?" asked Sarkis.

The salesman raised a finger to his lips by way of studying his customers. "Boxer for you and tights for the boy," he said confidently.

"Excellent. We'll take a pair of each right away."

"Any particular color?" asked the salesman, leading the way to the back of the store and a surplus heap of bathing suits on a table.

"Not for me," said Sarkis.

"I like orange," said the boy.

They had not been rummaging through the merchandise for

long when Hagop found just what he was looking for—a bright orange swimsuit, which he immediately hoisted into the air for approval.

"Excellent!" hailed Sarkis.

"Sunset Orange," said the salesman. "Our biggest seller this summer. You probably found the last one."

"Are you sure it fits?" Sarkis asked the boy.

"No problem there," said the salesman. "The suit has a circumflex, stretch-wear binding good for any size between 8 and 20. He'll be fine. And now let's see what we can do for you." Poring over the pile of suits, the salesman pulled one out from the bottom of the heap as if having saved it for just this moment. "Feast your eyes on this beauty." He held up a scintillating, aqua-colored pair of boxer trunks that bedazzled Sarkis. The true color of the trunks was indescribable, owing to the blend of various tints and the textural sheen of the material. "The color is unique," said the salesman. "It's called 'Archipelago Marine.'" He allowed the suit to cast its spell over Sarkis. "I guarantee you won't find another like it on the beach."

"I believe you," said Sarkis, squinting.

The salesman leaned closer and spoke in a tone of man-to-man candor. "It's our feeling that the suit combines the ruggedness of a desert island with the dashing savoir faire of a man about town."

"It does, it does," agreed Sarkis, blinking at the play of light on the satiny material.

The salesman leaned closer and spoke even more confidentially. "If you don't mind my saying so, the suit is you."

"I like it," declared Sarkis.

"I knew you would."

"Do you mind if I try it on?"

The salesman balked. "Well, eh, that's a bit irregular. As a rule, we don't fit men's bathing suits in the shop."

"I'd like to get the feel of it."

"Of course, but I can assure you ..."

"After all, buying a bathing suit is no trifling matter."

"I agree."

"I mean, I would hate to have any regrets once I got into the water."

"I understand completely," said the salesman, who wasn't sure he understood at all. "Well, if you insist ... There's a fitting room in the back."

"I'll be right back."

With his bathing suit in hand, Sarkis withdrew to a dressing booth and pulled the curtain closed behind him. Minutes later, the curtain was opened and out came Sarkis in his "Archipelago Marine" bathing suit. He cut a startlingly conspicuous figure in the sedate environs of the menswear shop. Somehow, the combination of a prominent belly, hairy torso and legs, and bare feet made him appear overexposed, if not butt naked. At the sight of him, Hagop was dumbstruck. He dropped his orange bathing suit and stared with a stunned curiosity. The salesman was agape. For a time, no one spoke.

"Sarkis, you're hairy," observed the boy.

The salesman was speeding nervous glances at the door. "I'm sorry, but this is highly irregular. I mean, did you have to remove *all* your clothes?"

"How else could I see how I looked?"

"Yes, of course, but I mean ... that is ... was it necessary to remove your shoes and socks as well?"

"Shoes and socks always look funny on someone wearing a bathing suit, don't you think? It's as if the person didn't know how to finish getting dressed—you know, like a patient in a hospital."

The salesman begrudged the point. "That's true. I've often thought that myself." "Well, tell me how I look!" said Sarkis, catching sight of himself in a triple-paneled mirror standing against the wall.

The salesman's attention kept shifting between Sarkis and the front door. "The suit is most definitely you," he said, "but it might be embarrassing if a customer were to come in and see you ... err ... dressed that way."

"There's nothing wrong with the way he's dressed," said Hagop. "He's just hairy, that's all."

Sarkis admired himself in the mirror. "You're absolutely right about these trunks. They do give a man a rugged, masculine look."

Sarkis flattered himself with several "rugged and masculine" poses, among them the three-quarter shoulder turn in the manner of a body builder, then a full frontal thrust. Finally, he took up a boxer's stance by hunching his shoulders and raising his fists to eye level. His expression was grim, combative. He began flicking his wrists in short, jab-like motions, then added a bob and weave to roll under imaginary punches being thrown at him. A few more hammer-like jabs, followed by a left cross, made short work of his imaginary opponent. Sarkis kept bouncing on the balls of his feet to advertise his fitness and eagerness for action. "Come on, Hagop. What say we go a few rounds? I feel in the peak of condition." The boy stared blankly at his friend. "Put up the ol' dukers. Let's see what you've got."

"Whoa!" said the salesman, stepping between the man and boy. "I'm afraid this is going too far. We simply can't permit this. I must insist you put your clothes back on."

Sarkis leaned aside and whispered into the salesman's ear, "This won't take long. I'll carry the kid for a round or two then ..." Sarkis flicked his wrist to indicate the bombshell he was holding in reserve. "He'll never know what hit him."

"Please!" exclaimed the salesman. "This is not a gymnasium. This is a menswear shop."

"No doubt about it," concurred Sarkis. "This may well be the best menswear shop in the world, and you, my friend, may well be the best menswear salesman in the world. Therefore, I can't see any reason why you would object to a little boxing match right here in your store."

The salesman looked to Hagop as if appealing to the boy for a translation, but Hagop only shrugged his shoulders in ignorance.

"Come on, Hagop, let's give it a go." Sarkis began circling his opponent and, with his hands, inviting him to make a move. Hagop, who hadn't any idea of what he was supposed to be doing, followed Sarkis's moves with a dull, uninvolved expression. "But first," said Sarkis, "some background on myself may be in order. I've had three fights in my life and lost them all, one to Harold Finger in elementary school, and one each to Tommy O'Connor and Nester Zapata in high school. They weren't very good fighters, but I was worse. I lost all three fights because I had the heart of a dormouse. The thought of getting hurt had me shaking in my shoes. Hagop, are you afraid of getting hurt in this match?"

"No."

"Then you're sure to win. My nerves are starting to go already."

As Sarkis and Hagop circled each other, the salesman alternated his looks between the front door and the two combatants. Gradually, he began following the others like a referee monitoring a bout.

"The boy has a classic style," said Sarkis to the salesman. "Notice the sullen eyes, the relaxed hands-down defense. He's a little slow on his feet, but I'll wager he strikes like lightning."

"He doesn't look the least bit interested in fighting," said the salesman, hoping to end this exhibition as soon as possible.

"Don't be fooled. He's just playing possum. First he lulls you to sleep and then, before you know it ..."

"Sarkis, how did you get so hairy?" asked Hagop.

"It's an ethno-genetic characteristic of my people."

"What people?" asked the salesman.

"Armenians," said Sarkis. "Armenians are known for their hair and big noses. They're also known for their dancing and for banging their fists on the table when arguing politics."

"I'm getting dizzy going in circles," said Hagop.

"Part of my master strategy," said Sarkis. "I'm setting you up for the Levonian haymaker."

"I don't think I like fighting."

"Neither do I. But what can we do? It's too late to turn back. It's a matter of saving face. Whoever gives in would look like a weakling."

"You can be the winner if you want. I don't care."

"That's very noble of you, Hagop, but I cannot accept your charity. A man's victories must be earned."

The salesman sighed in frustration. "Well, I hope one of you wins soon. We really must put an end to this."

"Looks like a standoff to me," said Sarkis.

"Good!" exclaimed the salesman. "Why don't we call the fight a draw?"

"No draws," said Sarkis. "A draw would be like saying you had no business fighting in the first place. Neither side gains any glory that way."

The salesman knit his brow intently. "Maybe we can stop the fight for other reasons. Let's say you're physically unable to continue, that you've aggravated an old injury to your heart and you're having trouble breathing. In fact you entered this fight against doctor's orders. That's how much of a champion you are." The salesman anxiously awaited Sarkis's reaction. "How does that sound?"

Sarkis needed only a moment to make up his mind. "I like it!" he said. "The idea has a gutsy, human interest ring to it. I can see the media running with the story: 'A Tragic Ending to a Short and Brutal Career.' Yes, I think you've hit on something." Sarkis stopped stalking the boy. Suddenly he clutched his chest as if stricken with a stabbing pain and cast a helpless, imploring look around him. The others watched intently. Sarkis staggered to and fro, and kept buckling his knees as if each step might be his last. Finally, he twisted full circle and dropped to the floor with a thud. He lay there outstretched and on his back, his arms opened wide.

For a stunned moment, the salesman stared at the fallen figure. Then by way of seizing the moment, hoisted Hagop's arm and declared, "The winner and new champion."

"Oh, no, you don't," protested Sarkis from the floor. "I'm not out until I've been counted out."

"The count—yes, of course," said the salesman, and he began the slow, rhythmic motion of his arm. "1 ... 2 ... 3 ..."

Sarkis rose to one knee as the count continued. "4 ... 5 ... 6 ..."

He lifted his planted knee off the floor, then let it drop again. On all fours now, and looking glassy eyed, he addressed an imaginary ringside crowd whose collective heart he had touched deeply. "Never wanted to get into the fight game. First love was always the violin, but I swore I'd never let mom scrub another hallway as long as these dukes could bring home the bacon." And giving up the fight, he collapsed like a dead weight to the floor again. "7 ... 8 ... 9 ... 10." And again the salesman hoisted Hagop's arm in victory, the boy looking a bit addlepated from all the excitement.

Just then a customer entered the shop, a middle-aged lady wearing a wide-brimmed straw hat and a summery cotton dress. Upon seeing the salesman holding up Hagop's arm, she stopped short in puzzlement. Moments later, seeing Sarkis slowly emerge from behind a table of miscellaneous menswear items, she blanked out altogether and gave an affrighted yelp.

Alerted to her presence, the salesman dropped Hagop's hand and came to the lady's side. He cleared his throat and fiddled with his tie, his way of assuming a proper, business-like demeanor.

"Good afternoon." He smiled. "May I help you?"

The lady could not take her eyes off Sarkis, who had come to his feet like a graceless bovine hulk. "My goodness, what's he doing?"

The salesman hemmed a bit. "Getting up from the floor, I think."

"Hairy, isn't he?" noted the lady, whose shock was mixed with just a hint of intrigue.

"An ethno-genetic characteristic of his people."

"I've no objection to hair, you understand, but there's a time and place for everything."

"He was trying on his bathing suit."

"Then why does his appearance strike me as so obscene?"

"I'm afraid I couldn't say, ma'am."

"He almost looks naked."

"He's been practicing for the beach."

"This is a menswear shop and not a beach," insisted the lady. "Is it your practice to allow people to parade around here with no clothes on, and in the presence of children, no less?"

The salesman took umbrage at the remark. "My dear lady," he said, with an air of condescension. "I think you should know this may well be the best menswear shop in the world, and I may well be the best menswear salesman in the world. Therefore, I see nothing wrong with a man's trying on a bathing suit whether he happens to be hairy or not."

"Bravo!" cheered Sarkis from the back of the shop, where he was posing before the mirror again yet able to hear the others.

"I don't know what you're talking about!" said the lady to the salesman.

"Was there something special you were looking for?" asked the salesman.

"Yes, there was." The lady frowned in confusion. "But I've forgotten what it was, what with all the commotion going on. Something for my husband, but I can't remember."

"Perhaps I can help you," said the salesman. "Swimming trunks, jockey shorts, garter belts, cuff links, ties, shoelaces, shirts? I'm sure we have whatever you might be looking for."

The lady's attention kept reverting to Sarkis. "He, at least, could have had the decency to keep his shoes and socks on."

"That thought did occur to us, but we decided against it."

"I'll take the trunks," called out Sarkis. "We'll need some towels, too."

The lady warily backed away. "I'd better come back another time."

"Are you sure I can't help you remember what you came to buy?"

"No, no," said the lady, flustered. "I can't remember a thing. My mind is a complete blank."

Sarkis chimed in from the rear, "Amnesia can be a very disabling condition. Is there anything I can do to help?"

"What in the world is he talking about?" said the lady, utterly exasperated at this point.

"He wants to help," said the salesman.

The lady addressed Sarkis emphatically. "I do not have amnesia!"

Sarkis turned away from the mirror and came forward in full view of the lady, who retreated as she might from a feral beast. Sarkis kept his distance to assure her that she had nothing to fear.

"Perhaps you don't know you have amnesia," he suggested. "After all, if you've forgotten something, it stands to reason that you would forget that you've forgotten, and therefore believe that you still remember."

"I'm well aware of what amnesia is," said the lady, "and I would be the first to remember if I were forgetting I had forgotten ... Oh, this is ridiculous. I don't even know what I'm saying."

"Please, I don't mean to pry, but is it possible that when you saw the menswear shop, you were reminded of some unhappy childhood experience, which you immediately buried in your subconscious?"

The woman glared incredulously at Sarkis. "I don't believe this conversation is happening. If you must know, you're the one who made me forget ... you ... getting up from the floor ... and the way you looked."

"Me?" said Sarkis quizzically. And then, as if he'd had a sudden burst of intuition, he exclaimed, "Aha! We may be getting somewhere. I reminded you of someone. A close family member, perhaps?" With utmost delicacy he added, "Your father, perhaps?"

"My father?" The lady was aghast. "The only thing you reminded me of was some kind of animal being let out of a cage."

"Fear of animals!" spouted Sarkis triumphantly. "I knew we'd get to the bottom of this."

"Oh, this is utterly insane. I'm leaving here before I lose my mind."

"But do you know where you're going?"

"As far from here as my legs will carry me!"

"If I might make one small suggestion," said Sarkis. "And believe me, I don't mean to interfere in your personal affairs, but might you consider the possibility of ... err... seeking ... professional help? There are people trained to handle this kind of thing."

The woman was beside herself. "If anyone here needs his head examined ... but why in God's name am I even wasting my breath! Sir! I don't know what zoo they let you out of, but the sooner they return you to captivity, the better off the rest of us will be." With that, she quickly turned away and, with one hand atop her hat as if it might get blown away, she hurried toward the door. By the time she exited from the shop, she was virtually in a trot. Sarkis caught sight of her through the front window and watched her disappear down the street.

"Do you think she'll be all right?" he said.

"I think so," said the salesman. "She just forgot what she came to buy."

"What was the name of that thing you said she had?" Hagop asked Sarkis.

"Amnesia. Loss of memory. Sometimes it's caused by a sudden emotional shock. That appears to be the case here."

"Your hair," said the salesman. "She saw your hair and forgot what she was doing."

"Hmm," mulled Sarkis, with a graver, more pensive look. "Her case may be more serious than I thought."

Hagop nudged Sarkis with his shoulder. "Time to go swimming, Sarkis."

"Right you are. I'll change and be right back."

Within minutes Sarkis was back in street clothes and at the checkout counter paying for the bathing suits and towels. The salesman rang up the sale and with a smile handed Sarkis his receipt.

"I'm almost afraid to ask this question," said the salesman, "but will you be staying long in Asbury Park?"

"That's hard to say. We've just arrived, and I'll be looking for work here."

"Oh? Any particular field?"

"I plan to get a job on a merry-go-round."

"A merry-go-round, you say?!" After a deliberative pause, the salesman thought the better of pursuing the subject. No telling where any further questions might lead. "Well, the best of luck to you, I'm sure."

"Thank you. I'm sure, too."

Upon leaving the shop, Sarkis and Hagop stepped into the glare of a bright lemon squash sun nearing its zenith. "Beautiful day, isn't it?" said Sarkis, squinting in the light.

"And getting hotter all the time. It must really be hot back in the city."

Sarkis took a deep, expansive breath. "I have a feeling Asbury Park is going to be good to us, Hagop. What do you think?"

"I like it already, but we still have a lot to do, don't we?"

"What we don't get done today we can always leave for tomorrow or even the next day."

"Right now I can't wait to be in the water cooling off."

"Neither can I. Let's get to that beach."

ON THE BEACH

On the beach, Sarkis and Hagop distanced themselves from a growing crowd of bathers and found an isolated spot to lay their towels. After a brisk plunge in the ocean, Sarkis stretched himself out upon his towel and basked in the sun while Hagop busied himself by building a fort in the sand. The construction was progressing nicely with few setbacks. The boy erected four sloping walls; then, with a discarded soda cup, he made molds for the towers, several of which crumbled for lack of adhesion. After many attempts, he finally succeeded in making two towers stand with a semblance of stability. The boy admired his work like a proud architect. Having accomplished as much, he decided to let the fort stand as it was for the present.

"Let's go in the water again, Sarkis."

"Didn't we just come out of the water?"

"No. We've been out a long time. It's time to go back in. Come on."

"Please, Hagop, not yet," begged Sarkis. "The sun is warm and the sand is like a feather bed. Let me lie here a little longer."

"Sarkis, sometimes you act just like a grown-up. Every time grown-ups come to the beach, they want to lie down in the sand all day and never go in the water."

"You're right, Hagop. You're absolutely right and it's a crime."

"Grown-ups are always the first ones to say, 'Let's go to the beach!' And then when they get there, they don't want to do anything.”

"I know. All they want to do is lay in the sand and sleep."

"They want to get a tan all the time."

"They're lazy and vain, Hagop."

"What's vain?"

"Vain is thinking how handsome or beautiful you'd be if you only had a tan."

"You're supposed to go in the water when you come to the beach. That's what the beach is for."

"You're right again, Hagop. The truth comes to you as naturally as breathing."

"So why don't we go in the water again?"

"Because I'm a grown-up, and I'm vain, and because the sun is warm and the sand is like a feather bed."

Hagop resumed the building of his fort. "When grown-ups go to the beach, they go in the water for ten minutes to let everybody think how much they love it. Then they don't go in the rest of the day."

"True, too true."

"I could stay in the water for hours."

"Why don't you go in now and I'll come later."

"If I go now, you won't come. You'll sleep in the sun all day."

"Hagop, how could you even suggest I would do such a thing? I'll be along in a minute, I promise."

"No, I'll wait," said the boy, and he continued working on his fort.

Sarkis rolled on his side and surveyed the boy's work.

"How's the fort coming?"

"Okay, I guess, but the sand isn't sticky enough."

Hagop was firming up the walls and smoothing out the groundwork.

"The towers are cracking a bit," said Sarkis, "but the fort is beautiful."

"The fort is a castle, too," said Hagop, who had been waiting for Sarkis to show an interest in his creation. "Here's where the king and queen live. Here's where the soldiers live, and over here is where the prisoners are locked up. Sometimes the prisoners are tortured. The king doesn't torture them. A mean prince does, without telling the king. The prince has a few soldiers who help him, and they're mean, too. The prince wants to take over the fort. He hates the king and queen. They're good and he's bad."

"Who attacks the fort?"

Hagop deliberated. "Indians," he decided. "Indians are always attacking the fort."

"Are they good or bad Indians?"

"The chief is a good Indian. The others are pretty good, too, but the prince makes the Indians attack. He tells the chief the king is going to kill them all and take away their land. That's why the Indians keep attacking. Oh, and I forgot: The prince keeps giving the Indians whiskey to make them act crazy. The Indians think the prince is their friend, but he hates them more than he hates anybody."

"Do the Indians take over the fort?"

"No. The king waves a magic wand and all the Indians go to sleep before they can climb the walls."

"And then what happens?"

"Every time the Indians fall asleep, the prince gets mad. So he tortures them while they're sleeping. When they wake up, he tells them the king did the torturing. That makes the Indians want to attack the fort again."

"The king certainly has his troubles. What happens at the end?"

"I'm not sure. I think the Indians find out how mean the prince is. They do some Indian magic and turn him into a frog. Then the Indians, the king and queen and everybody become friends and live together. They smoke the peace pipe and do the buffalo dance."

"And does the prince stay a frog all his life?"

"No, a crocodile eats him."

"Serves him right."

"The crocodile used to be a mean Eskimo until the other Eskimos did some magic and turned him into a crocodile."

"I didn't think Eskimos were mean."

"Some Eskimos are mean, but not many. This way, all the mean people go into the woods and eat each other up while everybody else lives together."

Sarkis reflected upon the boy's story. "Who do you like best?"

"The chief. He's the bravest, but I like the chief's son, too."

"The chief's son? Where did he come from?"

"He's not really the chief's son. When he was a baby, the Indians found him in the forest. He's a white boy, but he doesn't know it. The chief treats him like a son. The boy learns to hunt and shoot a bow and arrow like the Indians do. At the end, the chief tells him the truth, but the boy loves the chief anyway. When the boy grows up, he marries the king's daughter and they have queens and kings for babies."

"I'm glad no trouble started when the king found out a white boy was living with the Indians."

"No trouble," said Hagop. "Once you smoke the peace pipe and do the buffalo dance, you never have any more trouble."

"I like the ending very much."

"The fort's not finished yet," said Hagop. "I still have to make flags and rooms for the soldiers."

"What we need are sticks and cups to make flagpoles and rooms and whatever else we need."

"We'll put the flags on the towers."

"And we can dig a moat around the castle, too."

"What's a moat?"

"A moat is a ditch filled with water that protects the castle against enemies. But since the people in this castle have no enemies, the moat can be used for a swimming pool."

"Then everybody can go swimming and people can have diving contests off the towers."

"The castle sounds like a wonderful place, Hagop. How would you like to live there?"

"I'd like it fine."

"What would you do there?"

"I'd learn about the Indians and live with them for a while like the chief's son did. I'd learn Indian secrets, like how to follow a trail by looking at broken branches or dust on the leaves of a tree. Then I'd live in the castle too, because dungeons are fun."

"Sounds wonderful."

"I wish we were in the fort now. I wish it was real."

"It is real. I don't know anything in the world more real than your fort."

"I'm going to find some sticks and cups," said Hagop, jumping to his feet.

"Tell you what. I've got a better idea. Why don't we buy some Popsicles and Dixie cups and use them when we're finished? My stomach tells me it's about time to be eating something anyway."

"How many should I buy?"

Sarkis pulled out money from his change pocket. "Buy us three Dixie cups, two Popsicles and four Fudgsicles. I haven't had a Fudgsicle in years, and we'll need all the sticks we can get."

At a concession stand toward the rear of the beach, Hagop purchased the ice cream and returned with the treats. He and Sarkis had a Dixie cup, a Popsicle and two Fudgsicles apiece. By the end of this binge, though, Sarkis wasn't feeling any too well. Aside from a digestive rumble in his stomach, his complexion had begun to take on a wan, sickly look.

"Hagop."

"What?" said the boy, licking clean the last of his ice cream sticks.

"I don't feel so good."

"Do you want some more ice cream? My mother says ice cream is good for you when you feel sick."

"I think I have Fudgsiclitis." Sarkis fondled his stomach.

"Does that mean you want another Fudgsicle?"

"No. That means you must never mention that word again in my presence for as long as you live."

"Sarkis, you don't look so good."

Sarkis stretched out on the sand like a man on a stretcher. "I'll be all right if I rest and don't move for a week. I remember a time when I could eat four Fudgsicles and a banana split, and top them off with a bottle of cream soda, but that time will never come for me again."

"I feel fine. How come I'm not sick?"

"That's the beauty of a young boy's stomach. It's a human sewer system. You could swallow half the beach and come up smiling from ear to ear."

"I guess you want to rest then, don't you?" said Hagop, anticipating a disappointment.

"Just for a while. You go ahead and work on the fort. Later, you can show me what you've done."

"The fort won't be any fun if you don't help me."

"Would you rather go in the water?"

"No, I'll wait for you."

"I know what you can do," said Sarkis. He closed his eyes and let the sun warm him. "It's something I always loved doing. Go down by the water and stand in the sand and let the water rush over your feet. Don't move. Just stand there and let yourself sink into the sand little by little. As you watch the water come and go, some beautiful thoughts will happen to you. How would you like to try that?"

The boy seemed willing, if unenthused. "Okay, I guess."

Sarkis flopped his arms outward as in a cruciform. "Now you must let me die in peace—a victim of the Fudgsicle plague."

"Can we finish the fort later?"

"You bet we will. The fort will be a magnificent edifice—a towering monument to love."

Hagop was idly making circles in the sand with his finger. "Sarkis, would you be my father?"

Sarkis fell silent. For a moment, any trace of lightheartedness faded from his countenance. Quickly, though, he deflected the boy's words with an exaggerated bit of playacting.

"Every man in the world is a father to every child in the world," he croaked. "That's my deathbed speech, Hagop—famous last words by a dying man."

"Sarkis, you're not dying. You're faking."

"I wish I were," said Sarkis, looking weak and forlorn. "Take care of my little dog for me, Hagop. I leave you all my worldly possessions: one 'Archipelago Marine' bathing suit, a towel, a wallet, and house keys."

"Sarkis, you don't have a dog. Now I know you're not dying."

"Maybe not, but I have to rest now and let the sun melt the Fudgsicles in my stomach."

"Then can we go in the water?"

"Yes, of course. That's exactly what we'll do."

Hagop rose to his feet. "Okay, I'll wait for you by the water. Hurry up and rest so you'll feel better."

A restorative nap in the sun had Sarkis feeling like his old self. Sitting up and shielding his eyes from the glare, he looked around and spotted Hagop by the water's edge. The boy was standing still, his head lowered in what seemed deep contemplation. Sarkis rose and made his way to the boy's side. Hagop was watching the water rush in and recede across his feet, and though aware of Sarkis's presence, he never looked up as if doing so might break his concentration.

"I'm watching the water come and go," said Hagop.

"And what do you think about while you're watching?"

"Nothing much. Just how good it feels when your feet sink into the sand every time the water goes out."

"If you don't move, you can make a deep hole."

"I made a deep hole before, but then I pulled my feet out and started all over again."

"I like the way it feels when the water goes and pulls at your feet."

"So do I, but the water doesn't always reach your feet," said Hagop. "You have to wait each time and see."

"You can have fun guessing how far the water will come up on the sand."

"There's a lot to see, too—different pictures in the sand every time the water goes out."

"What else do you see?"

"Plants, weeds, and shells. I saw a snail before, but then the water went out and the snail was gone."

"Did the snail come back?"

"No, but there's always something different to see."

"Every time the ocean rushes in, a whole new world of life comes in with it."

"Does the ocean ever stop?"

"No, the ocean goes on forever. You could stand here for the rest of your life and you would always see something new the ocean brings in."

"Are the plants alive?"

"Yes, they are."

"Is everything in the ocean alive?"

"Yes, every inch of space in the ocean is alive. So is every inch of space in the world, and in the sky, which goes on forever and is so big that nobody can measure it. Every inch of space in all the worlds everywhere is filled with something alive. Can you imagine that?"

"No. That's too much to imagine."

"Neither can I. That's what God is, I think."

"What?"

"Everything we can't imagine, but know is there."

"Where were all the shells and seaweed and living things before they came here?"

"They may have gone around the world a million years before they came here. That's why everything you find on a beach is a souvenir of all the life that ever was, and all the life that ever will be."

A wave broke and rushed up the sand across their feet, and then retreated out to sea, leaving in its wake a farrago of shells, plants, and weeds glistening in the sun.

"I like standing still," said Hagop. "There's a lot to do."

"Yes, there is."

"Why don't more people do it?"

"Some people do when they're alone, but most people are so used to moving around, they don't know how to stand still anymore."

"Standing still is easy. I can do it without trying."

"When people are young, they can do things like standing still because it comes naturally to them. The trouble starts when they grow up and forget about everything that came naturally to them when they were young."

Hagop continued staring at the sand around his feet, but he was thinking more than watching. Finally, he looked up and asked, "If I can stand still and grown-ups can't, does that mean I'm smarter than grown-ups?"

"In a way, I suppose."

"If I told my parents that, I'd get a licking."

"Oh, but you wouldn't want to tell your parents that, anyway."

"Why not?"

"Well, because then you wouldn't be smarter."

"I don't understand."

"Look at it this way," said Sarkis, "don't grown-ups always tell you they're smarter than you?"

"Yes."

"Well? If you told grown-ups that you were smarter than they were, you'd be acting just like a grown-up, wouldn't you?"

"I guess so."

"And if you acted just like a grown-up, you couldn't be

smarter than a grown-up, could you?"

"I guess not."

"So you wouldn't tell them you were smarter, and that's why you would be smarter."

Hagop scratched his head. "Sarkis, you must be the smartest person in the world."

"You're probably right, but I wouldn't want to tell anyone."

"Because if you told them, you wouldn't be smarter, right?"

"Right."

"Then you'd be bragging, wouldn't you?"

"That's right, and bragging only means that you don't know enough about something, not that you know too much."

"But Sarkis, you brag. I hear you brag all the time."

"You're right. I'm probably the biggest braggart in the world." Sarkis paused. "So let that be a lesson to you."

"What's that?"

"Anybody who tells you how to be smart doesn't know what he's talking about."

"Now I'm all mixed up."

"Good! Come on. Let's go swimming."

Hagop was first in the water, the boy making a dash and giving himself up to the first wave that came by. In contrast, Sarkis exhibited a timid, long-suffering approach to getting wet. Advancing one step at a time, he cringed with each chilly rise in the water level. Finally, more out of desperation than daring, he dived headlong into a breaker, surfaced and swam vigorously to acclimate his body to the temperature.

Sarkis swam beyond the concentration of bathers in the shallow water and toward the farthest buoy lines. There, in the tranquil, lapping waters, he turned on his back and bobbed afloat over the water's gentle undulations. The only sound to be heard was that of ocean murmurs in his ears. The world seemed lifetimes away. The cloudless sky went on forever. Life, for the moment, was like a floating barge, drifting in no particular direction, but always smoothly, wherever the current might lead. Here in the deeper water, Sarkis experienced a perfect solitude. But, as with moments too rarefied to last, he could not maintain the balance. Soon his weight shifted, and in his effort to right himself, his legs began to sink. Sarkis's head dipped underwater, and a snootful of ocean had him gasping and spitting. Buoying himself, he looked toward shore, and was surprised to see how far out the current had taken him—well beyond designated boundary lines and into prohibited waters. Bathers along the beach dotted the shoreline like miniature figures. Anxiously now, he turned shoreward, gave a strong paddle kick with his legs and began swimming back to safer waters.

Meanwhile, Hagop was playing in the shallow water. The boy was battling waves by trying to hold his ground as they broke over him, but each time he braced himself against an attack, he would be knocked over backward. Growing more determined with each defeat, he began punching at the waves as if he could box them into submission. But any attempt to stand toe to toe with an onrushing breaker proved futile. Each one made short work of the boy by rudely dumping him on his behind.

Seeing Sarkis wading toward shore, Hagop waved and said, "I'm fighting the waves. Watch." A small wave swelled toward him and crested. As it broke, he began flailing away, only to end up, as always, sitting in the shallows and spitting up water.

"Looks like the waves are winning," said Sarkis. "Why don't you try riding them instead of fighting them?"

"I don't know how."

"I'm not much good at riding waves myself, but I think I can teach you how. Would you like to learn?"

Hagop shrugged as if to say, Why not?

Sarkis taught Hagop how to ride a wave. He cautioned the boy against launching out too soon or too late, and showed him how to catch the break at its peak and to keep his body extended and poised throughout the ride. All these techniques Hagop picked up quickly and soon he was riding waves with the ease of a seasoned surfer. He swooshed in their bellies, sailed in their curls, and knifed through the water with effortless grace.

After a number of successful rides, Hagop looked for a bigger challenge. He let pass several breakers until he focused on one ahead that promised to be the most formidable he had encountered thus far. He waited for the break, caught it perfectly and, feeling the propulsion driving him, bored through the water like a torpedo. But then suddenly the boy was thrown out of control, caught in an undertow that swirled him about like a leaf in a storm. Spun sideways and then flipped on his back, he had the dire sense of being in the throes of some final and irreversible calamity. At length, he came to a scraping halt on a shallow bed of pebbles near the beach. He rose slowly, wincing and cradling his bruised arms. As it happened, he was more stunned and confused than hurt. Hagop had never experienced anything of this kind before. That frightening sense of being at the mercy of a powerful, invisible force had left him shaken. "I started spinning around. I don't know what happened."

Sarkis finished checking the boy's arms. "You must have gotten caught in the undertow."

"What's that?"

"I'm not sure, myself. It sneaks up and grabs you sometimes, and pulls you in different directions, and you can't fight it no matter how hard you try."

Hagop shook his head apprehensively. "I don't think I want to ride any more waves."

Sarkis saw the fear lurking in the boy's eyes. "Hagop, will you do me a favor? You can say no if you like, but would you ride one more wave before we go in?" The boy pursed his lips in a pout. "It's not good to end on a bad ride."

Reluctantly, Hagop acceded to the request. He waded out a dozen yards or so. Upon sighting a breaker forming up ahead, he planted his feet and readied himself. Just as the mounting curl rose above his head like a crescendo, he came under its lip and caught the break perfectly. The wave sucked him up and propelled him faster and farther than any before it had. The boy sped through the water, past the shallow bed of pebbles and all the way to the beach, where he bellied onto the sand like some shipwrecked survivor swept ashore on a desert island. Sitting up, he looked back and, with a sense of elation, realized how far he had traveled. Meanwhile, Sarkis was coming up the beach right behind him. "How was that?" asked Sarkis.

Hagop was flushed and breathing excitedly. "It was like riding the wind."

Sarkis smiled slyly, savoring the boy's triumph. "Was it now?" He extended a hand and, with a playful yank, assisted Hagop to his feet. "Like riding the wind, you say?" The boy nodded, and the two headed off in the direction of their towels.

During their time in the water, the beach had filled with bathers. The once sparsely populated setting was now a panoply of beach umbrellas, blankets, ice chests, slatted chairs, radios, and sundry paraphernalia. Returning to their place, the man and boy found their towels mussed up and sandy, owing to the increased volume of traffic passing to and fro nearby. Amid the clutter of surrounding encampments, the towels looked diminished, even overwhelmed, by the encroaching populace.

Hagop came to a sudden stop. "Sarkis, look!" The boy was pointing, not to the towels, but to the lumpy mounds of sand and articles of refuse scattered nearby. "The fort is gone!"

So it was, or, more accurately, trampled underfoot. All that remained of the fortress was a portion of one tower and fragments of one wall. The Dixie cups and Fudgsicle sticks had been toppled or partially buried in the sand. Sarkis surveyed the ruins with a doleful eye. "Someone must have run over it on their way to the water."

Hagop was bristling with anger. "How could they do it? How could they do something like that?"

"They probably never saw it. It was an accident."

"I don't care!" cried the boy. "They had no business doing that! It was our fort. We built it and made it up ourselves."

"Hagop ..." Sarkis faltered. "Hagop, we can build another one. We can make it even better than the first."

"No, we can't make one better because that was the best one ever."

"You'll see. We can do it."

"It won't be the same." The boy hung his head over the ruins, the crushed remnants of his creation. At length, he dragged his foot across the sand and toppled the last remaining tower. He stood there brooding in silence. "The fort was going to be beautiful when we finished."

"It was beautiful."

Sarkis picked up their towels and shook them off. He held one out to the boy. Hagop did not respond. Sarkis kept his arm extended and jiggled the towel like an attention getter. The boy still made no move to take it.

"Tell you what," Sarkis said. "I'll race you to the bath house, and if you win, I'll buy you a giant ice cream sundae with walnuts and a mountain of whipped cream on top."

The boy still did not move or give the first sign of having heard the proposition. Then, with his gaze still downcast, he slowly reached out and took the towel. He mumbled, "Gimme a head start?"

"Sure, but it won't do you any good."

Sarkis hitched up his swim trunks, thumbed his nose in a competitive manner and took up a three-point sprinter's stance as evidence of the seriousness with which he was approaching this match. Hagop, in a less demonstrative mode, waited a few yards ahead.

"Are you ready, young fella?" said Sarkis. "On your mark ..."

At the count of three they were off and running. Hagop held the lead over the heavy, slow footing. Sarkis stayed in contention, but each time he threatened to overtake the boy, he stumbled and fell into the sand. Hagop opened up a wide lead and won handily.

SARKIS, MUMFRED LEWIS AND THE MERRY-GO-ROUND THAT WOULDN'T DIE

"Sarkis, are you really going to get a job on the merry-go-round?" asked Hagop as they were walking along the boardwalk with their towels and bathing suits tucked under their arms.

"I certainly am. We're going to Ocean Grove where there's an amusement park, and I should think a merry-go-round as well."

And so there was. The merry-go-round house at Ocean Grove stood apart from other amusements and alongside a man-made lake that featured paddle boat rides. The circular building had a roof that tapered into a crown of beaded lights, all of them currently blacked out, as were the decorative bulbs embroidering the eaves and windows. The pavilion appeared closed, the interior dark except for whatever slivers of sunlight filtered through the windows. Nevertheless, when Sarkis tried the front door, it was open. He and the boy cautiously stepped inside like wary interlopers. The pavilion was as quiet as a still-life picture. Immediately Sarkis's attention was drawn to the merry-go-round standing in the middle of the floor. At the sight of it his eyes took on a wondrous aura.

The animals posed under a tinsel-trimmed canopy; animals, it seemed, of every stripe and color. There were horses—orange, lavender, and yellow; tawny lions and tigers; a polka-dotted giraffe; two white swans; an ostrich; and one golden unicorn. Their bodies were polished to a lacquered sheen as they froze in suspended leaps and high-stepping canters. Some of the animals flashed startled eyes and bared teeth, while others carried themselves with a courtly air. Interspersed amid the animals were chariot coaches, decorated with winged cherubs blowing heavenly coronets. The entire pageant scintillated with the magic of a make-believe world about to spring to life.

Sarkis and Hagop approached the merry-go-round with the deference accorded to a sacred shrine. Then drawing closer, they realized they were not alone in the pavilion. They heard the tinkling sound of metal against metal, and moments later noticed a man lying on his side in the control booth at the hub of the platform. He was performing maintenance on the control box. At his side lay an assortment of tools and rags. He was a ruddy-faced man dressed in a plaid shirt and denim trousers. He seemed to take no notice of his two visitors when they came to the door of the booth. "Excuse me," said Sarkis.

The man never bothered to look up from his supine position. "I hear you," he said by way of dispensing with any small talk. "What can I do for you?"

"Are you the proprietor of this merry-go-round?"

"That's right. Mumfred Lewis, operator and sole proprietor."

Sarkis came right to the point. "Mr. Lewis, I would like a job on the merry-go-round."

Mumfred Lewis decided it was time to see with whom he was carrying on this conversation. He came to a sitting position and sized up his visitors. "You're a little old to be looking for a job on a merry-go-round, aren't you?"

"He doesn't want to be a tailor anymore," interjected Hagop.

"Well, that's very interesting, I'm sure," said the proprietor, "but I don't need any help right now. If you want to know the truth, I may be out of work myself before long. This merry-go-round has been on the fritz for three days now, and I've been going crazy trying to fix it."

"The merry-go-round is out of order?" said Sarkis, taken aback by the news.

"That's right. The maintenance department was supposed to send a specialist here three days ago and he still hasn't shown up. If this keeps up much longer, I'll have to start combing the beach for a living."

"Where do you think the problem lies?" asked Sarkis, with a

growing sense of urgency.

"Seems to be electrical," said Mumfred. "Thursday night the control box started sparking and everything stopped. The animals haven't moved since." Mumfred glanced worriedly at the motionless cavalcade. "She's an old machine, you understand— one of your earlier models that still run by throttle, not like those push button, cookie cutter jobs that manufacturers are turning out nowadays." He shook his head regretfully. "I kept her running as best I could but ...Well, let's face it; this old warhorse may have seen its last days."

"Mr. Lewis, you're telling me this testament to eternal youth may have withered up and died of old age? I refuse to believe that. What's more, I don't intend to stand by and let it happen."

"Oh?" said Mumfred, a glimmer of hope in his eyes. "You know a little something about these machines?"

"Not a thing," said Sarkis.

"Uh huh," muttered the proprietor with tongue roundly in cheek. "You should be a great help, then."

"But there must be something we can do."

"I'm open to suggestions."

"Do you mind if I take a look in there? You never know. Sometimes a pair of fresh eyes can see what a pair of overworked eyes has been missing."

"I guess it can't do any harm," said Mumfred, if a bit skeptically.

Sarkis sat on the floor in front of the control box and rubbed his palms in anticipation of an undertaking about which he knew nothing. One look inside the box, however, and his face went blank. He hadn't realized so many bolts, screws, and wires were needed to run a merry-go-round. At first he only stared at the maze of circuitry. Next, he poked around in places—much as a person who knows nothing about used cars might kick tires in a used car lot. Presently, though, abandoning all caution, he attacked the problem head on (Sarkis being a proponent of the adage that nothing so much breeds failure as indecision). Working at a non-stop pace, he called for tools, which Mumfred handed to him like an assistant in some complicated surgical procedure. Sarkis burrowed into the electrical configurations and began tightening screws, snipping, splicing, and re-circuiting wires, making sure no ends were straggling. At times he became so involved in what he was doing, his head would disappear into the box and not come out again until Mumfred or Hagop made him come up for air. It was all a mysterious process, and if Sarkis had inadvertently discovered what had incapacitated the merry-go-round, he wasn't sharing the knowledge. Whenever either of them asked how the work was going, he would pause with an evasive shrug or mutter some vagary like, "Hard to say in these matters. Never can be too sure." As a crowning touch to his efforts, he oiled everything in sight with a squirt can and wiped all the components clean so that if all else failed, this conglomeration of old and probably worn out parts would at least look as good as new.

By the time Sarkis laid down his tools, the shadows of a late summer's afternoon had stretched across the pavilion floor and over the backs of the wooden animals. He slowly rose to his feet, his fifty-year-old back creaking from having been stretched in ways altogether unfamiliar to it.

"Well, Mr. Lewis," he said after wiping his hands clean. "I'd say there's nothing more to be done except to give her a test run and see what happens."

Mumfred Lewis was understandably wary after having seen his control box overhauled and clumps of clipped wire strewn about the floor. "Maybe you two better stand aside," he said, "just in case this old warhorse decides to kick up its heels."

Sarkis and Hagop withdrew to the side of the platform while Mumfred took his place at the controls. He gingerly laid his hands on the throttle as if the slightest touch might set it off. He pushed forward. Nothing happened. He jiggled the throttle and still nothing happened. He tried maneuvering it every which way until finally a sound was heard—a low moan like a whiny, dyspeptic barrel organ. The music had begun, if still unrecognizable and lacking any semblance of a tune or tempo. And then the animals moved. Initially their motion was a source of elation, but soon became a cause for concern, if not alarm.

"Sarkis, look!" exclaimed the boy, pointing to the moving cavalcade of animals.

"I am."

"Do you see what I see?"

"I think so."

"The merry-go-round ..."

"I know."

"It's going backward."

Mumfred stepped out of the control booth and looked inquisitively at the animals moving from left to right instead of their customary right to left.

"What's going on here?" he said, squinting as if his eyesight had been temporarily impaired.

"The merry-go-round," said Hagop. "It's going backward."

"What do you mean it's going backward?"

"The merry-go-round," said Hagop. "It's going backward."

"That's ridiculous," said Mumfred, as his eyes bore incontrovertible witness to what his mind rejected. "A merry-go-round can't go backward."

"This one can," said Sarkis.

"Maybe we're standing wrong," said Mumfred, and he tried to reorient himself to the moving animals, but whichever way he turned, they were either beating a retreat or coming toward him by way of their hind parts. "This can't be happ— ... I mean, anyone with any common sense knows ..."

"It's happening," confirmed Sarkis.

Mumfred just threw up his hands and slapped them to his sides in a gesture of utter bafflement. "Well if this doesn't beat all."

Meanwhile, the garbled, dissonant sounds emanating from the merry-go-round had begun to unravel and find their true sequential pattern. A familiar melody was evolving, one that Sarkis immediately recognized as a popular standard. In fact the ditty was his favorite of all merry-go-round tunes, "The Daring Young Man on the Flying Trapeze."

"Hagop, listen to that music. Do you know what it is?"

The boy immediately recognized the spirit of the piece if not its name. "It's circus music."

"Yes, but not just any circus music. You won't find a happier marriage anywhere between music and a merry-go-round." Sarkis smiled approvingly over the harmonious collaboration of sight and sound. "Hagop, we just may have found the merry-go-round of my dreams."

Mumfred, standing outside the control booth with arms akimbo, kept shaking his head in wonder. "It's running pretty good, I'll have to say that, but still … we just can't keep letting it run backward, can we?"

"Why not?"

"Backward is not the way it's supposed to go."

"Look at it this way, Mumfred. It's probably the only merry-go-round of its kind in the world and should make for a fabulous amusement park attraction."

"It's unheard of."

"That's precisely the point."

Mumfred had his doubts. "Do you think it's safe? I mean a merry-go-round that starts going backward ... who knows what it might do next."

"Why don't you try stopping it, and let's see what happens."

"I'll give it a try," said Mumfred. The owner manned the controls again and shifted the throttle out of its present gear. Instantly the merry-go-round bucked and almost knocked him off his feet. It then gradually accelerated to full speed as if the animals had taken off on a stampede. "Sarkis, something's wrong! It's out of control!"

"You've probably got the throttle on 'Slow,'" said Sarkis, who showed a remarkable equanimity during these runaway movements. "Try switching to 'Fast' and see what happens."

"To 'Fast'?" And Mumfred checked the position of the throttle. "You mean slow could be fast and fast ...?"

"We probably got everything in reverse order. Just think backward and you'll be fine."

"This is all getting to be too much for me," said Mumfred as he reversed the speed, and sure enough, as Sarkis had suspected, the animals settled into a moderate cadence. Eventually, as Mumfred kept nudging the throttle in the opposite direction, the ride came to a full stop.

Mumfred weaved out of the control booth like a tipsy sailor and took a seat on the edge of the platform. He leaned forward with his arms upon his knees and a befuddled look on his face.

"Fifteen years in the business. I thought I'd seen a thing or two ..." He shook his head. "… but this beats all."

"I don't think you have a thing to worry about," said Sarkis. "It looks to me as if everything is in order, but just a different order than the one we expected."

"It'll take some getting used to," said Mumfred. "To tell the truth I'm not sure we should open our doors to the public yet. I mean we'd be taking a big chance if something should *really* go wrong." He began shaking his head again. "Oh, I don't know what to think."

Sarkis cast an affectionate eye around the darkened pavilion, first at the decorative wall trimmings, then the clown and jester motifs around the windows, and lastly the merry-go-round itself, motionless in the shadowy light as if under wraps. "Mumfred?" he said, still glancing around the room.

The owner looked up. "Yes?"

Sarkis smiled benignly. "It's time to turn on the lights."

News of the merry-go-round spread quickly through the amusement park, and by early evening people were dropping by to witness or to ride the novelty. By nightfall the curious minded had formed a line extending outside the amusement park and to the promenade alongside the artificial lake. Needless to say, Mumfred, Sarkis, and Hagop had all they could do to handle the landslide business, but handle it they did. Mumfred stationed himself at the cashier booth and sold the tickets; Hagop collected the stubs from the boarding passengers and monitored the number of customers for each ride. That left Sarkis to man the controls, a task he performed with all the ease and assurance of one who had been operating a backward merry-go-round all his life.

Never had the animals performed better. Never had these emissaries of the wild leaped with such grace and élan as if spurred by public adulation. Never had the music sounded so clear, so perfect in pitch and tone. The melodious sounds of "The Daring Young Man on the Flying Trapeze" floated outside the pavilion and across the amusement park grounds, where passersby heard it and often hummed or whistled along. Sometimes a passerby, drawn to the mellifluent strains of that music, came to the pavilion door and listened with his eyes closed as if revisiting some half-forgotten memory. Then reopening his eyes, he quietly went on his way again.

As the hour grew later and children were ushered off to bed, the crowds began dwindling until only a few customers wandered in for a ride. Given prolonged periods of inactivity, Sarkis found time to help clean up the pavilion, liberally scattered with candy wrappers, Styrofoam cups, and ticket shreds. He attacked his work with an industrial-sized push broom, while at his side, not to say under his nose, Hagop pushed right along with him. As for Mumfred, he was busily counting the receipts of this banner day, easily the most profitable day he had ever known as the owner of a merry-go-round.

As Sarkis and Hagop swept up the residue of litter, the boy suddenly remembered the reason he and Sarkis had come to the merry-go-round in the first place. Stopping short, Hagop wheeled in his tracks and dashed to the ticket booth where Mumfred was still tallying the day's receipts. The owner looked up expectantly through the window bars and waited for the boy to speak. Hagop, however, was too excited to speak just yet, his brain bursting with the events of this day. When words did begin spilling out of his mouth, they did so in such a rush he couldn't have stopped himself even if he had wanted to.

"Mr. Lewis, are you going to give Sarkis a job? Please, Mr. Lewis, you have to give him the job, because if you do he'll be the happiest person in the world. I mean I think he's the happiest person already, but this job will make him even happier. You see, Mr. Lewis, it's been a crazy day, and when Sarkis came out of his house this morning to buy the paper he didn't know he was going to Asbury Park and I didn't know I was going with him and all I can tell you is he'll be the best helper you ever had. Sarkis just wants to do happy things, even if they look crazy to somebody else. That's why this job is so important to him and that's why you have to do this for him if you can."

Mumfred Lewis was dumbstruck by this emotional outpouring, most of which he didn't even try to unscramble. Nevertheless, when the verbal dust had settled, and Hagop stood there, eagerly awaiting a response, Mumfred knew exactly what it would be.

"He fixed the merry-go-round for me, didn't he? I'd be out of business without him, wouldn't I? You tell him he can start work tomorrow afternoon at 3 o'clock. Tell you something else. We'll see if we can find a little work for you, too."

Hagop took a minute to process the full import of these words. Once doing so, he whirled around to the entrance of the booth and rushed toward Mumfred. The boy threw his arms around the owner's neck.

"Mr. Lewis, I love you! You're the best friend anybody ever had."

"Whoa! No need for all that," yelped Mumfred, flustered by such a demonstrative show of affection. The owner's arms hung awkwardly at his sides like those of someone unaccustomed to receiving a hug, much less reciprocating in kind.

Hagop relayed the news to Sarkis, who was still pushing his broom at the far end of the pavilion. "Sarkis, you got the job! We start tomorrow at three o'clock."

Sarkis acknowledged his good fortune with a wave and then, as if the outcome of his job search had never seriously been in doubt, continued sweeping the floor around the merry-go-round. Come closing time he thanked Mumfred personally.

"Mumfred, I can't thank you enough for giving me this job. You'll never know what it means to me."

"Don't be thanking me too soon. I can give you a job, but I can't afford to pay much."

"I wouldn't think of asking for a penny more."

"A penny more than what?" puzzled Mumfred.

"A penny more than you can afford to pay."

"Something tells me we're going around in circles," said Mumfred with a mock suspicious eye toward the merry-go-round. "Go on home, you two. I'll see you both tomorrow at three o'clock."

"You can count on us," said Hagop.

By the time they left the amusement park, most of the day's activities had come to an end. The rides had been put to bed, some under tarpaulin wraps, although the penny arcade and Pokerino gaming casino still attracted a late-night clientele. Nearby, at the man-made lake, a fleet of white paddle boats lay tethered to the dock, and around the perimeter of the lake, a necklace of overhanging lights cast dazzling reflections upon the placid waters.

"Sarkis, do you know where we're going? We don't have a place to stay yet."

Sarkis looked caught off guard. "You're right. I almost forgot. We'll have to take care of that right away."

They strolled along beach side streets, sparsely inhabited at this hour and only occasionally lit by a tall, goose-necked lamppost. Up ahead they saw the lights of a fast-food stand brightening the darkness like a beacon. Drawing closer, they caught whiffs of meat sizzling on the grill and French fries crackling in the deep fry. Sarkis smacked his lips with anticipation. "But we can't very well look for a place to live on an empty stomach, can we?"

"You mean we can eat first?"

"How does a juicy hamburger or two sound?"

"And French fries?"

"Wouldn't be a hamburger without French fries."

With appetites whetted, the man and boy put a spring in their step and headed straightaway toward the food stand. A cool breeze blew off the ocean; the heavens sparkled with a full array of stars, and behind them, in the distance, where the merry-go-round was hosting one last customer, the sound of "The Daring Young Man on the Flying Trapeze" wafted through the balmy, delicious night.

YOU'RE THE FUTURE OF THE WORLD

Hagop struggled to stay awake. Along a tree-lined street of bungalows and private homes, the boy came to a stop behind Sarkis, yawned, and dropped his arms limply to his sides.

"I'm sleepy," he said.

"Maybe we'll have luck on this street."

For the past several hours they had been looking for a room, but with no success. Either the ocean-front rentals were priced too high or, due to the lateness of the hour, people were not answering their doors. The time was well past midnight. As Hagop's eyelids drooped with fatigue, the man and the boy now looked for vacancies farther away from the ocean front.

"Why don't we just sleep on the beach?" suggested Hagop.

"If we don't find a room soon, we may have to."

They came to a private home with a room vacancy shingle hanging above the porch. The house was small, the roof and sidings in need of repairs. Still, the prospects of a room buoyed Sarkis's spirits as he led Hagop up the porch steps and to the door. Sarkis rang the bell, under which was posted the name Mrs. C. Lilly. Presently they heard footsteps approaching and then a woman's voice at the door.

"Yes? Who's there?" The voice was cautious and that of an older woman.

"Mrs. Lilly?"

"Yes, who's there?"

"We've come about the room."

A pause. "It's late," said Mrs. Lilly. "Couldn't you come back in the morning?"

"I realize it's late, and I hate to bother you, but we've been looking for a room for hours. I have a boy with me, and he can hardly stay awake."

Mrs. Lilly edged open the door and peeked out over the chain lock. Seeing Hagop sagging on his feet, she unhinged the chain and opened all the way. She was a white-haired woman, perhaps in her sixties, dressed in a drab print bathrobe and bedroom slippers. Despite her wariness at opening the door, and the drowsy look of interrupted sleep in her eyes, her face had a gentle aspect. She looked more timid than suspicious, her manner suggesting that of a woman who had lived a sheltered life and grown unaccustomed to dealing with strangers.

"Please excuse me," she apologized, "but I live alone and have to be careful about answering the door at night."

"I understand, and I appreciate your seeing us at this hour. We had almost given up trying to find a room."

"It is late," repeated Mrs. Lilly. She noticed Hagop again, the boy's head nodding and eyelids closing every few seconds. "But I suppose I can show you the room tonight."

Mrs. Lilly led Sarkis and Hagop to the basement and to a den-sized room. The ceiling of the room was no more than a foot or two above Sarkis's head. The width of the room was not much more accommodating, barely big enough to house a bed, a cot, and a gym locker that served as a clothes closet. Curiously, though, the quarters did not feel cramped. In part, this was due to an adjoining bathroom and a partially finished basement with a table and several sofas. But in part, too, the room had a relaxed, peaceful feel to it, one that made the usual considerations of space less important than they normally would have been. There was space here, but of a different kind. The feeling was that of a sanctuary where one could retreat, and, if one chose, travel great distances without taking a step.

"It's perfect," said Sarkis.

Mrs. Lilly appeared relieved. "I'm glad. This summer I rented the room for the first time. Two college boys shared it, and with the cot they seemed to manage well enough."

"We'll pay in advance, of course," said Sarkis reaching for his wallet.

Mrs. Lilly seemed discomfited at the mention of money. "The boys paid me 25 dollars a week. I hope that's not too much,"

"That's more than fair," said Sarkis, counting out the money for a week's rent. "That's downright generous."

Mrs. Lilly was relieved to have the financial arrangements settled, as if money transactions were awkward for her.

"I never know if I'm asking too much or too little," she confessed.

"You're very kind to take us in. I don't know what we would have done without you." Sarkis was feeling at home in his new environs. "Well, Hagop, what do you think of your new home?"

Hagop wasn't thinking much of anything at this point. The boy was half asleep on his feet and slouched against Sarkis. His lips were parted in a dull stupor as if he might be expecting a fly to enter his mouth at any moment.

"The boy can hardly stand up," said Mrs. Lilly. "Why don't you put him to bed?"

"Yes, of course." Sarkis lifted Hagop off the floor and cradled the boy in his arms. "Off you go to dreamland, young fella."

Sarkis laid Hagop on the bed and removed the boy's shoes and socks. When he tried to tuck the boy in, Hagop sloughed off the sheet as he would an unwelcome encumbrance. Turning on his side, he raised his knees in a crouch and hugged his pillow with both arms. Moments later he was fast asleep.

"You shouldn't keep the boy up so late," admonished Mrs. Lilly. "After all, he's only a child."

"I know," said Sarkis contritely. "Sometimes I forget."

"There are fresh towels and soap in the bathroom, and blankets in the closet if you need any." Mrs. Lilly had started for the door, then hesitated and said in a diffident, almost apologetic voice, "I suppose I should ask how long you'll be staying."

"That's hard to say. You see, we arrived in Asbury Park just this morning and we're not settled yet. Tomorrow I begin work on the merry-go-round, but I don't really know for how long."

"Oh?" said Mrs. Lilly. "You're a mechanic of some kind?"

"Oh, no, not at all. I'll be helping to run the merry-go-round and—just between you and me, Mrs. Lilly—riding on it as much as possible."

Mrs. Lilly didn't know quite what to make of that.

"My, my, that does sound interesting," she said evasively. Again she started to leave. "Well, if there's anything you need, please let me know."

"I can't think of a thing," said Sarkis, "except ..."

"Yes?"

Sarkis was reluctant to impose. "Please don't think me forward, but would you, by any chance, happen to have a typewriter I could use?"

"A typewriter? As a matter of fact I would. It hasn't been used in two years, but it's in excellent condition. It belonged to my late husband."

"Perhaps I should explain. You see, one of the reasons I've come to Asbury Park is to write a book. I haven't begun the book yet, but when I do, I'll need a typewriter."

Mrs. Lilly was pleasantly surprised. "Oh, I see. You're an author."

"Far from it," said Sarkis. "To be honest, I don't know the first thing about writing, but I'd like to learn."

Mrs. Lilly started to say something but then hesitated. Finally she overcame her self-consciousness and spoke.

"This may sound silly to you, but my husband, Wilbur, used to write in his spare time. He wasn't a professional writer or anything like that. He simply wrote for his own pleasure."

"I can't think of a better reason for anyone to write."

"Wilbur was an insurance salesman by profession, but poetry was his real love."

"Asbury Park must be a wonderful place for a poet to live," said Sarkis, captivated by the thought. "Solitary walks on the beach, the feel of ocean mist against your face, the sound of waves rushing in and rushing out. I imagine a poet on the beach in Asbury Park can feel himself a part of the natural order of things, a part of the universe itself."

"Saturday mornings," said Mrs. Lilly.

"Saturday mornings?" queried Sarkis, losing the drift of the conversation.

"That's when Wilbur would take his walks on the beach. Every Saturday morning he'd leave the house at six o'clock and would not return until nine or ten for his breakfast. He always took his notebook with him and scribbled notes and ideas for poems he wanted to write. In fact, Wilbur took his notebook with him wherever he went, even to the office every day. Some evenings he would come home from work with pages of ideas." Somewhat embarrassed, Mrs. Lilly added, "Wilbur was not a very successful insurance salesman, I'm afraid."

"He sounds like quite a man."

"He was quite a man," said Mrs. Lilly, feeling more and more willing to discuss her personal life. "And a very private man, too, I might add. Many times when we were together, he was really by himself; that is, his mind would be miles away. I would never ask him where, of course. I didn't think it was my place to ask him where his mind was."

Sarkis eyed Mrs. Lilly with a wry sense of admiration. "You're an unusual woman," he said.

"Unusual?" Mrs. Lilly blushed at the thought. "I'm afraid I've never done anything unusual. Wilbur and I lived a quiet, uneventful life in this house for forty-seven years. We were never blessed with children, you see, and so only had ourselves to make our way. Don't misunderstand me, I was very happy with our life together, but there was nothing unusual about it."

Sarkis mused aloud. "The action of quietness," he said softly.

"I'm sorry. I don't understand."

"Just a thought," said Sarkis. "In stillness there is action. In silence there is sound. The action and the sound are happening all the time, inside us as well as outside. It's something the boy and I were trying to learn on the beach today."

Mrs. Lilly was listening intently. "I think I understand you, at least where people are concerned. Between people, silences can be more important than words, can't they? I mean, if the silences are misunderstood, all the words in the world can't explain them, can they?"

A comfortable silence followed in which nothing needed to be explained. "Mrs. Lilly, I take back what I said a few minutes ago. You're a *very* unusual woman."

Mrs. Lilly smiled bashfully. She seemed to vacillate now between leaving and continuing their conversation. Then, braving the moment, she said, "I used to memorize many of my husband's poems. Would you like to hear one?"

"I'd be honored," said Sarkis, flattered to be asked.

"I don't know if this is a very good poem or not, but it's my favorite." Mrs. Lilly recited the words with care, ever mindful of doing justice to her husband's verse:

> "A poem is a shell in a crystal hall,
> And love a leaf in the golden fall.
> I bequeath to the world
> What the world can't recall. A shell. A leaf.
> My possessions all."

Sarkis savored the words as he let the last line trail off into silence. "A lovely poem," he said.

"He wrote many little verses like that," said Mrs. Lilly, her pride showing through a glint in her eyes. But now afraid she might have overstayed her welcome, she retreated toward the door again. "Here I am babbling away when you should be getting your rest." She glanced around the room by way of reminding herself of any accommodation she may have overlooked. "Of course you're welcome to the typewriter whenever you need it," she said, opening the door. "Have you decided what kind of book you will write?"

"An animal, hunting, and sea ship story, I hope."

"My, my, that does sound exciting. All that in one book?"

Sarkis couldn't help smiling in reaction to Mrs. Lilly's utterly ingenuous response.

"I'm going to try," he said.

"And I just know you'll do an excellent job of it, too." Then shyly Mrs. Lilly said, "Well, I've certainly enjoyed our little conversation, Mr. ... Mr. ..."

"Levonian. Sarkis Levonian. I've certainly enjoyed it, too."

"I'll be saying good night then, Mr. Levonian." And this time Mrs. Lilly did leave the room and gently closed the door behind her.

Sarkis was not sleepy, the excitement of this day still buzzing in his brain. For a while he gazed out the lone window in the room and listened to the crickets in the back yard. From time to time his attention turned to Hagop sleeping nearby, and on one occasion Sarkis removed a coverlet from the gym locker and draped it over the boy. Then he resumed his watch at the window, but only to look back on the boy again, sleeping so soundly not a muscle in his body had budged since being put to bed. He still lay on his side, arms hugging the pillow and knees folded to the waist. Presently from the window, Sarkis began speaking to the boy as if Hagop were awake and listening.

"Sleep tight, my friend. You're the future of the world, and you need your sleep. We only have a short time together, but we'll make the most of it if we can. You are teaching me so much, and I have so much to learn. Of course, I'll pretend to be teaching you, but I'll know better. You are teaching me that each of us in the world is born with the wisdom of the world inside him. You are teaching me that what we call truth lies not in what we learn but in what we have forgotten. You are teaching me that every soul is born in goodness and wants nothing more than to become more and more of its own goodness. I say this knowing full well there are barbarians loose in the world, but they cannot change what you are teaching me. I know the barbarians and their causes and their ideals and their speeches, but I know, too, they gave up the truth in their desire to become barbarians. A man was not born for hate. Hatred is what a man learns after he has been taught right from wrong and good from bad. But a soul cannot make these separations without declaring war on itself. If a man says he must hate in order to protect what he loves, he has declared war on himself and can no longer love what he seeks to protect. For that reason, the world's victories are only losses. But you know all this already. The beautiful thing is that you know all this without having to lift a finger, without having to waste a thought. That's why you are the teacher that you are. In a few years you won't be half the teacher you are today. In time the truths you know today will be buried under all that comes with growing up. But in this time we have together, perhaps we can help each other. If I can, I will teach you not to forget what you already know, and if you can, you will teach me to remember what I have forgotten. So sleep tight, young fellow. You're the future of the world and you need your sleep. By the way, I know what you did for me tonight at the merry-go-round. I couldn't hear everything you said to Mumfred, but I know it took courage to say what you did and that it had everything to do with us being hired. So thank you, friend. Sleep the good sleep. You're resting in the lap of God, and so long as you rest there, no harm can come to you."

A WEEKFUL OF SUNDAYS

Sarkis awoke feeling at least ten years younger. The sun rushed through the window between his cot and Hagop's bed and spread its wakening light across the room like a welcome.

"Hagop, are you awake?" said Sarkis.

"Yes."

"Hagop, do you realize what day it is?"

"No."

"Today is Monday."

"What's so special about Monday?"

"For twenty years I would wake up every Monday and go to the tailor shop, but today is Monday and I'm still in bed. Today is like Sunday all over again."

"Does that mean I have to go to church?"

"No, you don't have to go to church—unless you want to."

"That's good, because I don't like going to church."

Sarkis sat up in his cot and gave an expert imitation of a man alarmed.

"Why, I had no idea you didn't like going to church," he said.

"I only go because my parents make me."

"What don't you like about church?"

"I don't understand that much of what goes on. All I ever do in church is sit down and stand up. Just when I'm sitting down and resting the priest says something and I have to stand up again."

"Hagop, you surprise me."

"Church is boring and the time goes slow. Sometimes I stare

at people to make the time go faster. I pick out a woman with a funny hat and stare at her. Or I watch somebody sleepy trying to look interested. The men are the most fun to watch. They can never stand still. They look nervous, like they really want to pick their noses but they can't."

"Doesn't the priest tell you interesting stories about religion?"

"The stories are all about the Bible and the olden times. They're not too interesting."

"Your father likes to go to church, doesn't he?"

"He goes because my mother makes him go. He doesn't like church, either. He gets mad if I say I don't want to go, but he's the same way. Fathers are funny. First they say how you have to do good in school even if they never did good in school. Then they say how you should always go to church even if they don't like to go themselves. Fathers don't make much sense sometimes."

"Your mother likes to go to church. I'm sure of that."

"She's the only one who does. If it wasn't for my mother, we'd never go to church. But she's funny, too. Yesterday was the first time in months we didn't go, and do you know why? Because my mother said she didn't have anything nice to wear. Now that's a crazy reason not to go to church. I'm glad we didn't go, but it's still a crazy reason."

"I just thought of something," said Sarkis with a revelatory air. "Maybe church is more for women than it is for men."

"I don't know why anybody should have to go. Did God say that everybody has to go to church all the time?"

"Well, not exactly, but people go to church to learn about God and to worship him."

"Why should people have to go to church to learn about God? We learned about God yesterday on the beach and we didn't have to be in church to do it."

"That's true."

"We didn't need any statues to look at or Bibles to read. My mother says that God made the water and the sky. So if God made the water and the sky, that's what people should look at to learn about God. God didn't make statues, so I don't know why people have to look at statues. God didn't make churches, either. I know because my father had to give fifty dollars once to help build our church. He got a little mad when he did. My father doesn't like to show it, but he gets a little mad when he has to give too much money to the church.”

“Hagop, people build churches because they love God and want to please him.”

“If God made the water and the sky and the whole wide world and all the people, animals, trees, and mountains in the world, then I don't think a little church is going to make Him feel all that good.”

“What do you think would please God?”

“I don't know. Being nice to everybody, I guess.”

“Well, that's what going to church is supposed to do, make people feel nice to everybody.”

“It's hard to feel nice to everybody when you have to sit down and stand up all the time and not talk and get all dressed up. When I have to do all that, I just feel tired. I don't like getting dressed up. Did God say everybody has to get dressed up to go to church and learn about Him?”

“No, He didn't say you have to.”

“Girls are the only ones who love to dress up when they go to church because they want to look pretty. And do you know what they talk about when church is over? They don't talk about God or anything like that. They stand around outside and talk about how pretty and dressed up everybody else looks. I know because I listen to my mother talking to her friends after church and that's all they ever talk about.” A thought crossed the boy's mind. “Sarkis, you're right. Church is more for girls than for boys.”

“The idea never occurred to me before, but it may be true.”

“Do you go to church, Sarkis?”

“I can't remember the last time I went.”

“Why don't you go?”

“I guess I'm like you, Hagop. I don't understand too much of what goes on in church.”

“But you still try to learn about God, don't you?”

“More and more, the older I get.”

“Do you watch the water and the sky all the time to learn about God?”

“Not necessarily. I think I learn the most when a beautiful thought happens to me and I don't know where the thought came from. Whenever I have a beautiful thought, I feel like I'm in a church even if I'm only in Mrs. Lilly's basement. I guess a church is any place where you can have a beautiful thought."

"What's a beautiful thought?"

"That's a hard question, Hagop. I don't think I could make up a beautiful thought off the top of my head. For example, when you said that being nice to everybody would please God, that was a beautiful thought."

"I don't think it was so beautiful. Give me another one."

Sarkis looked stuck. "Hagop, a person can't start having beautiful thoughts as soon as somebody asks him. A beautiful thought has to come naturally. You can't make it happen. It has to happen by itself, like nighttime and daytime, and rain, and people, too, when they're not afraid to be themselves. When we see all these things that love to happen by themselves, why, then we have beautiful thoughts about them."

"Can you have beautiful thoughts about dogs, rocks, and turtles?"

"Of course you can."

"I like dogs, rocks, and turtles. Can you have beautiful thoughts about rats and cockroaches?"

Sarkis frowned. "Not as easily as you can about dogs, rocks, and turtles."

"Rats and cockroaches aren't beautiful, are they?"

"They're probably beautiful to other rats and cockroaches. We don't like them because they're dirty and spread germs, but the rats and cockroaches don't know they're dirty and spread germs. They're living the only way they know how, like everything else lives."

"When I see a rat or cockroach, I scream."

"I don't blame you. Whenever I see a snake, I scream and run for the hills. If we're afraid of something, we can't think it's beautiful, but if we weren't afraid, who knows, we might think differently."

"It's no good to be afraid, right?"

"Everybody is afraid of something. The important thing is to admit you're afraid when you're afraid, and not to pretend you're not. Once people start pretending they're not afraid, they begin to hate what they're afraid of. Once they start hating, the trouble starts. They're liable to do things like killing. And even worse."

"What's worse than killing?"

"Giving yourself a good reason for doing it."

Hagop rose from bed, stretched his arms as far as he could and yawned leisurely. "Well, I'm sure glad today is like Sunday and I don't have to go to church."

"Tomorrow will be like Sunday, too, and the next day, and the next. We'll make the week a weekful of Sundays, Hagop. How does that sound?"

"Saturday is my favorite day. I like Saturday because I can hang around and do whatever I like and wear old clothes when I go out."

"Good. Then from now on, every day will be Saturday for you and Sunday for me. Every day will be whatever day we want it to be."

SO WHO'S IN THE CRAZY HOUSE?

Sarkis, of a sudden, had a desire to know as much as he could about his traveling companion. Sitting forward on the edge of the cot, he said, "Hagop, I want you tell me everything you do on Saturdays."

"Well, I get up in the morning and go to the schoolyard with my friend George, and we bat the ball around. After a while, the big guys come and kick us off the field and they play choose-up games all day. George and I watch the games and get sodas for the big guys, but the big guys let us keep the deposit on the bottles, so afterward, we buy sodas for ourselves at Teller's candy store. Then I go home and copy or trace pictures out of a magazine and color them. Then maybe I'll look at my baseball chewing gum cards and memorize all the batting averages and stories about the players. I make believe I know all the players and they know me. Sometimes I make believe I'm the batboy of the team or one of the star players who'll get his picture on a chewing gum card someday. Then my cousin Dewey'll come over the house and we'll play the baseball game we made up with dice. We have teams and players and we keep batting averages and make uniforms for all the team. After Dewey goes home, I usually eat dinner, and then cut out sports pictures for my scrapbook or do something with my Tinker Toy set, like make a steering wheel or crazy shape. Then I read a library book if I have one, and after that, I go to sleep."

"Remarkable!" exclaimed Sarkis. "That's the busiest day I ever heard of. How do you find time to do everything?"

Hagop was nonchalant. "Oh, I find time," he said, "if my mother doesn't find silly things for me to do."

"Hagop, if you can find as much to do every day of your life, you'll be a very happy man."

"I never thought I was doing so much. I thought grown-ups were the ones who were so busy and kids were the ones with nothing to do."

"That's not true," said Sarkis. "That's a make-believe story grown-ups tell to make you think they're doing important things. Grown-ups like to think they're doing important things or else they'll start wondering why they ever grew up. Sometimes they know they're making believe, too. Every once in a while a grown-up will get a feeling or a hunch that what he's doing may not be so important, or even make sense, but when he does, he usually has enough friends to tell him his hunches are babyish and don't count for much. If his friends keep telling him enough times, he'll forget his hunches little by little until he doesn't have any more. He'll go on doing whatever he does and never think about it again. Do you understand what I'm trying to say?"

"A little bit. Not much."

"Well, anyway, the point I want to make is that grown-ups aren't as busy as they look. Now I've made a careful study of this problem. Being a grown-up, I'm naturally interested in the subject. A couple of months ago, when I had nothing to do, I stood outside the Moosehead Tavern and watched everybody who passed by, just to see what they were doing. Now, the women who passed by looked like they had someplace to go, so we won't count them in this study. God bless the women. They always look like they know where they're going. But the men! Ah, that was a different story. The men were like lost and confused puppies. They didn't know what to do or where to go. One man I watched walked to the corner, stood there, watched the light change to red or green, then turned around and walked back. Another man had a newspaper in his hand and kept tapping it against his leg as if he didn't know what to do after he had finished reading the news. Another man was looking through the window of the Moosehead Tavern and trying to decide whether he should go in or not. Another man walked to the corner and actually couldn't make up his mind whether to cross the street or stay where he was. So help me, he walked up to the curb three times and came back three times. He never did cross the street. Another man was standing outside of Schultz's delicatessen and looking at his watch every twenty seconds as if something important was supposed to happen every twenty seconds. All of this is true, Hagop, every word of it. Now here's the important part. A good many youngsters passed that corner, too, children your age and even younger. Now, every youngster who passed by knew exactly what he was doing. In one way or another every boy and girl was having a good time. One boy was doing nothing more than bouncing a ball, but he wasn't just bouncing a ball because he had nothing better to do. He was bouncing a ball as if it were the most important thing in the world he could be doing at that moment. Other youngsters were kidding and laughing with each other. Another youngster ran by and jumped over a hydrant. Then another whizzed by on a skateboard. Every young person was making some kind of fun happen, and that's what was so important and beautiful to see—the young people in their playfulness. For them, the day could go on forever because they would never run out of things to do. For the grown-ups, though, the day was over before it began. You see, Hagop, the day I watched these people was a holiday, and the grown-ups didn't know what to do on a holiday. Holidays are for hunches, but the grown-ups had gotten rid of their hunches a long time ago, so they were waiting for the day to be over and for tomorrow to come so they could go back to work or do whatever they did to make themselves feel important. What I'm trying to say, Hagop, is that every day of a person's life should be a holiday as much as possible. Every day should be filled with playfulness, not just when you're a boy, but when you're a man. I know it's important to grow up and to do what grown-ups have to do, but growing up shouldn't stop your life from being a holiday. It shouldn't stop you from having hunches and doing happy things. You know what I'd like to see one day? I'd like to see all the grown-ups in the world walking down the street and bouncing a ball. That's what I'd like to see. Now wouldn't that be something?"

"They would all go to the crazy house if they did something like that, wouldn't they?"

"Probably. But think of those grown-ups I watched on the corner. Now they were in a kind of crazy house already. Nobody locked them up in a room—everybody was in the same crazy house, so nobody had to get locked up. Everybody could stand around and tell each other they weren't crazy. Then if somebody did something that really wasn't crazy, do you know what would happen? Everybody would lock the person up and call him crazy."

"Is that what would happen?"

"I've known it to happen."

"So then everybody in the crazy house isn't crazy, and everybody outside the crazy house is crazy."

"Sometimes it works that way."

"Sarkis, that's crazy!"

"I know."

"Everything's backward!"

"Very often."

"It's like the merry-go-round."

"A little bit."

Hagop gave up on the discussion because he couldn't decide who was crazy and who wasn't. "Let's go eat," he said. "I'm hungry."

"Good idea," said Sarkis. "Let's go to the boardwalk and have pancakes for breakfast. On the way we'll think of nothing but food. By the time we eat, we'll be so hungry that the pancakes we order will be the most delicious pancakes in the world."

"What else will we do before we go to work today?"

"I don't know. We'll just let the day happen by itself. Right now I can't think of anything but food, can you?"

"No. I'm thinking about those pancakes and juicy syrup all over them."

"Good. From now on we'll think of nothing but food. Let's get dressed."

While Hagop donned his clothes, Sarkis washed himself in the bathroom, all the while singing or humming songs, the words to which he had forgotten, the melodies of which he altered to suit his falsetto, baritone voice. While scrubbing his face, he called out to the boy, "Hagop, look outside and tell me what kind of day it is."

"A beautiful day," said Hagop. "Just like yesterday."

"Do you know what a day like today is perfect for?"

"No, what?"

"Pancakes, Hagop. Pancakes. I told you we weren't thinking

of anything else."
    "Ooooops! I forgot."

SARKIS'S THEORY ON CLOCKS

After leaving their basement apartment, Sarkis and Hagop walked toward the boardwalk along a tree-lined street of bungalows and private homes. As Hagop had observed, the day was as beautiful as yesterday when their adventure together had begun.

"Hagop, are you thinking about food?"

"Yes, I am."

"Good. So am I. Nothing excites me more than the thought of food. Some people get excited when they think of a new idea, or when they design a house, write a poem, or paint a picture, but food is what excites me the most. To think about eating and then to eat what you've been thinking about is enough to make me dizzy. A point to remember, though—food always tastes better when you're hungry. I know that sounds foolish, but you'd be surprised how many people don't enjoy food because they're not hungry when they eat." Sarkis deliberated and came to a conclusion. "Clocks are the problem there," he said. "Yes, clocks are the problem."

"Clocks?"

"Clocks telling us what time we have to eat."

"People have to have clocks, don't they?"

"Yes, but clocks are tricks, too."

"What kind of a trick is a clock?"

"Clocks are tricks by telling us it's time to do the same thing we did when it was that time the day before. Now, regular clocks are important, but they're not the most important clocks we have. Our bodies are clocks, too, and our minds and feelings are clocks, and sometimes, when we listen hard to the clocks inside us, they tell us that we don't want to do the same thing we did the day before just because the time is the same. If I ate at six o'clock yesterday, maybe I don't want to eat at six o'clock today. Or if I went to work at eight o'clock yesterday, why should that mean I'm supposed to go to work at eight o'clock today? The trouble with regular clocks is that they make people think it's time to do certain things when it may not be the time at all. Just because the hands of a clock went in a circle twenty-four times doesn't mean I'm supposed to do the same thing as I did twenty-four circles ago."

"Sarkis, if people didn't do the same things at the same time, nobody would know what anybody else is doing. Everything would really be crazy then. Nobody would know when to go to work. Suppose my mother went shopping and all the stores were closed because people didn't feel like opening up? What would happen then?"

"I know everybody has to work and find each other when they have to, but if we do everything by regular clocks just because they go around in circles so many times, then that's a little crazy, too. If a person really believes that a clock is telling him what time it is, if he really believes his life has to be doing what the clock tells him—a clock, a machine with two hands going around in circles— well, that has to be a little crazy, doesn't it?"

"So then we're crazy if we look at clocks and crazy if we don't. Here we go again!"

"Who knows? Maybe we are and maybe we aren't. If we're all crazy, I guess the only important thing is whether we're happy crazy or unhappy crazy. Which would you rather be?"

"Happy crazy."

"Good. And if you're happy crazy, who's to say that you're crazy at all?"

"Sarkis, every time you talk, I never know if I'm crazy or not."

"Let me put it this way, Hagop. Remember that man I told you about outside of Schultz's delicatessen, the man who was looking at his watch every twenty seconds? Now he was expecting that watch to tell him something, but the watch can't tell him anything.

He had to keep looking at his watch because his inside clock wasn't working. His inside clock broke down when people made him get rid of his hunches. So he was looking at his watch as if he couldn't do anything without it. The watch had to tell him when to eat, when to wake up, when to go to work. A machine was telling him that. It's like when you talked about not going to church because God didn't build it, or looking at statues that God didn't make when we should be spending more time looking at what God did make. Well, why should a man spend his time keeping time to a clock that God didn't make when he has one inside him that God did make and which keeps better time?"

"I don't know about any clock inside me."

"You know more about it than I do. In a few years when people start telling you to look at your watch more, you'll have to listen harder to the clock inside you, but the clock is there if you want to hear it."

"All I can say is that it took me a long time to tell regular time, and now you're saying not to look at clocks anymore."

"How did we get on this subject anyway? I thought we were going to think about pancakes and nothing but pancakes."

"We were. Then you started talking about food and clocks and God."

"Good. I guess that means God is telling us it's time to eat."

HAGOP FALLS IN LOVE

On this sunny Monday morning in Asbury Park, one customer was sitting at the counter where Sarkis and Hagop went to have their breakfast. The customer was a stocky man in his forties, with a tan and thinning sandy hair. He was hunched over a bowl of cereal and reading the morning paper. Behind the counter, a waitress was rinsing glasses, and behind her, at the griddle, a young girl was making pancakes and sausages for customers sitting at tables in the rear dining room. The girl hovered over the griddle with a spatula in her hand and flipped the pancakes carefully. She handled the spatula with a tentative, awkward motion—like someone unaccustomed to short-order cooking. She perspired freely, too, and occasionally stepped back from the heat to wipe her brow.

Sarkis and the boy took seats near the customer at the counter. The waitress pulled out a pad from her apron pocket. "What'll you have?"

"Pancakes," said Sarkis. "Golden brown Aunt Jemima pancakes, if you please."

"Me, too," said the boy.

The waitress smirked. "You wouldn't consider Betty Crocker pancakes in case we happen to be out of Aunt Jemima, would you?"

"Betty Crocker would be fine," said Sarkis. "I don't think she's the woman Aunt Jemima is, but they're both fine ladies and we'll settle for either."

"Well, that's very sporting of you," said the waitress facetiously. She placed the written order on a spike holder near the girl at the griddle and resumed rinsing her glasses.

"What's the difference between Aunt Jemima pancakes and Betty Crocker pancakes?" asked Hagop.

"Probably none, but when I was a boy, Aunt Jemima's laughing face on a box of pancake mix always made me feel I was getting a happier breakfast. Betty Crocker's picture never gave me that feeling. She looked too serious. I kept thinking she ought to be somebody's mother or grandmother but I couldn't picture her as part of a family, just a person who made pancake mix all day."

"Everything smells good in here," said Hagop, whiffing the aroma of food from the griddle.

Sarkis snapped his fingers in a revelatory flash. "That reminds me—I want some oatmeal, too."

"What reminds you?"

"Things that smell good. You know, Hagop, I haven't had a bowl of oatmeal in maybe twenty-five years. I'm craving some right now." Sarkis motioned to the waitress. "Miss, would you please add a bowl of oatmeal to my order?"

The waitress said guardedly, "Any particular brand?"

"Quaker Oats if possible."

"Really?" piped the waitress with mock surprise. "Quaker Oats, you say! Why, it so happens we wouldn't think of serving any other brand. Would you like some tomato juice with your oatmeal, say by Sacramento, or some corn flakes by Kellogg's?"

"No thank you, but I'd like the oatmeal to be as gloppy and ugly as possible."

"Gloppy and ugly. Of course," said the waitress patronizingly. "Why, we serve the gloppiest and ugliest oatmeal on the Jersey shore. It's a specialty of the house."

"Good. That's how my mother used to make it, and her oatmeal was the most delicious I ever tasted."

"Well, isn't that sweet of you to remember your mother that way. Of course we can't guarantee our oatmeal will be quite as good as hers, but we'll do the best we can."

"Thank you," said Sarkis, smiling and beginning to feel at home in the restaurant.

Hagop's extraordinary experience took place about this time.

The precise moment of the event is impossible to determine, except to say it occurred between the time Sarkis turned away to glance out the restaurant window at passersby along the boardwalk, and when he turned back to say something to the boy. One look at Hagop and Sarkis was slack jawed. The boy looked spellbound. His eyes were riveted straight ahead. At first, Sarkis could not determine the object of the boy's fixation. However, upon closer investigation, it became clear that Hagop was staring shamelessly at the girl making pancakes at the griddle.

"Hagop, what's the matter?"

"The girl."

"What girl?" said Sarkis nervously. "Oh, that girl. What about her?"

"Look."

Sarkis looked, but saw nothing unusual or eye-catching about the girl, just a pleasant, everyday-looking girl. In fact, strictly speaking, her face was too round, her eyes too large, and her hair too short. It was set in bangs that were not as evenly cropped as they could have been. And yet, while each separate feature may have lacked a refinement that would have qualified her as attractive, the whole of her conveyed an appealing and unaffected charm.

"I'm looking, Hagop. What am I supposed to see?"

"She's pretty."

"I agree, but do you think it's polite to stare so hard?"

"I can't help it."

"What else do you see?"

"She has nice hair."

"What else?"

"She's working too hard."

"That's her job. She's young and the work won't hurt her."

"She's sweating, too. I don't like her to sweat so much."

Sarkis was beginning to sense a significant turn of events here.

"Hagop, are you still hungry?"

"No."

"Do you know what day it is?"

"I'm not sure."

"Can you tell me the most important thing that ever happened in your life before now?"

"Nothing important ever happened in my life."

"That's what I was afraid of."

"Sarkis, what's happening?"

"Hagop, I think you've fallen in love."

"Sarkis, I'm only ten years old!"

"I realize that."

"What should I do?"

"Nothing. Just keep staring. Nothing else you can do right now."

The customer nearby, eating his cereal and reading, noticed something amiss out of the corner of his eye.

"Pardon me," he said to Sarkis. "Is anything wrong with the boy?"

"He's just fallen in love."

"Oh," said the customer, nodding absently as if he might have been told the time of day or been asked to pass the sugar. Finishing his cereal, he wiped his mouth with a napkin and leaned toward Sarkis again. "Um, eh ... he's a little young, isn't he?"

"He's ten."

"I see," said the customer, nodding again as if no further explanation were necessary. He resumed the reading of his newspaper, but now kept sneaking glances at the boy. Finally he couldn't restrain himself. Rising from his stool, he leaned over the counter and looked Hagop squarely in the eyes. The boy's gaze went right through him. "He looks hypnotized. He doesn't move a muscle."

"He'll probably stay that way awhile. Right now, he can't see anything but the girl."

"And the girl?" said the customer returning to his seat. "The one over there making pancakes?"

Sarkis nodded. "At this moment she's a vision of loveliness in his eyes."

The customer sized up the boy's love interest. "No offense intended, but she doesn't look so special to me. I mean, I wouldn't call her a knockout or anything."

"Who's to say?" mused Sarkis. "We'll never see her as the boy must be seeing her at this moment."

The customer gainsaid any such notion. "The kid's going through a crush, that's all. I was the same way when I first met my wife. I couldn't take my eyes off her. If I couldn't be with her, I'd have to phone her four or five times a day and then once more before going to bed. Otherwise I couldn't sleep. I'm telling you, I had a bad case of the love bug. It's like an infection. Believe me, though, marriage cures it in a hurry."

The waitress now came forward with Sarkis's oatmeal and two orders of pancakes. She was moving with brisk efficiency when she glimpsed Hagop in his mesmerized state. She stopped and frowned in puzzlement.

"What's the matter with the boy?"

"He's just fallen in love," said Sarkis.

"Really!" said the waitress, who at this point would not have been surprised by anything Sarkis said. "How exciting. Anyone I know?"

"The girl over there making pancakes," said Sarkis.

"Ellie Prentice? Well, who would have guessed? And how long has this romance been going on?"

"About five minutes."

"Five minutes! My, my, that long? The boy just came into the restaurant, watched Ellie flipping pancakes, and flipped himself, hm?"

"That's about the size of it," said Sarkis. "You being a woman can surely understand how unpredictable these affairs of the heart can be."

"Listen, mister, I haven't understood a thing you've said since you walked in here. First you sit down at my counter and order Aunt Jemima pancakes and 'gloppy' and 'ugly' Quaker Oats oatmeal. Then, after I turn my back for two minutes, you tell me the boy has fallen in love with the girl making pancakes."

"Now hold on," interrupted the customer. "The man's telling you the truth. I saw the whole thing myself. The kid was taken by surprise. He never knew what hit him." The waitress eyeballed the customer suspiciously as if he and Sarkis might be in cahoots. "And another thing," added the customer. "There's nothing wrong with Quaker Oats oatmeal. I used to eat it all the time myself as a boy."

"You don't say!" The waitress leaned upon the counter and in her most mockingly sugar coated voice said, "And tell me, did your mother make oatmeal 'gloppy' and 'ugly' like his mother did?"

The customer jumped to his feet and wagged an indignant finger in the waitress's face. "You'd better not be making any cracks about my mother, miss."

"It's all right," Sarkis interceded. "I was only telling her before how my mother used to make oatmeal."

"Well, if your mother made gloppy and ugly oatmeal, that's the way it was supposed to be," said the customer. "Anyway, oatmeal has to look gloppy and ugly. That's the only way it comes."

"That's true," said Sarkis. "Oatmeal is one of those naturally ugly cereals that no one can really do much about."

The customer closed his eyes and smiled dreamily. "Sometimes my mother would spice it up with a dash of cinnamon." He paused, savoring the reminiscence. "Now that was a treat! Mm, I can taste it now."

The waitress threw up her hands. "I think you both have bats in your attic." The customer turned sharply to the waitress. "Have you got anything against mothers, miss?"

"No, but I think some of their sons belong in little padded rooms with no windows."

"Oh, that's witty, very witty. You're a regular comic, aren't you? "

The waitress ignored the customer and turned her attention to Hagop, who had been forgotten during these preemptive exchanges and who, through them all, had remained as rigid as a statue.

"Why doesn't he move?" she asked. "He looks paralyzed."

"He's been smitten by his love object," said Sarkis. "Wave your hand in front of his face and see what happens."

The waitress passed her hand in front of Hagop's eyes and the boy never so much as blinked.

"He may be sick," she said. "Do you think we should call a doctor or the rescue squad?"

"That won't be necessary," said Sarkis. "He's only suffering from love sickness. There's nothing much we can do except wait until he snaps out of it."

"I have an idea," said the waitress, her eyes brightening. "Maybe if I brought Ellie over, she could talk to the boy and sort of bring him out of it."

"You know, that just might work," said Sarkis. "But the girl will have to be very careful with him. He's in a delicate state right now, and we all have to be mindful of what we say and how we say it. One slip and he could come undone."

"Call the girl," said the customer. "Let's see what happens."

The waitress summoned the girl, Ellie, who promptly set aside her spatula, wiped her hands on her apron and came forward. She looked a shade nervous, as might a girl being called to the front of the class by a teacher.

"Ellie, we've got a little problem here," said the waitress. "See this boy?" Ellie gave a start at the sight of Hagop staring at her. "It seems he's developed some kind of attachment to you. He's love struck or lovesick or something. I'm not sure what's going on here myself. We thought if you could talk to him and make him talk to you, he might snap out of it."

Ellie was nonplused. "Is this a joke or something?"

"No joke," said the customer. "Look at the boy. Does he look like he's joking?"

Ellie peered at Hagop more closely without detecting the least movement in the boy's face. "I don't get it," she said. "He looks hypnotized."

"He's fallen pretty hard for you," said Sarkis. "We just thought you might be able to help."

Ellie still half expected a joke to be made of the matter, but no one gave any hint of one. "You're serious," she decided.

"Quite serious," said Sarkis. "The boy hasn't moved a muscle in ten minutes."

"But what should I say?"

"Anything," said Sarkis, "but handle him gently. He's in a very delicate state right now."

Ellie turned toward Hagop and immediately grew flustered under the boy's unwavering gaze. She nervously looked to the others who, with smiles of encouragement, prodded her to continue. Ellie took a deep breath, stood face to face with Hagop and smiled uneasily. "Hello," she said.

The others leaned closer, anxiously awaiting Hagop's response. When the boy said nothing, they huddled over the counter and exchanged worried glances. "No reaction at all," said the customer. "Do you think he heard her?" "I'm sure of it," said

Sarkis, "but we can't tell what affect the girl's voice may be having on him."

"Shh!" The waitress quieted the others down. "Go on, Ellie, say something else." Everyone huddled closer.

"My name is Ellie. What's yours?"

Hagop still didn't speak or indicate that he had even heard. He was sitting upright, his gaze fixed, intractable. But then he moved, or rather, was moved. Without any warning, he tipped backward and began keeling over. He would have fallen on his head had not Sarkis and the customer caught the boy from behind.

"Oh my!" yelped Ellie.

"I don't like this," said the customer nervously.

"It's all right," said Sarkis, sitting the boy upright again as if propping a dummy. "Keep talking to him, Ellie."

The girl needed a minute to collect herself. The others looked on supportively. "Now I told you my name," she said. "Shouldn't you tell me yours?"

Another silence. But then, to everyone's surprise, the boy responded. "Hagop," he said.

"He spoke!" exclaimed the customer. Sarkis motioned for silence. "That's a funny name," said Ellie.

"My name is really Jack, but Sarkis changed it to Hagop because it sounded better."

Sarkis whispered excitedly to the others. "We've made a breakthrough! Ellie, you did it, you did it."

"How old are you?" asked Ellie. "I'm ten. How old are you?"

"Seventeen. I'll be eighteen in November."

"Are you a mother with babies?"

"No. I still go to school. I start my senior year in high school this fall."

"I go to school, too. I'm in the fifth grade."

"Do you like school?"

"No, do you?" I like it. School is a lot of work, but you make friends and have fun, too."

"I don't have any friends."

"Oh, I don't believe that."

"Except Georgie and my cousin Dewey. And Sarkis, too— he's my friend."

"There you see. That makes three friends already."

"Why do you like school?"

"Because I go to dances and belong to different clubs. Also, I'm a cheerleader. That's the most fun of all."

"What's a cheerleader?"

"A cheerleader goes to football games and basketball games and helps the crowd cheer for the school team. We sing songs and do dances. We have special uniforms, too."

"I like uniforms."

"Ours are red and gold. We wear short skirts and jump around a lot."

"Why do you have to wear short skirts?" asked Hagop, a note of disapproval creeping into his voice.

"So we can kick our legs high and put on a good show. All cheerleaders wear short skirts."

"Uh-oh," said Sarkis, noticing a sullen change in the boy. "She may have said the wrong thing."

"When you kick your legs high, all the boys look at you, don't they?" said Hagop.

"Well, a cheerleader is supposed to get everybody's attention. That's the whole point."

Hagop fell silent. A pouting scowl came over his face.

Sarkis annotated the moment for the others. "Jealousy syndrome. Public exposure of physical attributes on the part of the love object produces strains of melancholia in the lover."

"Do you like making pancakes?" asked Hagop.

"I don't mind. I'm only working until I go back to school. I'm saving money to buy a car next year."

"You sweat when you make pancakes, don't you?"

"The griddle gets pretty hot, especially in the mornings when people come for breakfast. It's not so busy in the afternoons."

"If I had money, I'd buy you a fan so you wouldn't have to sweat so much."

Ellie blushed. "Why, that's sweet. That's about the sweetest thing anybody ever said to me."

"Then you'd be cool all day."

Ellie smiled shyly, at a loss for words. And then, unable to let this moment pass without a more demonstrable show of appreciation, she rose on her tiptoes, leaned across the counter, and planted a kiss on the boy's forehead.

Hagop stiffened like a board. His eyeballs froze. Sarkis and the customer, anticipating another swoon, came off their stools and readied themselves for the fall, but this time Hagop held his seat. His would-be rescuers heaved a sigh of relief. "Are you all right?" asked Ellie, nervously. Hagop's nod allayed the girl's concerns. The two fell silent, shyly avoiding each other's eyes. Their awkwardness made for a fragile, even intimate, moment as if in the preceding scene, each had bared a secret part of himself, a part never to be reclaimed and now entrusted to the other for safekeeping.

"Don't you want to eat your pancakes?" asked Ellie. "They'll get cold." The boy shook his head without as much as a glance at his plate.

The customer was observing this scene with a sardonic eye. "See what falling in love can do to you? Loss of appetite, staring sickness, fainting spells, and who knows what else? Next thing you know a man has a leash around his neck and is being led around like a puppy dog."

The waitress waved off the contention. "No woman ever led a man around on a leash unless he wanted to be led around on a leash."

"Now what man in his right mind would want that?" said the customer sitting up in his seat.

The waitress curled her tongue in her cheek and studied the customer with an appraiser's eye. "Do you know what the trouble with men is?" she finally said. Her glance shifted to Sarkis, then back again. "I'll tell you what the trouble with men is. Oatmeal! That's what the trouble with men is."

The customer screwed up his face. "Now what in God's name is that supposed to mean?"

"Oatmeal!" repeated the waitress. "That's what it means. Too much of their mother's oatmeal."

"There she goes making cracks about my mother again." The customer bounced up from his seat and again wagged a finger of rebuke at the waitress. "I'm warning you, miss—you're asking for trouble."

"Oh, sit down and drink your coffee," said the waitress, and with a flick of the wrist, as if brushing off a fly, motioned the customer back to his seat.

Meanwhile Hagop and Ellie were fumbling for words, each sensing their time together was drawing to a close. At length, Ellie dimmed her eyelids and said demurely, "Well, I guess I should be getting back to work now." The boy's face sagged with disappointment. Ellie lowered her head under his downcast eyes. "Will you come back and see me soon?"

Hagop nodded obsequiously.

The customer flashed a look to the others. "Did you see that? Did you see how he gave in without a struggle? That's how women get to you. They say something sugary sweet like, 'Will you come back and see me soon?' or, 'Gee, I had a wonderful time tonight. I hope we can do it again.' And the men melt like butter. My wife was the same way. Do you know what she said to me at the end of our first date? She looked at me with those innocent, baby blue eyes and said, 'Be careful driving home. The roads are a little wet tonight.' And that was that. I was done. Life as I knew it was over. Don't ask me how they do it, but women have a way of getting their hooks into you with just a dewy-eyed look or a sugar-coated word." The customer shook his head in befuddlement. "You know something? I don't even think it was raining that night she told me to be careful driving home."

"Oatmeal," said the waitress.

The customer slapped his knees in exasperation. "I don't understand this woman. I'm talking about one thing, and she's talking about oatmeal."

Meanwhile, Hagop was saying to Ellie, "You could visit us, too, whenever you want. Sarkis and I work on the merry-go-round. It's not far from here. I forget where."

"Ocean Grove," said Sarkis.

"And do you know what?" continued the boy. "The merry-go-round goes backward."

"Backward?"

"That's right. There's no other merry-go-round like it in the world."

"This is one merry-go-round I've got to see. I'll come and visit you soon."

"Can you come tonight?"

Ellie balked. "I'd love to, I really would, but I can't tonight. You see, I have to meet somebody. I promised already."

Hagop was crestfallen.

"Ellie can come another time," said Sarkis. "We can't ask her to change her plans, can we?"

"I'll come and see you soon, I promise." She fumbled for more words, but faltered. "But I really should be getting back to work now." Hagop's eyes remained downcast and his chin tucked glumly to his chest. Ellie tried to perk him up by mimicking his pout, but the boy kept sulking. The girl stepped back from the counter and looked to the others apologetically.

"I'm afraid I wasn't much help."

"Oh, no," said Sarkis, "you did a beautiful job. You worked wonders with him."

"I really will try to come and see him," said Ellie. "He's just about the sweetest kid I ever met." She waited for any further instructions. "If there's ever anything I can do ..." She let the words trail off.

"I don't see there's anything more to be done right now," said the waitress. "Thanks so much, Ellie. You've been a great help." And with a nod she gave the girl leave to return to her station. "Nice young lady," said Sarkis, setting his plate aside and turning his attention to the boy. "Hagop, how do you feel?" The boy shrugged apathetically. "How about a breath of fresh air? I think we both could use one about now."

"I guess so," said Hagop, then as an afterthought, "Can we come back again soon?"

"Of course. We can come back whenever you want."

"And I'll tell you what," said the waitress, leaning on the counter. "Next time you come, you can have a free order of pancakes because you didn't eat yours today." Hagop seemed oblivious to the waitress's offer, food obviously nowhere in his thoughts at present. He came off the stool and waited for Sarkis to pay the bill.

The customer leaned aside toward the boy. "Take care of yourself, young fella." With a wag of his index finger he motioned for Hagop to come closer and into his confidence. "And where women are concerned, take my advice. Show them who's boss right from the start. Remember this—once you give in to a woman, you can never make up the ground you lose. So if you have to beat your chest like a gorilla to get your way, you go ahead and beat your chest like a gorilla. Believe me, in the end, they'll respect you for it."

The waitress was flabbergasted by this discourse. "What kind of craziness are you putting into this child's head? He's only a baby, and you're trying to turn him into an animal."

"I'm just telling him the facts of life, that's all. A man is never too young to learn the facts of life."

"Facts of life? You wouldn't know the facts of life if you fell over them." The waitress leaned over the counter again and clasped the boy's hand in both of hers. "Don't even listen to him, hon. He's only running off at the mouth because he has nothing better to do with his time. Whenever you have a problem, you come back here and we'll take care of you." The waitress gave the customer a scathing stare by way of daring him to say another word.

"I'm sure the boy knows he has two good friends here whenever he needs them," said Sarkis in a conciliatory tone. "We appreciate your concern." He held out his hand for the boy to take. "Ready, Hagop?"

An exchange of goodbyes and well wishes followed, whereupon, Sarkis and Hagop headed toward the door. One last goodbye was in order as they looked back to the others. Ellie waved from the griddle, her spatula hoisted high in hand. The waitress and the customer waved as well, the customer topping off his wave with a broad wink and a flip hand salute.

In the wake of this eventful Monday morning, the restaurant settled down to a leisurely, business-as-usual routine. The customer resumed the reading of his newspaper, while the waitress busied herself soaking cups and glassware in a tubful of soapy water. Presently, the customer nudged his empty mug toward the waitress. "Another cup of coffee," he said without looking up from his newspaper.

"Any particular brand?" quipped the waitress. "Sanka? Maxwell House? Chock Full O' Nuts?"

"Oh, funny, very funny. Just pour the coffee please. Black, no sugar. Wife thinks I may be developing early signs of diabetes." The customer cast a weary, beleaguered sigh. "I'm telling you, there's no end to a man's troubles."

EVERYTHING BEAUTIFUL HAS A LITTLE LONELINESS IN IT

The fresh air did little to relieve Hagop's mood, which could be described as a mixture of tenderness, melancholy, and a sense of detachment from his surroundings. In the extreme, such a mood subjects its host to a kind of sweet anguish, to an almost painful sensitivity. One becomes susceptible to the most acute feelings should the occasion arise. Or is much of an occasion needed—a billowing cloud above the horizon, a child picking shells on the beach. Indeed, any event that calls attention to the singularity of its existence is apt to have an effect out of all proportion to the event itself. In the extreme, Hagop's mood was that of the great poets whose sensibilities are so attuned that life becomes for them a series of revelations, each one filled with a surfeit of joy, sadness, and sympathy—sometimes all of them at once. For such people the most commonplace occurrence is invested with the extraordinary. For them, the richness of life may be experienced in a lover's smile, a leaf fluttering to the ground, a bird warbling in a still wood.

"Do you think she'll come to the merry-go-round?" asked Hagop as he and Sarkis sauntered along the boardwalk.

"I know she wants to," said Sarkis. "She can't tonight, but one night soon ... I think there's a good chance she will." After a prolonged silence, during which Hagop seemed miles away, Sarkis made the only sensible suggestion he could think of. "Hagop, I think you should be alone for a while."

"Why?"

"You'll want to think about Ellie and remember your talk with her. Sometimes you'll remember it one way, sometimes another. You'll never be sure what everything means, but you should be alone when all these thoughts come to you."

"Where should I go?"

"Anywhere. Just take a walk."

"The only walks I ever took were around the block or going to the schoolyard."

"This could be an important walk for you, then."

"Will I be hungry afterwards?"

"Probably not."

"I don't think I'll ever be hungry again."

"You will. I promise you."

When they came to a ramp leading off the boardwalk to the local streets, Sarkis stopped. Hagop knew the time for his walk had come. The boy had mixed feelings about the venture yet he also recognized an obligation to undertake it.

"I guess I should start my walk now, huh?"

"Do you know the way back home?"

"I remember the house. I won't get lost."

"If you do get lost, just go to Ellie's restaurant and wait for me there."

"When should I come back?"

"Whenever you finish your walk."

"You mean I don't have to be back at a certain time?"

"I can't tell you when to come back. It's your walk."

"That's right; it is."

"No clocks to worry about except the clock inside. You'll know when to come home."

"I guess so."

"See you later, then?"

"Uh-huh," muttered the boy, and he watched Sarkis depart down the ramp and to the street.

In the quiet of the morning Hagop began his walking and his being alone and his thinking of Ellie the pancake girl. The boardwalk and the beach were sparsely inhabited at this hour, it being early in the morning, and a Monday morning at that. The weekend visitors had gone home. Most shops and concession stands were still closed, so the beachfront had the feeling of an isolated landscape, even though an occasional bather appeared on the beach or a passerby on the boardwalk. Somehow the presence of a few scattered people made the beachfront feel more desolate than if there had been no people at all, and Hagop wondered why that should be true. As he sauntered past the concession stands and viewed the displays behind the barred windows, Hagop's thoughts turned to cotton candy, frozen custard, popcorn, and orange drinks, but also to Ellie and their talk together and how she had kissed him on the forehead. And remembering that kiss, he smiled—then frowned, remembering, too, how she was a cheerleader and went to games and danced in front of people, and how being a cheerleader meant that she probably had a lot of friends. Hagop wondered if Ellie would ever kiss him if she were with her friends or would she ignore him or just say hello and act polite? That would be worse than ignoring him. Above all, Hagop thought how nice today would be if Ellie were taking this walk with him and they were looking at the beach and into shop windows together. He imagined all the things they would talk about and what a wonderful walk they could be having if she were here. But she wasn't. She was working, and who knew if they would ever take a walk together.

Part of Hagop's walking and being alone engendered a feeling of loneliness that he had never known before. He disliked this feeling. What was the good of it if you wanted somebody with you? On the other hand, he thought, feeling lonely was not so bad. He could do the kind of thinking that a person could only do when he was by himself. Hagop thought about how Ellie liked school and he didn't, and he was sad that Ellie should have a different opinion from his about anything. Ellie was almost twice as old as he was and maybe when he reached Ellie's age he would like school, too, but he doubted if he ever would.

As he passed people on the boardwalk Hagop noticed children his age with their parents. Today he felt much older than children his age. Today he felt as old as if he had lived before, maybe more than once—over and over—and all his lives added up to how old he felt today. And Hagop wondered if other people ever felt the same way or if they only felt the age they were.

Part of Hagop's walking and being alone was to feel the sun

on his face and to hear the ocean and to see the waves breaking across the sand. Sometimes he followed a wave from the time it was a bulge in the water until it rose, curled, crashed, and then swarmed over the sand and receded out to sea. The monotonous sound and formation of the waves made Hagop feel that everything in the world was a little lonely like himself today, even though he had never thought of the ocean as being lonely. Maybe it was from always doing the same thing over and over again. Hagop had always thought of the ocean as fun, but today, so many of his feelings were new that nothing was the way it used to be. Today the ocean was something lonely. But the ocean was beautiful, too, and Hagop thought maybe everything lonely was beautiful or everything beautiful was lonely. He didn't know which came first, but he knew the two feelings belonged together somehow. He had the same feeling about the beach, the sky, and the boardwalk, and the people he saw, and himself as well. These feelings were all converging in a beautiful, sad, and mixed up way. He felt that way about Ellie, too, because Ellie was included in everything Hagop thought about, whether she was the subject on his mind or not. Hagop knew Ellie was the reason he had these new feelings. He knew Ellie was the reason he would never be the same again, and the thought of never being the same again scared him a little. For as long as he could remember he had always been the way he was. He did not know what to do with these new feelings. Not being hungry scared him a little, too, and he wondered how long he would go without feeling hungry. Suppose he went the rest of his life without eating again? His parents would be furious and spank the daylights out of him, but then he realized his parents would first have to find a way to keep him alive before they could spank the daylights out of him. The prospect of never eating again made him feel sad, so he didn't think about anything for a while.

Walking along the boardwalk, Hagop felt the sun and the breeze on his face, and he watched the ocean and the sky. Sometimes while his mind was resting from his many thoughts he felt he *was* the sun and the breeze and the ocean and the sky, not Hagop or Jack or somebody with a name, but an inseparable part of the air and the light that surrounded him.

Part of Hagop's walking and being alone was to walk the length of the boardwalk to where the beach ended and a white restaurant stood on stilts in the sand. Around and underneath the restaurant sea gulls were pecking at garbage and Hagop stopped to watch the scavenger birds foraging for food. They were like visitors from another world, and Hagop watched them like someone spying on the movements of alien creatures. At the same time he recognized that their world was as real to them as his world was to him, and this recognition was both revelatory and natural. After watching the birds nourish themselves he began his walk back. On the way he made a study of the boardwalk planks under his feet and the splinters on the boards and the gaps between the boards, and he separated in his mind the older boards from the newer ones, and he imagined things buried under the boardwalk like treasures and forgotten items that people left there. He thought about being a beachcomber and surviving on whatever money he could find in the sand, and selling key chains and combs that people left in the sand, and at night sleeping under the boardwalk where he would be sheltered from the summer rains, even though the cracks in the boardwalk would let some of the rain through. Looking out to sea he saw boats anchored in the ocean. He wondered what kind of people were on the boats and whether or not they lived there, and if he had a boat how far would he have to go to reach the other side of the ocean. He wondered what people were doing right now in lands across the sea while he was here in Asbury Park walking and being alone.

In the distance Hagop saw a man fishing off a reef. The boy climbed over the rail guard and jumped down to the sand and trudged to the water's edge, where he watched the man casting his line and waiting for the fish to bite. Hagop considered talking to the man but changed his mind because at least for today, talking to people did not seem like an important thing to do. Instead he continued his walk along the water's edge, where he found a snail shell. He picked up the shell and studied its endless curves, which were difficult to follow but which always seemed to know where they were going without ever making a mistake, and he remembered yesterday when he and Sarkis stood by the water's edge. He thought how maybe years and years ago when the world was young somebody picked up this shell and how years and years from now when the world was old somebody would pick up the shell again. Hagop studied the shell from all sides and smelled the ocean on it, and he held it to his ear and listened to a mysterious hum inside. Then he threw the shell as far as he could into the ocean because he knew the shell did not belong to him. Heavy-legged in the sand, he crossed the width of the beach now and hoisted himself over the rail guard and onto the boardwalk, where he continued his walk.

At no time during Hagop's walking and being alone did he feel he had to go home, and this feeling of having all the time in the world was one of the best parts of his walk. Thanks to Sarkis, the boy did not have to think about clocks except for the clock inside, which he didn't know much about and wasn't sure existed—even though Hagop tried to believe everything Sarkis told him. Hagop was glad he didn't have to think about being anywhere but where he was. Sometimes he felt he could continue his walk forever, but as the morning grew later and the sun rose higher and more people began appearing on the beach and on the boardwalk, Hagop knew that his walk was coming to an end. He was not saddened the way people often are when they leave a place they have enjoyed being. This departure would be different because Hagop did not feel he was leaving anything behind, but that he was taking something with him. Hagop also knew that he could return to the beach whenever he wanted and that each time he came back his walk would be different and maybe even better than the time before. When Hagop left the beach he did so with a feeling of having become acquainted with something that would always be with him, and this feeling, amid the many sad, funny, and confused feelings he had, was also part of Hagop's walking and being alone.

Back in Mrs. Lilly's basement room, Sarkis was reclining on his cot with his eyes closed and his hands clasped behind his head. He heard Hagop enter the basement by way of the backyard door, but never bothered to open his eyes—as if the boy's arrival had been expected at precisely this moment.

"How was your walk?"

"Okay," said Hagop, taking a seat on the bed. For the present, he did not know how to describe his walk, with all its discoveries and special thoughts about Ellie. "What did you do?"

"I went to the store and bought us some things we needed, like toothpaste and toothbrushes. Then I came back here and took myself a nap." Sarkis finally opened his eyes. "But tell me more about your walk. Where did you go?"

"Up and down the boardwalk. And on the beach, too."

"Do you remember anything special?"

"Not too much right now."

"Nothing at all?"

"No, I remember some of it."

"Like what?"

"Everything beautiful has a little loneliness in it."

Sarkis gently closed his eyes like a silent affirmation, then re-opened them. "I'd say you had a good walk."

"I'm still not hungry."

"Don't worry about it."

Hagop flopped across the bed and hugged his pillow. "Can we go to the merry-go-round early today?" he asked.

"I don't see why not," said Sarkis. "Why don't you wash up and we'll go."

The boy withdrew to the bathroom and commenced washing. While water ran from the tap, he suddenly appeared at the door, his face brimming with excitement. Water was dripping off his cheeks and chin.

"Sarkis, it was the best walk I ever had!"

Slowly a smile came over Sarkis's face. The eyes crinkled and the cheeks swelled until there was no room on his face for anything but the smile. "It surely must have been," he said. "It surely must have been."

"I didn't know how to tell you before."

Hagop returned to the bathroom to finish washing. Meanwhile Sarkis, remaining on the cot, removed his hands from behind his head and placed them upon his chest. He interlaced his fingers as in a prayerful repose. He never stopped smiling.

LIFE, LIBERTY AND THE PURSUIT OF INNOCENCE

Mondays are idle days in an amusement park. Weekend visitors have returned to the city, while those vacationing longer have migrated to the beach for the day. In the evening the park livens up with customers, but during the day the grounds are like a vacated playpen. Mondays are also maintenance days in an amusement park. At a merry-go-round, the animals are wiped clean, the brass poles polished, the controls checked and oiled, and the burnt-out lights replaced around the hem of the carousel's canopy and along the eaves outside the pavilion. Today then, Sarkis, Hagop, and Mumfred tended to these and other chores, all of which were completed by early afternoon, whereupon Mumfred, for want of anything to do and with the boredom of the day weighing upon him, said he'd be getting a bite to eat and would return in due course.

"Don't rush," said Sarkis. "We'll take care of everything while you're gone."

"There won't be much happening today," said Mumfred. "Monday is always a slow day."

By way of passing the time on this Monday afternoon, Sarkis and Hagop rode the merry-go-round, thus showcasing its most distinctive feature, an inexplicable insistence on going the opposite way. Soon a visitor appeared at the door. He was a soldier, a tall, gangly youth of 20 or 21 years of age. The youth was looking the worse for wear, partly because of an immoderate consumption of alcohol that day and partly because of the ungainly look of his class A uniform. The pants hung a size too small on his lanky frame and lacked anything resembling a crease. His shirt was unbuttoned at the collar and his garrison cap tilted over one ear in an exaggeration of that rakish angle worn by World War II combat veterans.

After pausing a moment to focus on his immediate surroundings, the soldier came forward at a slightly oblique angle, as if each step were a challenge to his equilibrium. Upon seeing Sarkis and Hagop galloping backward, he stopped short, blinked in puzzlement and cast a befuddled look around him as if he had stumbled through the wrong end of a revolving door. He attempted to gain his bearings by standing straighter, but the rigor of assuming an erect posture lay beyond his capabilities at the present. "Something fishy going on here," he mumbled. He ventured forward again, but when the animals passed in reverse, he backed off. "Maybe I should go out and come in again." He backtracked toward the door now, but when turning to leave, made a full circle and missed the exit.

"Come in," called Sarkis. "You were going the right way before."

"Okay, if you say so." The soldier looked to the door and then to the merry-go-round as if to establish, beyond a shadow of a doubt, his physical existence somewhere between the two points. Then he took his garrison cap and reversed it on his head, a maneuver that immediately seemed to rectify any directional problems he was having. With a cocky smile now, he proceeded toward the merry-go-round, his legs still wobbly but his confidence immeasurably bolstered. "Simple adjustment needed, that's all."

Sarkis, seeing that the soldier was none too steady on his feet, brought the ride to a halt and came to the young man's side. "Are you all right?"

"Absolutely. Situation under control."

Sarkis introduced himself and the boy to the soldier. The serviceman reciprocated, barely keeping his balance in the process. "Pfc. Orville T. Briggs," he said, with a less than snappy salute. "U.S. 51407571, E Company 10th Engineers, Fort Monmouth, New Jersey."

"You looked confused when you came in. Are you sure you're

all right?"

"No confusion," said Orville. He burped. "I see you can't get your merry-go-round straightened out."

"I suppose it does look funny, but it's doing just fine."

"Even so, it's my duty to tell you that you may be in violation of regulations here. I just don't know which ones yet." Orville puckered his lips pensively. "Unless, of course, the merry-go-round is going forward, and everything else is going backward."

"I hadn't thought of that."

"In which case, when I came in the front door, I was really going out the back door. Or—not to put too fine a point on it— when I woke up this morning, I was three sheets to the wind, but after drinking all day, I'm starting to sober up. Am I on the right track?" Sarkis appeared none too sure, but Orville looked smugly pleased with his own analysis. "I knew there had to be a logical explanation." The soldier hiccupped as if to punctuate his exegesis.

"Where you from, soldier?" asked Sarkis.

"Akron, Ohio—rubber capital of the United States. I'm on a merit pass today because my work detail had the cleanest lavatory in the battalion." He leaned closer to Sarkis. "Do you know what my job was? I had to polish all the spigots and the shower drains until you could see your face in them."

"I'd say you deserved a merit pass after that."

"I'll tell you something else. The colonel who inspected this morning said we did such an outstanding job he wants the Inspector General to see the lavatory tomorrow. Do you know what that means? That means no one can use the lavatory until after the Inspector General sees it tomorrow." Orville cozied up to Sarkis's ear. "Do you know what would happen if anyone tried to use the lavatory before the Inspector General arrived?" Sarkis shook his head. "He'd be slapped with an Article 15 and made to get on his hands and knees and scrub the whole lavatory clean with a toothbrush."

"He would?" squeaked Sarkis.

"Shh, keep it down." Orville looked furtively about as if the walls might have ears. "I'll tell you something else," he said. "Now this is strictly confidential between you and me." He huddled closer and said in a hushed voice, "Everybody in the Army is crazy!"

"Crazy?"

"Shh. Crazy as a loon. You see, everybody has to be crazy or else nothing gets done. Now you and I know that anybody who gets up at 4 o'clock in the morning to polish spigots and drains is missing a few screws in his tool chest. But the Army trains you that way. If they can make everybody crazy, then everybody will do what he's supposed do, get it? I mean one normal guy can mess up everything. That's why I have to be careful how I think in the Army. I can't afford to have any normal thoughts. Take this morning, for example. While I was polishing one of the shower drains, I began thinking how crazy it was to be on my hands and knees doing this at 4 o'clock in the morning. I got scared because I was having a normal thought. I had to tell myself—quit thinking like that, Orville. Remember, crazy is normal and normal is crazy. Don't start turning things right side up. It wasn't easy, but I'm all right now. You see, when I got my merit pass today, I decided to go on a little binge because if I got drunk I'd start acting crazy again and get myself back to normal, if you know what I mean. So that's what I did, and here I am."

Sarkis scratched his head. "Orville, I'm not sure I understand what you just said, but you sound like a man thinking backward but in the right direction."

Orville eyed the merry-go-round with a newfound respect. "Oh, I'm starting to get the picture. Interesting toy you have there."

"We think it's a symbol, but we're not sure of what."

"There's no question it's making a statement," said Orville. He pulled out his wallet and after making a myopic inspection of his funds, handed Sarkis several bills. "I'll take eight rides."

"Eight rides?"

"Why not?" Orville teetered. "I don't have any place to go and my pass is good until midnight. God knows I don't need another drink."

"Well, then, welcome aboard, young man."

Orville now joined the others on the merry-go-round, the soldier's choice of carrier, a burnt orange stallion with one foreleg raised in a high-stepping canter. After mounting with some difficulty, he took hold of the reins and assumed the erect, imperious posture of those statues of military heroes found in public parks. The impersonation, however, fell short of the mark once the ride got underway. What with his hat cocked backward and his direction reversed, Orville looked less the military gallant than a survivor beating a hasty retreat from a frontal attack.

As the three passengers sailed along on their rhythmic, undulating course, a second visitor appeared at the door, a boy of no more than six or seven years of age. He was a serious looking child, to the extent of a furrowed brow and a glum, intensely inquisitive face. He was dressed in shorts, sneakers, and a T-shirt illustrated with the tawny head of a Bengal tiger. Standing at the entrance, he gazed intently at the merry-go-round, and then, bent on taking a closer look, approached the circling animals. Only then did Sarkis notice this latest arrival, and notice too that no adults accompanied him. When no one followed the boy into the pavilion, Sarkis again brought the ride to a halt and came to the boy's side.

"Anything the matter?"

"I'm lost," said the boy, matter-of-factly.

"Lost?"

"I can't find my mommy and daddy."

"Do you remember where you lost them?"

"No."

"Do you know where we could look for them?"

"No."

"Were you all together in the amusement park?"

"We were in a store."

"What kind of store?"

"A store for clothes."

"Near here?"

"I don't know."

"I see," mulled Sarkis, who decided he wasn't much good at knowing what to do with a six- or seven-year-old boy who had misplaced his parents. "What's your name?"

"Jared."

Sarkis scratched his chin. "What do you think we should do, Jared?"

"I don't know."

"Would you like me to go with you so we can look for your mommy and daddy together?"

"They always find me."

"Oh, you've lost them before?"

"Sometimes."

"Do they tell you what to do when you lose them?"

"They tell me to call home."

"Is anybody home now?"

"No, they're looking for me."

"I see." Sarkis pondered further. "Do you think they'll find you here if you wait for them?"

"I suppose."

"Would you like to stay awhile?"

"Okay."

Sarkis had noticed how the boy's attention kept shifting toward the merry-go-round as they talked. "You like the merry-go-round?" The boy's shrug amounted to saying yes without his wishing to appear overeager. "Want to take a ride?"

"Okay."

"What kind of animal do you want to ride?"

The boy looked over the offerings and headed straight for the golden unicorn, posed on its hind legs with its horn protruding from the head. "Excellent choice," said Sarkis, who saw to it that the boy was properly mounted and secured. "Standby, everyone," he added en route to the control booth. "We're ready to roll." And so it was that the child, Jared, joined the others on the merry-go-round.

In the absence of any other visitors, the four passengers rode for uninterrupted hours into the late afternoon. As the light of day shifted and shadows edged across the floor, none on board noticed the man and the woman standing at the door and surveying the premises. The woman, wearing white cotton slacks and gold sling backs, looked distraught, so much so that she looked right past her son on the merry-go-round. By contrast the man, a lean, bespectacled figure with a prominent shock of gray hair at the temples, affected a more controlled, not to say austere, demeanor. He bore himself erectly, armed, it seemed, with the kind of rectitude that stood ready to do battle at the first sign of opposition. Once spotting Jared, he started toward the merry-go-round pointing his finger in the direction of the boy.

"All right, son, let's get down from there and let's make it snappy."

The mother, alerted to her son's presence, hurried to the apron of the merry-go-round. She gasped in relief. "Jared, thank God you're safe! We've been going out of our minds the last two hours looking for you."

Jared passed in front of his parents, but gave no sign of acknowledging their presence. "Jared Klinger!" barked the father. "Did you hear me? I said get down from there. I've taken about all the nonsense I'm going to take from you for one day."

"I thought we had really lost him this time," said the mother.

"What he needs is a paddling he'll never forget," said Mr. Klinger. "He's run away for the last time. I'll see to that."

"He doesn't run away," objected the mother. "The boy wanders off because he's adventurous, that's all. He can't help it."

"Adventurous?" Mr. Klinger gave a dry, facetious laugh. "You certainly have a flair for the euphemistic, Elaine. I suppose he was just being adventurous when he stole away on that train to Coney Island this winter, and the police found him wandering on the beach. Or when he and the dog hid in a junkyard until the night watchman found them scrunched up in a tractor tire? These, I suppose, are innocent little adventures to you."

Sarkis said in passing, "The boy told us he was lost. I don't think he was running away."

Mr. Klinger gave Sarkis an insinuating look. "If you don't mind, I'm fully prepared to handle this without your assistance." He turned again to his wife. "Anyone who makes a career out of getting lost the way he does needs either a jailor or a psychiatric counselor to look after him."

"Harold!" said the mother indignantly. "I won't have you talking about our son as if he were abnormal."

"I wouldn't call disappearing from his parents every chance he gets normal behavior, would you?"

Sarkis loped by again and said, "He tried to remember where he lost you, but he couldn't."

Mr. Klinger, annoyed by this second, unsolicited interruption, gave Sarkis an even more acidulous look than before.

"Are you in charge here?" he said, raising his voice to be heard above the music.

"Just until the owner returns."

"Well, if you don't mind, I'd like my son off that damned ride right now. Do you understand me? Let's be quick about it." No sooner had Mr. Klinger issued his order when he realized the direction in which the merry-go-round was going. He gave a confounded start. "What in the name ... Why the blasted thing ... What's going on here, anyway?"

"What's the matter now?" said his wife wearily.

"Look for yourself. The damn thing is in reverse." Mr. Klinger addressed Sarkis in an affronted tone, "What's the meaning of this?"

"That's what we've been trying to find out," said Sarkis as he passed by.

Mr. Klinger watched the motion of the animals as if the sight were offensive to his sensibilities. "Is this somebody's idea of a joke or some cheap publicity stunt?"

"No, nothing like that. It just happened. The merry-go-round was broken and we fixed it as best we could."

"Fixed it? This is what you called fixed?" Mr. Klinger scowled. "May I ask by whose authority you are running this cockamamie ride in the wrong direction?"

Sarkis looked stumped. "I wasn't aware we needed any."

"Really! How convenient for you. And how do you know you're not violating a local ordinance or licensing regulation, not to mention standards of public safety here?"

Sarkis was feeling the pinch of questions that didn't invite answers so much as stifle them. "We haven't had the first problem so far," he said.

"That's not the point!" bristled Mr. Klinger.

"Harold," pleaded the woman on the verge of tears, "what difference does it make which way the merry-go-round is going? Let's take our son and go."

"Hold it right there, Elaine. It happens to make a difference to people with a grain of sense left in their heads. This ride was designed to go forward, in the direction the animals are facing. It is presently going backward, in the direction their hind parts are facing. *That,* it seems to me, is a matter of elementary logic. I would hope so simple a point would not be lost on you."

Sarkis interjected as he sailed by, "The owner said the ride has never performed better."

Mr. Klinger railed, "I wouldn't care if the blasted thing did pirouettes in space. It happens to be going the wrong way! Now I want my son off that machine and I want him off it now. I won't be telling you again."

Spurred by Mr. Klinger's directive, Sarkis brought the merry-go-round to a halt and ushered all passengers off the platform. With the boy Jared's first step onto solid ground, his mother smothered him with a hug and kisses.

"Oh, darling!" she sobbed. "Your mother had a fit worrying about you, an absolute fit." The boy allowed himself to be held but never reciprocated with a hug or even tentative touch.

"Step aside," said Mr. Klinger, moving in front of his wife. "Don't baby him, for god's sake. The boy's got to learn to answer for his actions." Mr. Klinger folded his arms like a one-man tribunal and stared his son straight in the eye. "Well, Jared, what do you have to say for yourself?"

Jared looked blankly at his father, as did Sarkis, Hagop, and Orville, who had come to the boy's side in a timorous show of support.

"Mr. Klinger," interceded Sarkis, "has the boy really done anything to warrant ..."

"The boy can speak for himself," said Mr. Klinger irately. "You don't seem to understand that your advice is not wanted in this matter."

"Do we have to discuss this here?" entreated the woman. "Can't we just take the boy and go?"

"No, we cannot!" insisted Mr. Klinger. "And yes, we have to discuss this here and now. I'm not going to let the boy think he can just walk away from his acts without immediate reprisals." He faced his son again. "Well, Jared, I'm waiting for an answer. What do you have to say for yourself?"

"I don't know."

"That's not an answer. That's an evasion of an answer."

Jared glanced to the others for assistance, but received only meek looks in return. "I don't know," repeated the boy.

"You don't know what?" pressed Mr. Klinger. Then, addressing his wife: "And you mean to tell me there's nothing wrong with this boy? On top of everything else we may be dealing with some kind of cognitive deficiency here."

"My son is not deficient, handicapped, or anything of the kind!" snapped the woman. "Now that's enough! I won't listen to this kind of talk again."

Orville, having strayed to the fringes of the group, raised his head as if addressing an invisible magistrate on high. "Your Honor, this boy is entitled to a fair trial. Under the Articles of War, section 142 ..."

"What in the world is that bubble head babbling about?" said Mr. Klinger. The father shook his head and resumed the interrogation of his son. "What I want to know, Jared, is why you repeatedly disobey your mother and me when we tell you not to leave our sight? I want to know what goes on in that head of yours when you disappear from us every chance you get."

"Nobody knows that," piped Hagop before he could stop himself. The words immediately drew the reproachful eye of Mr. Klinger. The boy retreated to the protective custody of Sarkis's side. "Nobody knows what goes on in somebody else's head."

"Young man," said Mr. Klinger, straining to curb his annoyance with these repeated interruptions. "If and when your opinion is wanted, I shall ask for it. Until then, I'd like my son to speak for himself."

Orville, still meandering outside the group, had resumed tinkering with his garrison cap, eyeballing it at arm's length, then trying it on frontward, backward, and every which way.

"Rocks, shapes, colors, and stories," he said.

"Would someone please tell me what he's talking about?" said Mr. Klinger, eyeing the soldier incredulously.

"Things that used to go on in my head when I was a boy," said Orville.

Mr. Klinger kept staring at the soldier as he would an alien species that had just alighted on the planet. "God help us," Klinger said. "If that's a soldier, God help us if we ever have to ship that off somewhere to defend our country."

"Daddy," said Jared, "I saw the house and Josh."

"The house? The dog? What are you talking about?"

"On the merry-go-round. I was flying on top of the clouds and I could see everything."

"Is that so?" said Mr. Klinger with mock indulgence. "And then, I suppose, you floated down to earth in your little parachute?"

"For heaven's sake," said the woman, "the boy was only

having a playful fantasy."

"Some might call it a full-blown delusion."

"Oh, I can't stand this anymore!" cried the woman through tears welling up in her eyes. "Please! May we take the boy and go! I want to go right now."

"All right, all right," grumbled Mr. Klinger. "It's obvious we can't get anything done in this setting."

Jared jumped up and down. "Can I ride on the merry-go-round again?"

"You're not going near that contraption," growled Mr. Klinger. "I'll deal with you when we get back to the hotel." Mr. Klinger turned to Sarkis. "And as for you, you haven't heard the last from me either. Oh, I've seen your kind before, mister— overgrown adolescents who look at life as a kind of joyride, free of responsibilities. No cares, no worries, isn't that right? Nothing pleases you more than thumbing your nose at respectable society. Well, I've got news for you, mister. I don't intend to stand by and watch you behaving like some middle-aged delinquent. I'm warning you, I'm a man of action. When my civic conscience is aroused, I do something about it." With that, he took his son by the hand and started pulling him away. The boy resisted by planting his heels on the ground and letting himself be dragged.

"Where are we going?" the boy whimpered.

"To put a ball and chain around your feet, if that's what it takes to keep you from running away."

"Daddy's only joking," said the woman. "We promised to take you on more rides and we will."

"Over my dead body," declared Mr. Klinger.

"We promised, and we'll keep our promise," insisted the woman, with a sidelong, incriminating glance at her husband.

While Mr. Klinger kept yanking Jared toward the door, Mrs. Klinger made no move to leave yet. For a perceptible moment she hesitated, as if being pulled in opposite directions. It was a curiously unguarded moment, one of those blips in the continuum when defenses fall away and the fragile recesses of the heart lay exposed. There, in the misty mirror of her eyes, lay traces of old wounds that had not healed, of choices made that could not be undone, of paths taken that had led to tangled, prickly crossings. She sped a rueful, apologetic glance toward Sarkis and the others as if to say that could she have stayed longer, she would have, and for reasons so cloudy, she herself did not understand them. "It's a beautiful merry-go-round," she said wistfully, then turned and followed her family out the door.

Toward evening, when Mumfred returned to work, the only visible change at the merry-go-round was the sight of Orville, slouched in the saddle of his burnt orange stallion and humming along to the music. As for Sarkis and Hagop, they passed most of the day in the cashier booth in the event any customers happened by. None did. This left Sarkis slouched in a chair, fending off recurrent bouts of drowsiness, and Hagop hunched over a pad of notebook paper, idly sketching figures of animals with long beards and floppy ears.

"Well, I see we have one customer anyway," said the owner, stopping outside the booth.

"That's Pfc. Orville T. Briggs," said Sarkis. "He's paid for eight rides, but to be honest, we're letting him have a few extras on the house."

Upon a closer look at the soldier's unkempt appearance, Mumfred frowned. "Are you sure he's all right? He looks a little frayed around the edges to me."

"He's a long way from home and feeling a little homesick, but otherwise, he's doing just fine."

Mumfred shrugged lackadaisically. "Well, I suppose, one customer is better than none. Like I say, Monday is a slow day. Nothing much ever happens on a Monday."

"SARKIS DOESN'T ANYTHING WORK RIGHT IN THIS PLACE?"

Dusk had settled over the amusement park when Sarkis and Hagop took a break from their duties at the merry-go-round and strolled alongside the lake. The twilight hour marked a transitional time between the beach-side outings of the day and the glitzy club entertainments of the evening. It was a time when people were finishing their dinners or taking leisurely constitutionals along the boardwalk. At the amusement park, all the rides had opened for business, though were only sparsely frequented, most of the activity being elsewhere. A few youngsters were carousing about, spending their allowances at the penny arcades, gaming parlors, or food stands. In the artificial lake, all shimmery with the reflection of fairy tale lights, a single paddle boat manned by a teenage couple glided across the water like a swan.

As Sarkis and Hagop crossed the promenade beside the lake, something caught the boy's eye. Stopping short, he tugged at Sarkis's arm and pointed to a solitary figure standing at the far side of the lake by the water's edge. "Sarkis, look. It's Ellie."

She was standing under a row of strung colored lights. Her head hung dolefully, and even her shoulder bag seemed to sag at her side. Upon seeing Sarkis and Hagop drawing nearer, she shied her head to one side so as not to expose her tear-stained eyes. As they approached, though, her resolve weakened and she burst out crying anew. "Ellie, what's the matter?" said Hagop, hurrying to her side.

Ellie shrugged as if doing so could shield her hurt, or else attribute it to some trifling irritant. "I was coming to see you both tonight," she said, "but I thought I'd wait awhile first."

"What's wrong?" asked Sarkis. "Is there anything we can do?" Ellie shook her head, discouraging any questions. There was an awkward pause, punctuated by tentative, self-conscious glances. Sarkis broke the silence. "We were taking a walk. Would you like to come along?"

Without a word, Ellie joined Sarkis and Hagop on their walk around the lake. Along the way she said little, other than to make a few halting, perfunctory remarks on the loveliness of the evening or her fondness for paddle boats, several of which now navigated around the lake. For the most part, though, they were silent, creating an awkward and uncertain mood. The three came full circle around the lake and to an impasse in the evening's agenda.

"Hagop," said Sarkis, "I have an idea! Let's not go back to work just yet. Let's spend a little time with Ellie—maybe show her around the amusement park."

"Won't Mumfred be mad if we don't go back?"

"I think Mumfred will understand." Sarkis paused. "But maybe you should go back and explain the situation to him."

"Situation?"

"Yes, tell him there's been an emergency. Tell him ... let's see ... tell him it's a matter of life and death, and if he needs us, we'll be somewhere in the amusement park having a good time."

"Sarkis, that doesn't make any sense."

"You'll know what to say, Hagop. You always know what to say. Anyway, business is slow right now and he won't mind."

"I'll do my best," said the boy, his brow knitted and his brain cells already churning over ways to best handle this assignment. "I'll be right back."

In the mellowing afterglow of day, Sarkis and Ellie repaired to a bench by the lake, under the necklace of lights that encircled the water. Neither spoke for a while, both still unsure of how to break the conversational ice. Clearly, though, Ellie was fighting back tears, and soon they began wending their way down her cheek again. She huddled closer to Sarkis, bringing her head into the crook of his shoulder. For the present she seemed to find a refuge there.

"The person you were supposed to meet tonight ..." Sarkis hesitated. "He didn't come?"

"You knew?"

"In a way. I guess I've been stood up enough times to know the look when I see it."

"I knew he wouldn't come ... I was just hoping ..." Ellie sniffled between words. "But in my heart I knew. He was nice. He was different from other boys I know. He didn't try to show off or act smart like so many of them do. He was just himself." She raised her head and looked Sarkis in the eye. "I guess he just stopped liking me, that's all. Can people's feelings just change that way? I don't understand. People's feelings shouldn't change, not true feelings, anyway."

Sarkis's eyes pled ignorance. His only response was to hold her securely around the shoulder and steady her faintly trembling body. For a time, the two gazed at the water, which reflected a shimmering tapestry of images from the surrounding rides and arcades. "Girls are lucky in one way, I think," said Sarkis. "They seem able to trust their feelings sooner than boys can. With boys, I don't know; there always seems to be confusion, a war going on inside between the boys they want to stay and the men they want to be. I don't know if that war ever ends, no matter how old we get." Sarkis tilted Ellie's face toward his and brushed aside a stray hair near her eye. "You see before you a perfect example."

"You're a man, you're a beautiful man."

Sarkis smiled wryly. "I can think of four or five people who at this very moment would sharply disagree with you."

"I don't care," said Ellie, who then cloistered herself into the protectiveness of Sarkis's shoulder again. But soon her feelings gave way to more uncontrollable tears and sobbing. Sarkis could feel the tense heaving of her body against his own. "Everything hurts," she said.

Sarkis anchored her with a firmer grip until her tensions eased. "Yes, for a while everything hurts," he said. He took her hand and turned it palm up. He scrutinized it like a fortune teller. With one finger he traced a crease from the heel of the hand to the joint of her index finger. "But things change," he said, intensifying his attention on the hand. "Hmm, what have we here? Most interesting indeed. Long lifeline. Much happiness—so much you won't know what to do with it all."

"Do you read palms?"

Sarkis gently closed her hand as if having given her something to hold. "This one I can."

Presently, in the distance, they saw Hagop coming off the promenade and running toward them. Upon his arrival the boy was panting and eager to deliver his message.

"Everything's okay," he said. "I just told Mumfred we had to help a friend, and he said we could take our time coming back."

"Good, let's get started," said Sarkis. He pulled out his wallet and counted his money. Then he checked the change in his pocket. "Our worldly possessions come to a grand total of $16.38. We'll spend every penny of that money no matter how long it takes."

"Where should we start?"

"Penny arcade," said Hagop.

"The penny arcade it is," said Sarkis. And off they went.

With the assured step of an adventurous team, the three companions strode toward the amusement center. Up ahead they could see the flashing lights of the arcade and hear the rattling sounds of the gaming tables and the gun shots from the shooting gallery. People had begun arriving at the park as marquees lit up everywhere and musical invitations rang out from the rides and entertainment concessions.

At the penny arcade Hagop and Ellie both won prizes. Ellie captured a souvenir bracelet by manipulating a mini forklift in a glass case filled with trinkets and baubles. To Hagop, though, went the spoils of the evening. After rolling championship scores on a Skee-Ball machine, he came away with a black and white panda bear almost as large as the boy himself. Leaving the arcade, he waddled forward, his arms so full of bear the boy was barely visible behind it. The smile on the bear's face—wide, dopey, imperturbable—was matched only by Hagop's supercilious grin when he showed off his prize to the others. "How do you like him?" asked Hagop.

"He's beautiful," said Ellie, breaking into a smile herself.

"Does he have a name yet?" asked Sarkis.

"Skeezix," said Hagop. "I knew his name was Skeezix as soon as I saw him."

"Skeezix. Why, he's a perfect Skeezix," said Ellie.

"We're off to a good start," said Sarkis. "Where to next?"

"Can we take a ride on the Ferris wheel?" asked Ellie.

"Say no more. We're on our way."

At the center of the amusement park stood the giant Ferris wheel, a formidable structure that loomed above every ride in the park as well as every edifice in the township just beyond. Once purchasing tickets at the booth, the three companions handed them to the operator, an amiable lumberjack of a man who ushered his passengers to their compartment. The seating was snug, especially with Skeezix sitting as large as life on Hagop's lap. But no one seemed to mind. Awaiting lift-off, all were brimming with anticipation, like neophytes on the brink of a maiden voyage.

Soon the big wheel began moving. It slowly lifted Sarkis, Hagop, and Ellie to the apex of its arc, from where they overlooked the expanses of Asbury Park. Its snaking shoreline spread out before them like a vast diorama. The giant wheel dipped and rose again. This time at its apex the three friends pointed out familiar landmarks that when seen from this height took on a magical remoteness. There! See the merry-go-round house lit like a crown. And there! The penny arcade. And way out there! The anchored boats offshore. All these sights were viewed now from a kind of Olympian perspective.

The wheel came full circle again, paused at the top of its arch, tipped teasingly forward and back with a stomach-churning swoop before continuing its descent. Again it lifted our three companions to the heights, but this time it came to an unexpected stop. Sarkis, Hagop, and Ellie began looking below to see if they could determine what was causing the delay. Surely the ride could not have ended so soon; besides which, no passengers were getting off. The only clue to the holdup was a scene at the control station where the operator and two bystanders were studying the apparatus and pointing to various parts as if engaged in a mild difference of opinion. "Uh-oh," said Sarkis.

Hagop grew anxious. "Sarkis, don't say what I'm thinking."

"Uh-oh, what?" queried Ellie.

"I think we're stuck," said Sarkis.

"Oh, no!" moaned Ellie.

Hagop yelped, "I knew it, I knew it!" The boy began shaking

his head in hopeless exasperation. "Sarkis, doesn't anything work right in this place?"

"What'll we do now?" asked Ellie.

Sarkis again looked to the men studying the control apparatus. "Those men down there look like they know what they're doing. I'm sure they'll figure out what's wrong and fix it soon."

Just then, a belligerent shout boomed out from a compartment somewhere below them. "What's the matter with you people down there! Why isn't this contraption moving?"

Sarkis and Hagop turned to each other. "I know that voice," said the boy.

"I know it, too."

"You don't mean ... uh-oh."

"Jared's father."

"What's he doing on the Ferris wheel? He said he wouldn't go on any more rides."

"Maybe he changed his mind and wanted to do something nice for Jared."

"Not him. He wouldn't do anything nice for anybody."

"Don't be too hard on him," said Sarkis. "He's had a rough day and it's not getting any easier."

Onto the scene now strode the burly operator of the Ferris wheel to check on the stranded passengers. He conducted a surprisingly high-spirited, not to say inspiriting tour. Circling the wheel, he extended to each stranded party an encouraging word. He indulged questions, placated anxieties, boosted hopes, and assured all that everything was being done to get them down as quickly as possible. The last passengers to whom he spoke were those at the top of the wheel. He cupped his hands like a bullhorn.

"You people up there all right?" he shouted toward Sarkis.

"We're fine," said Sarkis. "What seems to be the trouble?"

"Probably a short circuit somewhere. We're not sure yet. We've called for the maintenance specialist and he's on his way." The operator pumped his fist in an exhortative, never-say-die gesture. "We'll get you out of this. Don't you worry about a thing." And on this uplifting note, he turned and headed back to the control station.

Ellie sighed. "Well, at least we know someone is coming to fix the Ferris wheel."

"They should have us going again soon," said Sarkis. "In the meantime we'll just have to make ourselves as comfortable as possible." With a collective sigh, they adjusted their bodies to the restricted space and resigned themselves to an indeterminate delay.

In what seemed the blinking of an eye, darkness fell over the New Jersey shore and the heavens were transformed into a canopy of light. The stars in their regalia shone like an imperial regency on high. Viewed from atop the Ferris wheel, they seemed close at hand as if clusters could be snatched by merely standing up and reaching out for them.

"I wonder how many stars are in the sky," said Hagop, transfixed by the limitless expanse of light.

"Trillions and trillions," said Ellie.

"More than the highest number in the world," added Sarkis.

"What's the highest number in the world?" asked Hagop.

"Nobody knows," said Sarkis. "If somebody knew, then the number wouldn't be the highest anymore."

"Why not?"

"Because you can always add one more to the highest number in the world and make it one higher."

"And that's how many stars are in the sky?" said Hagop. "Always one more than the highest number in the world?"

"As far as anyone knows," said Sarkis.

Ellie pondered aloud, "When you think about it—I mean how everything goes on and on forever—our lives become small and unimportant, don't they?"

"Or maybe," said Sarkis, "our lives become small and unimportant when we stop thinking how everything goes on and on forever."

An unearthly hush fell over the three, as if each could sense in the grandiloquent night a mystery beyond all knowing, a mystery so awesome that to contemplate it too long was to feel uneasy and even captive in its presence.

Hagop broke the silence when he propped Skeezix upon his lap and addressed the pet bear. "Say something, Skeezix. You sit there smiling, dumb and happy all the time, but you never say anything." Skeezix's sparkling eyes seemed to beam right through the boy. "Look at him, Sarkis. He doesn't care how long we get stuck. He keeps smiling no matter what happens."

Just then, a voice from ground level cried out their names. "Sarkis! Hagop!" The man and boy gave a start, then scanned the increasing number of people who had gathered around the Ferris wheel. Who should they see sidestepping through the crowd but Mumfred Lewis, making his way past bystanders and waving to his friends with broad, windshield wiper strokes of his hand. "Are you guys all right?"

"Mumfred, how did you know where we were?" said Sarkis.

"I took a guess. When I heard the Ferris wheel got stuck, I figured that's where you'd be."

Sarkis looked flummoxed. "That's uncanny," he muttered.

"Are you sure you're all right?" shouted Mumfred. "Is there anything I can do?"

"Not much anyone can do except to get us down from here."

"Now don't get nervous," cautioned Mumfred, sounding a bit jittery. "The main thing is to keep calm."

"We're doing fine," said Sarkis. "The maintenance specialist is on his way."

"That's what I wanted to talk to you about," hollered Mumfred.

Sarkis squinted in puzzlement. "What's that?"

"Maintenance specialists. I've been doing a lot of thinking lately."

"What do you mean?"

"I've been thinking about maintenance specialists. Do you know what I think?"

"No, what?"

"They don't exist!"

"Who doesn't exist?" said Sarkis, increasingly confused.

"Maintenance specialists. I'm fairly certain of that now."

"Mumfred, what are you talking about?"

"Just what I'm telling you."

"Mumfred, make sense! The operator ... he just now told us ..."

"Oh, that's Harvey Tweed," said Mumfred flippantly. "He always calls for the maintenance specialist when something goes wrong, but they never come for him, just like they never come for me."

Sarkis was utterly confounded. "Mumfred, are you all right?"

"I'm fine," hollered Mumfred. "Listen, I know what I'm about to say will sound crazy, but just hear me out. I think maintenance specialists are people we make up in our minds. It's important for us to believe there's somebody out there, a Mr. Fixit, who has all the answers whenever anything goes wrong. As long as we believe that somebody's out there with the answers, we're fine. But there's no one out there, Sarkis. That's what's becoming so clear to me. There's just us doing whatever needs to be done. Do you get what I mean now?"

"I think so," said Sarkis, looking nonetheless perplexed. "I just never heard it put that way before."

"But Mumfred," interjected Hagop, "if nobody can fix the wheel, how will we get down from here?"

"Don't worry about a thing. Harvey Tweed will fix the Ferris wheel. He's a good man and you can count on him to do the job. As long as he believes the specialist is on his way, he'll work hard and fix the Ferris wheel himself."

Hagop wagged his head in stupefaction. "This is the craziest place I've ever been in my life."

"I've got to get back to the merry-go-round now," said Mumfred. "Your soldier friend, Orville, is still with us and somebody needs to keep an eye on him. Are you sure there's nothing I can do for you?"

"Not a thing," said Sarkis. "We'll see you when we get down."

In the compartment behind our three companions a commotion had broken out. A tyke of about five or six had begun bawling, "I wanna go down! I wanna go down!" while his two sisters tried to allay his fears of being stuck on the Ferris wheel. At the same time, the older sister was conversing with their mother, who was strenuously keeping open the lines of communication from ground level.

"Now Carolyn," cried the mother, drawing upon all her vocal reserves, "hold onto your brother tight and don't let go."

"He's perfectly safe," replied the girl. "He just won't stop crying."

"Stephen, do you hear me?" called the mother. "Now Stephen, listen to me. Big boys don't cry. Only silly little boys cry, do you understand? Now are you going to be a big boy or a silly little boy?"

Stephen did not need long to choose. After eyeballing his close surroundings and the presence of a sister on either side of him, he sat up, threw back his head and howled like a banshee, "I wanna go home! I wanna go home!"

"Stephen," implored the mother, "you have to stop crying because crying won't get you down one second sooner than the man can get you down. There's been an accident, and we have to wait until the Ferris wheel is fixed."

"Mother, we've explained that to him a hundred times already."

"Well, you have to make him understand what the problem is," insisted the mother. "If he understands what's happening, he'll stop crying, I'm sure."

"Yes, Mother."

"And behave yourselves while you're up there. Act like grown-ups, for goodness sake."

"Yes, Mother."

"I'll be back as soon as soon as I find out how long this awful situation is expected to last."

Hagop, overhearing Stephen's complaint, turned around in his seat to face the boy through the back window flap. "Don't worry, nothing bad's gonna happen." Hagop, then, in an effort to divert the boy's attention, propped up Skeezix to face out the back of the compartment. At the sight of the smiling bear, Stephen's eyes lit up and a smile of his own began to emerge. "This is Skeezix," said Hagop. "You don't see him crying, do you? And you know why? Because he doesn't care if he gets stuck on a Ferris wheel or up in a tree. He has fun wherever he goes."

The boy looked mesmerized, as if Skeezix were some magical creature dispatched from an enchanted forest. But then the boy's mood gave way to a pout, and the pout gave way to a snit, and the snit to a bumptious display of foot stomping. "I wanna bear like that! I wanna bear like that!"

Anxious to mollify the boy, Hagop resorted to flapping the bear's arms faster and wiggling him in a simulated dance, but these clownish gyrations only fueled Stephan's fascination with the pet bear. Nor could the boy's sisters do anything to quiet him, their remonstrations and appeasements falling upon deaf ears. At length

Hagop made what might be deemed the ultimate sacrifice. "Would you like to have Skeezix?" he said. "I'll give him to you when we get down."

"Oh, no!" intervened the sister, Carolyn. "We couldn't allow you to do anything like that."

"It's okay. He can have him."

"No, no, we couldn't," said the girl. "Stephen? Tell the boy thank you but that you wouldn't think of taking his bear."

"Why not?"

The girl sighed and virtually threw up her hands in frustration. "Oh, God, why do I even bother?"

"Hagop," said Sarkis, "your offer is very generous, but are you sure you want to give Skeezix away?"

"It's okay."

"You don't have to do anything like that. Skeezix is yours."

"It's okay," repeated Hagop.

The conversation was cut short when Harvey Tweed, the operator of the Ferris wheel, came forward to make another announcement. Taking his place in full view of the stranded passengers, the burly operator again cupped his hands to his mouth and spoke out in a reassuring voice. It was a voice that resonated with authority, a voice that could inspire confidence in the midst of any adversity.

"Ladies and gentlemen, may I have your attention, please! We believe our technical difficulties have been corrected, and we're ready to bring you down. "Please keep your seats and make sure your safety bars are locked in place. The descent may be slow going because of a power shortage, but be patient and we'll have you back on the ground with your friends and families before you know it. Thank you."

Harvey Tweed returned to the control station, where a number of other concerned spectators had gathered. The operator deliberated over the main lever like a scientist at the crucial stage of an experiment. He edged the throttle forward and waited. Moments later the control apparatus reacted with a shiver and a hiccup, then fell silent. Suddenly a shrill squawk escaped from the box, followed by a whistling sound that started in a low register but gradually grew sharper, more piercing. When the sound rose to a deafening pitch, approaching a decibel capable of shattering glass, Harvey Tweed dropped everything and bolted from the control station. "Everybody clear out! Take cover!"

What followed was a concatenation of backfires that kept repeating in no particular order. Sparks fired from the control box, the Ferris wheel gave a jerk forward, forcing passengers out of their seats, and then an eerie rattling sound, like the early warnings of a transmission blowout, vibrated through each compartment on the wheel. Finally, a small explosion brought everything to a stop while smoke smoldered from the operating apparatus like fizzled fireworks. "My God!" exclaimed Hagop, half out of his seat. "What happened?"

From below somewhere came the caterwauling voice of Jared's father. "That's it! That's the last straw! I'll be taking names, the names of every one of you involved in this. I'll have you all behind bars before I'm through!"

Bystanders, having fled the scene, gradually made their way back to re-establish contact with their friends and relatives. Among the more distraught, not to say frantic, groundlings was Stephen's mother, strong-arming her way through a crowd that had swelled in size as more people from around the amusement park gravitated to the scene of the aborted rescue attempt. Making her way to the front, she called to her children, outshouting the voices of others around her. "Children, are you all right?"

"Yes, Mother, we're fine," yelled the girl, Carolyn. Her brother Stephen was gleefully bouncing in his seat, apparently believing the fireworks and explosion to have been calculated special effects of the ride. "Again! Again!" he cheered. "Let's do it again!"

"Oh my God!" gasped the mother. "This is becoming treacherous!" She then issued the following directive: "Now children, listen to me very closely. I don't know how long before this Ferris wheel is fixed, but in the meantime, do you know what I want you to do? Stephen, Carolyn, Joyce—are you listening? Do you know what I want you to do?"

"What, Mother?"

"Pray! I want you to pray harder than you've ever prayed in your life. Pray to Mary, Joseph, and all the saints for blessing and safekeeping. Do you understand?"

"Yes, Mother."

"Good," said the mother, and she crossed herself, relieved to have prepared her children for the ultimate doomsday emergency.

Meanwhile, Harvey Tweed, after a careful examination of the operating apparatus, came forward to address the stranded passengers again. In the wake of the ill-fated rescue attempt, he elicited the first signs of distrust from the anxious gathering. Discontented mutterings had begun spreading through the crowd. Some people were casting aspersions on the operator's competence and ability to bring the stranded passengers to safety. Amid these rumblings, Harvey Tweed took up his customary position and motioned to the crowd for silence.

"Ladies and gentlemen, your attention, please," he said. He repeated the request several times until the fractious crowd quieted down. "We've had a slight malfunction, but nothing serious, I promise you. Two detonator circuits have blown out, but they'll be replaced as soon as possible. Also, we've been assured the maintenance specialist is on his way. So please be patient a while longer. In the meantime, we're doing everything we can. Now is everyone up there all right?" Receiving no answer and not able to detect anyone in distress, Harvey Tweed assumed everyone had survived the turbulent ordeal. "Thank you," he said, and returned to the control station where trails of smoke were blowing through the shell plate.

Notwithstanding Harvey Tweed's reassuring prospectus, the delay dragged on and the situation at ground level deteriorated in rapid degrees. People were becoming increasingly tense and at times volatile. With the crowd's patience wearing thin, tempers grew short and sometimes flared up. Bystanders elbowed one another while jockeying for positions closer to the Ferris wheel, or got into shouting matches with others trying to communicate with stranded passengers. Two park policemen arrived and cordoned off the area around the wheel; however, the crowd, ignoring the restraint, soon began pressing forward and eventually toppled the rope as if it had never been there.

At the control station, under a lantern light, Harvey Tweed continued his unflagging efforts to repair the generator. His task was not made easier by people crowding around him and telling him what to do or second guessing whatever he had done. These self-appointed advisers were often vociferous in their opinions.

Some blamed the operator outright for the mechanical breakdown, while others went so far as to threaten legal action for the pain and suffering inflicted upon stranded family members, not to mention persevering friends waiting at ground level. Under the constant peppering of kibitzers, contentious meddlers, and prospective plaintiffs, it was a wonder Harvey Tweed managed to concentrate at all, much less get anything done.

Hagop had been observing the hubbub below with a detached, almost clinical air. "You know what's so funny?" he mused. "The people on the ground are more nervous and scared than we are. I mean, we're the ones who are stuck and in trouble, but they're the ones who are nervous and scared."

"But suppose they can't get us down?" whined Ellie. "What'll we do then?"

"Not much we can do except make the best of it," said Sarkis.

Hagop turned around in his seat and said, "Sarkis? If we had to sleep up here, would we see the sun come up in the morning?"

"The sun? Oh yes, I would think so. The view from up here should be spectacular, too."

"That would be something!" enthused Hagop, envisioning such a moment.

The prospect of witnessing a sunrise was more than just a passing fancy for the boy. In all his ten years on the planet Hagop had never seen a sunrise. He had seen pictures of them in books, movies, and magazines, but these vicarious experiences had only whetted his appetite for the real thing. "That would be something," he repeated. "Really something."

Presently, Harvey Tweed came forward to make what would be his final announcement of the evening. His appearance this time was met with boos and catcalls from many bystanders, as well as derisive, finger-pointing accusations from those close enough to make them. The evening's tribulations had taken a toll on the stalwart operator. His walk was slower, more measured; his shoulders slumped with a kind of Lincolnesque gravity. There was about Harvey Tweed now a tempered demeanor as in those whose untutored passions have given way to the lessons of experience. Stepping through the crowd, braving the stings of public rebuke, Harvey Tweed brought to mind those historic personages whose characters were forged by the trials of office and the solitary burdens of decision making.

The operator took his customary place and cupped his hands to his mouth. "Ladies and gentlemen, may I have your attention, please! We believe we've finally straightened out our electrical problems, and we're ready to bring you down. Please be sure your safety bars are locked and hold on tight. You may feel a jolt at the start, due to a defective pulley circuit, but don't be alarmed. Everything will be fine. The ride may be a little bumpy, that's all. We're sorry for the inconvenience we have caused. We want to thank you for your patience and cooperation during this difficult time. As a token of our appreciation, we invite you all to come back any time for a complimentary ride on the big wheel. Bring your friends and family, and we'll make room for them, too."

"Over my dead body!" cried the familiar voice of Mr. Klinger.

Back at the control station, Harvey Tweed stood at the operating lever, gave a sigh of hopeful expectation and pushed the lever forward. After a few silent seconds, a weak, electrical whirring buzzed through the control box like a wheeze. The sound faded. Everyone waited. Suddenly the Ferris wheel gave a violent jerk, shaking up passengers and evincing yelps and screams throughout the compartments, as well as from bystanders retreating from the scene. Then the wheel stopped. Then it jerked again. Stopped. Jerked. And it continued in this manner until all the passengers were rattling in place and holding on for dear life. All the while, however, the wheel was turning, struggling for every inch like some wounded giant limping along, needing every ounce of strength to make the smallest gain. At length, after a series of discombobulating rumbles, the first compartment touched down, and a group of shaken passengers disembarked.

With each successive landing, the electrical power was cut off, then turned on for another series of jarring fits and starts. Sarkis, Hagop, and Ellie bumped and bucked their way toward the ground. Behind them, the boy Stephen clamored, "Again! Again! Let's do it again!" He alone of all the passengers was actually relishing this jarring, nerve-jangling descent.

The evening's travails finally came to an end, and the three companions were earthbound creatures again. Their first steps upon touching down were wobbly, like those of newfound legs, but in short order their steps grew confident and their pace brisk.

Behind them, in the distance, the Ferris wheel sputtered and jerked as it delivered the remaining passengers to safety. Cast against the emerald night, the big wheel looked like a foundering but indomitable vessel—battered, it might be said, but unbowed.

After Sarkis, Hagop, and Ellie had distanced themselves from the scene of their latest adventure, Hagop stopped short. "I forgot something," he said. Sarkis and Ellie exchanged knowing glances but refrained from saying a word. "I'll be right back." And holding Skeezix around the waist with both arms, the boy headed back toward the Ferris wheel.

When the boy returned empty handed, neither Sarkis nor Ellie knew what to say, both unsure as to how Hagop was taking the separation from his pet bear. For a time the three walked across the fairgrounds in silence. "I'm okay," said Hagop, sensing the uneasiness of his companions. "If I ever play Skee-Ball again, I'll just win another Skeezix, that's all." And with that the subject of the pet bear came to a close. The trio would soon part company for a while, Sarkis to the merry-go-round and Hagop and Ellie to whatever adventures they could find in the amusement park. Accordingly, Sarkis emptied his pockets and entrusted to the boy all remaining money, a grand total of $7.33. With the transfer of funds, though, came specific conditions, which Sarkis set down with the straightest of faces.

"Hagop, I want you to spend every last penny of this money and show Ellie the time of her life. Remember, she's been crying, and when a woman has been crying, a man must do everything in his power to make her smile again. He must cater to her every whim. He must ply her with compliments. No consideration is too small, no generosity too big. In short, he must be as a prince to her. Hagop, do you understand what I'm saying?"

Hagop gulped, "I think so."

Ellie did nothing to allay the boy's self-consciousness when she sidled up to him and cooed, "My shining prince," whereupon, Hagop blushed a hot shade of red.

Sarkis waved them off. "When you're all done, meet me at the merry-go-round, and we'll all go for a walk on the beach."

* * *

Here, reader, given a pause in the evening's occupations, the moment seems appropriate for that time-honored literary device known as an author's digression. This one concerns Pfc. Orville T. Briggs, the sole passenger on the merry-go-round when Sarkis returned to work. Some notation would seem in order both as to the soldier's outward appearance and—dare we suggest it?—his inward appearance as well. Physically, he was more unkempt than ever. His shirt was open at the collar, his tie wrapped around his neck like a scarf, and his cap tilted backward over one ear at an angle that defied the law of gravity. From head to toe he bore all the earmarks of one who had been shipwrecked and had survived to tell the tale. Yet, while his physical appearance had deteriorated markedly, another kind of change was manifesting itself, too—and here, reader, admittedly, we may be treading in areas better left uncharted in narrative matters. Orville's face was imbued with the kind of beatific radiance often depicted in the paintings of medieval mystics and saints. The change was noticeable in his smile—an ethereal smile that, while less than a grin, was considerably more than a crinkle. Indeed, when viewed in a certain light, the smile bore an uncanny resemblance to that of Hagop's pet bear, Skeezix. So much for comparisons. Who can say for sure what these signs may or may not have portended? One thing alone was fairly certain. Orville T. Briggs was not the same man who had stumbled into the merry-go-round that afternoon.

***

After closing time, Sarkis stood outside and waited for Hagop and Ellie. Before long, he spotted them in the distance, and they, spotting him, waved and broke into a run. Reaching Sarkis's side, both were panting for breath and bursting with further adventures to relate. "We did it!" said Hagop. "We spent every last penny we had."

"Wonderful. Where did you go?"

"We went to the Fun House," said Ellie, "and then to the Chamber of Horrors, and on more rides, too."

"At the Fun House, the air machine blew Ellie's dress up and she turned red," Hagop said.

"And what did you do when the air machine blew Ellie's dress up?" asked Sarkis.

"I laughed—what else?"

"Shining prince, indeed," said Sarkis.

"He was a perfect date," said Ellie. "He was everything you wanted him to be."

"Then we took a ride in a paddle boat," said Hagop. "It was all right, except people get pretty mushy in those boats. They go way out on the lake and mush it up."

"You won't think it's so mushy in a few years," said Ellie.

"Who needs all that mushy movie stuff, anyway?" said Hagop.

"I do," admitted Ellie.

"You do?" said Hagop.

Ellie sighed romantically. "Except when I'm with you, of course. You're so perfect, I don't need any of that mushy stuff."

And Hagop felt so good he could kick cans at the moon. "Come on," said Sarkis. "Let's go for a walk on the beach."

NIGHTSONG

They ended the night with a walk on the beach ... and oh, what a night it was! The stars burst above them like shattered crystal on a velvet dome.

They had slipped through the boardwalk rail guards and tramped across the sand to the water's edge.

And the water rippled in luminous waves of moonlight. Along the way, Ellie said, "I thought tonight would be the worst night of my life, but it's been a beautiful night."

And Sarkis was glad when Ellie said that. "I wish," said Ellie, "that life could always be this way. No worries, no time schedules, no tomorrows to think about."

And Hagop wanted Sarkis to talk about clocks again. "No clocks tonight," said Sarkis. "Look up at those stars. Do you think they care what time it is?"

And Ellie said that she learned in school how people on Earth could still see the lights of dead stars.

And Hagop didn't understand how people could still see the lights of dead stars, and Ellie explained how people could. But the more she explained, the less he understood. And Hagop came to a conclusion about himself—namely, that he didn't understand much of anything. And Sarkis told him not to worry about what he didn't understand. But Hagop wanted to know everything.

And Sarkis scooped up a handful of sand and said to the boy, "Hagop, do you understand this?"

"Understand sand?"

"Yes."

"How do you understand sand?"

"I don't know," said Sarkis. "You said you wanted to know everything."

"You can't understand sand."

"What do you do with it, then?"

"You walk on it, let your feet sink in it, or build a fort like we did yesterday."

"Good."

"Good how?"

"Good that you can find so many ways to enjoy sand without understanding it."

And the mystery of sand made Sarkis think about mysteries that no one understood but which books described and pretended to understand. And Sarkis knew if he read many books, he could describe sand and air and the composition of the ocean, and he could show how days became nights and nights became tomorrows and how light traveled from dead stars and how atmosphere became stratosphere and stratosphere became ionosphere and how cells multiplied and how life perpetuated itself in an eternal collaboration with death. And Sarkis knew when he had finished describing all there was to describe, he still would be reduced to the mystery of a grain of sand, and all the descriptions in the world would not bring him any closer to the mystery than he was now, feeling the sand and letting it sift through his fingers.

And Hagop and Ellie walked by themselves and took off their shoes and let the cold water rush over their feet. And both loved the tingling wetness of the water against their skin.

And Ellie challenged Hagop to a chase, and Hagop chased Ellie in circles around the beach until Ellie fell, exhausted and heavy-legged from running in the sand while Hagop was as fresh as when he had started.

And Ellie panted, "Don't you ever get tired?"

And Hagop said, "No, I can run for days without getting tired." For proof, he said she could ask any of his friends back in Washington Heights and they would tell her how long he could run.

And Hagop and Ellie continued their walk by the water's edge.

And Ellie became intrigued by the off-shore lights of gambling boats anchored beyond the two-mile zoning limit. And she imagined parties and romantic adventures taking place on those boats at this very moment.

And dreaming of adventure and romance, Ellie made up a story about a gambler who risks everything he owns in a game of dice for the love of a beautiful countess, who is prepared to run away with him if he wins.

And Hagop waited anxiously for the outcome of the story as it mounted to a tense climax. "He rolls the dice," said Ellie, who then paused until Hagop was breathless with anticipation, "… and he loses."

"Then what happens?"

"He joins the French Foreign Legion," said Ellie. "That's what they do in the movies, anyway."

And Hagop wondered if things that happened in the movies ever happened in real life.

"Sometimes they do," said Ellie. "People fall in love in the movies and they fall in love in real life, too."

"That's what Sarkis said happened to me this morning."

And Ellie was wistful yet happy when Hagop said that. "You looked awfully funny this morning," she said.

"I guess it was a stupid thing to do."

"It wasn't stupid at all," objected Ellie. "There isn't a girl alive who doesn't feel beautiful when she's admired by someone nice."

"But I'm only ten years old," said Hagop. "I'm too young to fall in love."

"Well, I don't care," said Ellie. "You made me feel awfully important this morning even though I was a little scared the way you kept staring."

And Hagop confessed to Ellie that he was a starer, and that he stared more than anybody else he knew. Sometimes, he said, he could sit on the front stoop of his apartment building and stare for hours at anybody or anything, like a man washing his car in front of the house or people going to a wake at Gribbins' Funeral Home across the street, or Frank Corregio, the fruit market owner, weighing vegetables on the sidewalk at the corner of St. Nicholas Avenue. Hagop said he could probably stare all day if his mother didn't call him in to eat or make him run an errand somewhere.

And Ellie confessed that she, too, was a starer, especially on trains and buses when she could look at different faces and wonder what kind of lives people lived behind those faces. And Ellie said that most people's faces were sad, and often she felt sad to think of all the unhappy people who must be in the world.

But Ellie also insisted that staring was impolite.

And Hagop said that whenever his mother caught him staring, she would tell him not to think so much. "She doesn't know I'm not thinking," said Hagop. "I'm only staring, but I guess I fool a lot of people that way."

And when Hagop and Ellie were not making confessions or talking about movies or love or staring, they did other things every bit as good. They did crazy things like making dizzy tracks in the wet sand or dodging the tide as it rushed at their feet or high-stepping and splashing barefoot in the shallow water or swaggering like drunken beachcombers or doing nothing at all but just walking and thinking to themselves. Which was good, too.

And Hagop took Ellie's hand as they sauntered on the beach because it was impossible not to think of taking Ellie's hand.

And sometimes, hand in hand, they would begin rocking and swaying and tipping each other off balance.

And they were like playful fawns in the moonlight.

And Sarkis, walking behind them, picked up a crooked limb of driftwood and trailed it in the sand. And he remembered how as a boy he had enjoyed picking up stray things like branches, corrugated boxes, wires, or scraps of metal—but mostly branches, which he used as walking sticks when he went exploring with his cousin Garo through the wilds of Fort Tryon Park or the Amsterdam woods. And he remembered peeling the barks and admiring the greenish-white pulp beneath the skin. And he also remembered the sense of loss when he would have to discard the branch before going home. And the crooked limb of driftwood felt good in Sarkis's hand and trailing it in the sand felt good, as did the night breeze and the mists of ocean spray against his face. And Sarkis loved the ocean more than he did any other phenomenon of nature. He loved its vast and brooding depths, a world in which other worlds thrived and still others disappeared into eternity. He loved the ocean, but with a fierce respect that made his love different from his love of trees, mountains, and lakes. He knew the ocean was neither his friend nor his enemy. The ocean was neither good nor evil. The ocean was a paradox, as nature itself was a paradox. The ocean was kind and the ocean was cruel. The ocean created and the ocean destroyed. The ocean healed and the ocean wounded. The ocean was all things manifest and made no compromises for being all things manifest. To love the ocean was dangerous, as much a risk of death as a promise of birth.

Sarkis knew there was no other way to love.

To Sarkis the ocean was unadulterated life.

And both Hagop and Ellie felt they could stay on the beach forever as they traipsed along the sand.

And the sandy beach stretched out like shifting, wavy patterns of a moonstruck terrain.

And Ellie said, "Isn't the moonlight on the water scary?"

And Hagop was reminded of movies in which loveless heroines took their lives by walking into the ocean like sleepwalkers.

Yes, he said, the moonlight was scary, but the moonlight was beautiful, too, especially when the beach was empty. "I like empty beaches," he said.

"So do I," said Ellie. "I don't feel lonely on an empty beach. I guess that sounds crazy, doesn't it?"

And Hagop told Ellie of his walk this morning and how he had not felt lonely even though no people were around.

And Ellie made another confession to Hagop, tonight being a night for confessions and for thinking about things most people never think about. "Most of the time I'm an extrovert," she said. "That means a person who likes being with other people more than being alone. But I don't feel that way tonight. I feel by myself in a good way tonight, even though you and Sarkis are with me. I feel very close to myself, like I was meeting me for the first time. 'Ellie,' somebody is saying, 'How do you do? Nice to meet you.'" And Ellie laughed because she knew she had to be sounding foolish. "I'm talking crazy, but I don't know how else to explain it."

And if Hagop knew anything after ten years of living on this planet, he knew Ellie was not talking crazy.

And the stars trembled above, teetering in place as if one push would send them shimmering down to earth in a shower of light.

And Ellie did not want this night to end.

And Sarkis, Hagop, and Ellie walked as far as the beach would take them, down to where the sand disappeared and the shallow water beat against a concrete wall that bridged into the next township. And going as far as they could go, they ended their walk and left the beach. And on the boardwalk, Hagop and Ellie brushed the sand off their feet. And while they lingered on the boardwalk, Ellie had mixed feelings about leaving, as if she were being pulled away from where she most wanted to be.

"I don't want to go," she said.

And Hagop understood her feelings from his own walk on the beach that morning.

And Sarkis asked Ellie, "Are you sad?"

And Ellie said, "In a way I am. I feel good in one way, but sad in another."

"Maybe you're sad because you're afraid you'll lose the good part of your feeling."

"I guess so," said Ellie. "Tomorrow I'll be working in the restaurant and tonight will seem like a long time ago."

"But you can always come back," said Hagop.

"Maybe I'm afraid I won't come back," said Ellie. "Once a new day starts, you get so busy doing things, you forget what you enjoy doing most, or you pretend you don't have time. You make important things unimportant and unimportant things important."

And Hagop told Ellie not to make that mistake. "I hope not," said Ellie, and then she said to Sarkis, "It's important not to make that mistake, isn't it?"

And Sarkis said he knew of no mistake in the world more important not to make.

And Sarkis and Hagop walked Ellie home to a bungalow that she shared for the summer with two girlfriends. And when the moment came to say goodnight, Ellie resisted the thought of leaving because her feelings were so mixed and unsorted. And she hugged Sarkis and Hagop with all her might, and thanked them for being with her tonight when she most needed to be with someone. And Ellie's confusion was the confusion of being human, of having lost something precious and fearing it would never be found again, yet at the same time discovering something, too, within the pain of her loss—a sympathy for things alive and suffering to grow. And Ellie was weak with these feelings, which would ease in time but which she would not understand maybe for years to come. "Thank you," she said again.

And Sarkis said, "Thank you, too," but Ellie said she couldn't imagine why anybody would want to thank her for anything.

And Sarkis said, "For being you."

And if Ellie had not turned and run into the bungalow at that moment, she would have burst into tears and cried her eyes red again.

And Hagop was worried about Ellie and asked, "Is she going to cry again?"

"Yes, she'll probably cry again."

And Hagop wanted to know why Ellie cried so much.

And Sarkis said, "People cry when their feelings have no place else to go."

And on the way home, Sarkis carried the crooked limb of driftwood in his hand. And he diverted himself by tapping the limb on the sidewalk like a cane and tapping it against lampposts, trash cans, hydrants, and picket fences, which made a washboard sound when the limb rattled across the palings.

And Hagop asked Sarkis why he had not thrown the wood away.

And Sarkis said, "I'm going to keep this one."

"What are you going to do with it?"

"I don't know yet," said Sarkis. "I may peel the bark or carve a design on it. Or maybe I'll leave the wood alone and stand it up in a corner of our room."

And Hagop was puzzled that Sarkis would want to keep a piece of wood that was mostly rotting away.

And Sarkis said, "If we keep the wood long enough, we won't notice how old or rotten it is. We'll begin to learn more and more about it. Each day we look at it, we'll notice shapes and designs we didn't notice before. We'll discover where the wood is darker and where the wood is lighter, and where the bark is soft or hard. We'll see how the grains change direction and where the wood is knotty and where the wood is smooth. We'll come to know every twist and curve of this wood like we know the palm of our hand. In time, we'll come to appreciate the miracle of this piece of wood and how it is different from every other piece of wood in the whole universe."

And Hagop was amazed that so much could be learned from an ordinary piece of wood, especially one that was mostly rotting away.

And Sarkis said the same could be learned from anything: leaves, cans, rusty spikes, and rocks. "Would you like to carry the wood for a while?" asked Sarkis.

And Hagop felt self-conscious and at the same time privileged at being asked if he would like to carry the wood. "If you think it's all right," he said. "Of course."

And Hagop carried the limb of driftwood as if it were a special gift, even though he had seen prettier pieces of wood.

And Sarkis told Hagop not to expect miracles right away.

And the longer Hagop carried the wood, the more he grew accustomed to the feel of the bark in his hand until he had to admit he was beginning to like the wood, too.

And when Hagop felt he had carried the driftwood long enough, he said, "Here Sarkis, you carry it now. It's your piece of wood."

"All right."

And after they had walked in silence for a block, Sarkis said, apropos of nothing in particular and everything in general, "Funny, isn't it?"

And Hagop, apropos of the same, said, "It sure is."

And that night, each slept a sound sleep, interrupted once when Hagop awoke and called Sarkis's name.

"What is it?" asked Sarkis..

And Hagop said, "I'm starved."

WRITER AT WORK

Sarkis began the writing of his book that morning at 7:30. Aroused from his sleep by the gestations of creative labor, he sat up in bed, fed paper into the typewriter that he had borrowed from Mrs. Lilly the day before, and began writing in a non-stop burst of energy. Employing a three-fingered key punching technique, he plunged headlong into his narrative. He allowed the story to unfold spontaneously, adding whatever flourishes his impulses dictated, brewing and tasting as he went (like a literary gourmet), being as much amused by what never happened as by what did; in fact, not caring where the truth of his narrative ended and where the lies began, but caring only for what he could make happen to the characters in his story. At 8:21, Hagop was awakened by the typing. Seeing Sarkis at work, the boy immediately sensed the magnitude of the occasion.

"The book!" cried Hagop.

"The book," said Sarkis, banging away at the keys. "About an hour ago I felt the labor pains coming and I knew the time had come."

"I didn't know you could type so good," said the boy.

"I can't type at all," said Sarkis. "My fingers are moving but I have no control over them. I'm listening, and my fingers are typing whatever I hear."

"Listening?" said Hagop, his eyes darting around the room. "Listening to who?"

"The voices. They must be mine but I can't be sure. Writing is a mysterious business, Hagop. No one knows what really happens when a writer writes."

Hagop squirmed a bit. "It sounds scary."

"What worries me is that I may be as crazy as a bedbug. If this is what a writer goes through every time he sits down to work, I'm not sure I'd want to be one."

Hagop shook his head in bemusement. "How can you write and talk at the same time? How do you know what you're doing?"

"I don't know what I'm doing. The story is writing itself. I could be eating an apple off a tree and the words would still be coming out of my fingers. I'm afraid I can't take any credit for this book." The boy was watching in rapt curiosity when Sarkis proposed, "Would you like to see me type with one hand and pick wax out of my ear with the other?" And before the boy could answer, Sarkis was crossing his legs, picking at his left ear with one hand while rattling the typewriter keys with the other. Following this eye-popping demonstration, Sarkis sat up and said, "Once the creative juices start flowing, nothing can stop them."

"I don't believe it," gasped Hagop.

"Easy as falling off a log," said Sarkis, his fingers tripping over the keys like those of a virtuoso pianist.

"What part are you writing now?" the boy asked.

"Let's see," said Sarkis scanning the paper. "Oh, yes, the conductor on the train. We just finished talking to him. That part didn't come out as well as I had hoped, but I can't do anything more with it. One thing I'm learning about writing, Hagop, is that no matter how hard a writer tries, nothing he writes comes out as well as he had hoped. A writer is always struggling with the truth and losing. Every word, every sentence, every comma defeats him. By the time he finishes the book, he's bound to feel like a fool for having tried to write it in the first place. In fact, the closer he comes to writing a good book, the worse he must feel. It's a losing battle all the way."

"Writers sound like sad people."

"A miserable breed. Misfits, every last one of them."

"Are you going to write about everything that happened to us?"

"Yes, I am. I'll have to lie and exaggerate a lot, but I don't know how else I'll be able to tell the truth."

Hagop frowned. "How can you lie and tell the truth at the same time?"

"To a writer, there's no difference, Hagop. Sometimes, the bigger the lies the better."

"Really?"

"No doubt about it."

For a while Hagop watched Sarkis type away at breakneck speed. "If you're writing about us, then you don't know how the book ends yet, do you?"

"No, but I have a pretty good idea."

"Is the ending happy?"

"Hard to say. I think I know what happens at the end, but I don't know whether what happens is happy or not. We'll have to wait and see."

"I can't wait to find out."

"We shouldn't worry too much about the ending," said Sarkis, his attention never wavering from the page. "Endings have a way of taking care of themselves. That's another thing I'm learning. A writer should only worry about what he's writing at the time he's writing it. Each part he writes should be the best and most interesting part of the book to him, so that if he dropped dead in the middle of the book, he would still have half a book worth reading and not just a beginning and a middle that needs an ending."

"I know your book won't be dull."

"I'll try to make it the best hunting, fishing, and sea ship story ever written. I know I'm bragging, Hagop, but if a writer didn't brag, he'd never have the courage to keep writing. Somewhere in the back of his mind he has to keep telling himself, 'I can write a book better than the last book I read or the last fifty books I read.' A part of him must never stop bragging about the book he thinks he can write."

Hagop was getting excited. "What part are you writing now?"

Sarkis consulted the page again. "Looks like we'll be arriving in Asbury Park soon."

Hagop sighed disappointedly. "The book has a long way to go yet, doesn't it?"

"I'm afraid so," said Sarkis. And with this realization a change came over him. His enthusiasm flagged. The pace of his typing, once so nimble and spritely, slackened like a battery running down and threatening to stall out altogether. The realization that so many people, places, and events remained to be described in the book seemed an insurmountable task. "Hagop, I may never finish this book," he despaired. "It just may be too much for me to handle."

"Sarkis, don't talk that way."

"I know I'm feeling sorry for myself, but I can't help it. The more I write, the more I find to say. The subject matter is inexhaustible."

"You can't give up now," urged Hagop. "You have to keep going."

"I once read somewhere how writers are very sensitive people, and how they're likely to get depressed over any little thing. One of those depressions must be hitting me now."

"Then start bragging," exhorted Hagop. "Think of all the books you read and how your book is going to be better."

Sarkis nodded weakly. "Yes, that helps. Thank you, Hagop."

"Think of what those books didn't have to make them good and what your book is going to have."

"Yes, that helps, too. Thank you, Hagop."

"Now start bragging."

Sarkis tried to rally his spirits but kept faltering. "Oh, what's the use?" he said. "Words, words, words. The world is drowning in words. Why should my words be any different?"

"Because you're different!"

Something in the boy's voice—in its spontaneous declaration of faith—had Sarkis sitting up in his seat again.

"You're right," he said. "Maybe that's all a writer wants to say when he writes. 'Hey world,' he's saying, 'I'm here to tell you there's never been another like me.'"

"Now you're bragging!" cheered Hagop. "Keep going."

Sarkis felt his spirits reviving. "Some people scribble graffiti on building walls. Other people write books. But the message is the same to all who read this: 'I was here!'"

"Attaboy! More."

"Every writer is a man who never took time to scribble on building walls as a boy."

"Now you're talking."

"I think I'm back on the beam now," said Sarkis typing with his customary élan. "Thank you, Hagop."

Hagop sighed with relief. "That was a close call."

"It certainly was. I had no idea a writer's depression could sneak up on him so fast."

"What part are you writing now?"

Sarkis glimpsed the typewritten page. "We're in the menswear shop, and what a time we're going to have before I'm through."

"Will you lie a lot?"

"Giant lies. Lies bigger than whales if I have anything to say about it."

In the excitement of the morning Hagop had forgotten how hungry he was, but given time to catch his breath now, he felt anew the pangs of a big appetite. "Sarkis, I'm so starved I could eat a horse."

"Tell you what. Why don't you go to Ellie's restaurant and have breakfast? The waitress promised you free pancakes, remember?"

"Aren't you coming?"

"I'll eat later. Can't stop now while the writing is going so good."

Only after dressing and making ready to leave did Hagop think to mention, "Sarkis, you have no money, remember? How are you going to eat if you have no money?"

"Can't stop eating because we have no money," said Sarkis, zinging the typewriter carriage back to the margin. "A person could starve to death that way."

"Uh-huh," uttered Hagop with a vacant nod. He didn't even try to unravel the meaning of Sarkis's pronouncement. "I guess I'll see you later, then."

"Say hello to everybody at the restaurant for me."

"I will."

"And don't rush. I'm bound to be at this a while longer."

"Okay."

As promised by the waitress at Ellie's restaurant, Hagop had his free breakfast, one comprised of juice, pancakes, bacon strips, and all the milk he could drink. Between mouthfuls of food, he kept up a running conversation with Ellie, stationed at the griddle. He told her how Sarkis had begun the writing of his book, and how he could type, talk, and pick wax out of his ear at the same time, none of which came as a surprise to Ellie, who had come to believe that Sarkis could do just about anything he put his mind to. Upon finishing his breakfast, Hagop said he couldn't stay because he had to get back to the room and keep an eye on Sarkis before he did something really crazy like standing on his head and typing. Or who knows what else.

Upon his return to the basement apartment, Hagop found Sarkis pounding away at the typewriter and showing no signs of letting up. At the sight of him, the boy grew concerned. There was about Sarkis now the pale, feverish cast of one stricken with an exotic malady. Hunched over the typewriter, his brow knitted, his unshaven face fuzzy with stubble, he looked the prototype of the addicted artist, the obsessive creator for whom time, health, comfort—indeed, the world-at-large—had ceased to exist.

"Hagop, I can't stop writing. I'm like a machine that's out of control."

"Sarkis, you have to rest sometime."

"I know, but as soon as I come to the end of one sentence, another one starts, and then another and another ..."

"You can't write everything in one day. You have to save some for tomorrow, too."

"You're right," said Sarkis, but his resolve quickly dissipated. "But who knows what kind of mood I'll be in tomorrow? I may forget everything I wanted to say today, or else, what I wanted to say today may not seem important tomorrow."

Hagop was nonplussed. "I never knew being a writer was so much trouble. Whenever I read a book, I think writing is easy because the books are so easy to read."

"Ah! Now you've put your finger on the heart of the problem," said Sarkis. "The agony of every writer is to make his book read as if it never had been written. Already I can see the mistakes I've been making."

"What kind of mistakes?"

"The worst kind—the kind that tell a reader he's been reading a book made up by someone at a typewriter instead of a book that happened by itself. I'll be able to correct some of the mistakes but not all of them."

Hagop sighed haplessly. Writing, he decided, must be like a sickness, except that with a cold or measles you could take medicine and get better. Who knew what medicine you took for this?

"When do you think you'll stop?"

"Don't know, but it's a cinch I can't go on this way much longer."

"Maybe I'll just wait for you outside."

"Good idea. No point in your staying here and watching me suffer." Hagop reluctantly headed toward the door when Sarkis asked, "How's the weather today?"

"Beautiful."

"Good. If anything can make me stop working, it's the thought of a beautiful day outside. I'll keep that in mind."

"Can we take a walk when you're finished?"

"You bet. We'll take a marvelous walk," promised Sarkis, "a walk you'll never forget. Wait and see."

"Okay. I'll wait for you in the yard."

Hagop left the room and started through the basement toward the back door. He had gone about half the distance when suddenly there erupted from the room a burst of howling laughter, the sound like the hooting of an animal. Hagop wheeled in his tracks and dashed back to the room, fearing that the strains of creative labor may have taken some final, irreversible toll on Sarkis. The boy stopped at the door and looked in apprehensively. Sarkis was whooping and hee-hawing in side-splitting guffaws. He kept rocking to and fro, slapping his knees, and laughing so hard that tears were streaming down his face. "Oooweeeee! Oooweeeee!" he squealed like a stuck pig.

"Sarkis, what's going on?"

Sarkis, barely able to catch his breath, pointed to the page in the typewriter and cackled, "The salesman in the menswear shop ... he just counted me out for the knockdown."

The boy was not amused. Having been scared out of his wits by a false alarm, he stood at the door, arms akimbo, and scowled like a reproving parent who had reached his limit with an incorrigible child. Hagop waited until the laughing subsided and Sarkis appeared, more or less, under control. Without another word, the boy turned away and started through the basement again. He had gone no farther than before when another burst of laughter erupted from the room, these hoots and cackles even louder and more sustained than the earlier ones. This time, however, the boy never broke stride, much less raised an eyebrow. With a composed, unperturbed air, he headed straightaway toward the back door. "That must be the lady coming into the men's shop," he muttered to himself. "I wonder whatever happened to her."

AN ODD PREDICAMENT

What an odd predicament Hagop found himself in while waiting for Sarkis in the front yard.

The boy had been playing with a clothesline that he had found under another one strung with Mrs. Lilly's wash. He had engaged in various activities with the rope such as lassoing fence palings and imitating how girls in his neighborhood skipped rope. In this latter effort he fared poorly; he kept tripping over himself and falling to the ground. Finally he decided just to lie there and do nothing. But presently he began twining the rope around his body to see how many crisscrossing loops and patterns he could make.

That was the beginning of Hagop's odd predicament.

When he tried to free himself of the rope, he discovered to his chagrin that he couldn't get loose. He began yanking at whatever slack he could get hold of, but the more he tugged and pulled, the tighter he made the knots until there was no slack left to grab. He had bound himself up tight like a package ready for shipping.

Lying on his back, Hagop stared at the sky and moaned, "Oh, God!"

Presently Sarkis emerged from the cellar, yawning and stretching his arms in the sunlight, after his period of creative incubation. Seeing Hagop lying on the ground and bound like a captive, he approached to see what the boy was doing.

"What's going on?" he asked.

"Oh, nothing," replied Hagop, too embarrassed to make mention of his predicament.

"Just playing, I see."

"I was."

Sarkis closed his eyes and bathed his head in sunlight. "Certainly is a beautiful day."

Hagop couldn't pretend any longer. "Sarkis, I tied myself up in a rope and I can't get out."

"I beg your pardon?"

"The rope. I tied myself up in it."

"How did you manage that?"

"I don't know."

"And you can't get free?"

"That's right."

"You're sure?"

"Yes."

"And you did this all by yourself. No help from anyone?"

"There's nobody else here except me."

Intrigued by this turn of events, Sarkis slowly circled the boy to examine his predicament from every possible angle. Upon completing his study, he stood contemplatively over the boy and weighed his findings. "Extraordinary," he concluded.

"Can you help me?"

"Of course I can help you. You don't think I would ever leave you in a predicament like this, do you?"

"Sarkis, this is impossible. Nobody can tie himself up in a rope."

"Hagop, nothing is impossible. Remember, you've done it, so we know it can be done."

"I can't even get my hands free," said the boy, wriggling in place. "Now how did I tie up my hands when I needed my hands to tie up the rest of me?"

Sarkis shook his head in amazement; whereupon he circled Hagop again, this time tugging on the rope here and there as he went. Convinced beyond a shadow of a doubt that the boy was bound securely, Sarkis again reflected upon the matter. "Outside of a few shamans and witch doctors, I don't know who else could accomplish such a feat."

"I don't care. I just want to get out of this rope."

"Of course, but in the meantime we shouldn't overlook the magnitude of your achievement."

"Why don't you try getting the knots out?"

"Let's have a look." Sarkis squatted beside the boy and studied the configuration of knots. He frowned at all the overlapping loops and underhanded twists the rope had taken. Deterred by this maze of entanglements, he had no idea of where to begin. "The tricky thing about knots," said Sarkis, "is that once you start monkeying around with them, you never know if you're making them tighter or looser."

Hagop wriggled some more, but gave up in frustration. "Every time I move, the rope gets tighter."

"That's the sign of a good knot."

"This is the stupidest thing I ever did in my life."

"Nonsense. Anyone can tie himself up in a rope and get free, but can you name me one person who can tie himself up and stay that way?"

"I don't know," said Hagop, who had given up trying to make any sense of his predicament. "I just want to get out of this rope."

"Of course you do, and I'm going to do everything in my power to help you."

"Why don't you get a knife and cut the rope?"

"Hagop, are you sure you want me to do that?"

"What do you mean am I sure? Sure I'm sure."

"Hmm," hedged Sarkis. "Sounds like cheating somehow."

"What are you talking about, Sarkis? Just get me out of this rope. Who cares about cheating?"

Sarkis gave the boy an avuncular look. "Hagop, you really don't mean that."

"Sarkis, just get a knife and cut the rope. *Puhleez!*"

"All right, if that's what you want. But I want you to know there may be more involved here than the simple cutting of a rope. You want my help, and I'm going to give it to you. If I cut you loose with a knife, you would think I was helping you, but I wouldn't be. I'd be showing you the easy way out. I'd be undermining your ability to rise to a challenge and overcome obstacles. What I'm saying to you, Hagop, is this—you owe it to yourself to free yourself."

A blank stare from Hagop. "That's it? That's your help?"

"In so many words, yes."

"Sarkis?"

"Yes, my boy?"

"That's the dumbest thing I ever heard."

Sarkis flinched defensively. "I put a lot of thought into that."

"I don't care. It's still the dumbest thing I ever heard."

"Hm," mulled Sarkis, raising a finger thoughtfully to his lips. "This problem may be knottier than I thought."

"So? Get the knife."

"Let's not be hasty," admonished Sarkis. He pondered the boy's predicament with appropriate expressions of concern such as pursed lips and a knitted brow. Suddenly struck by a brainstorm, he slapped his hands enthusiastically. "I've got it!" he cried. "Why didn't I think of this before?"

"What is it?"

"What you're supposed to do."

"Which is what?"

"Nothing! Do absolutely nothing."

"Sarkis, what do you mean, 'Do nothing'?"

"You've been struggling to get free, Hagop. That was your first mistake. You must stop struggling at once. The more people struggle, the more complicated they make their lives, and the more they have to struggle about. So the first step is to relax and do nothing."

"I don't know how to do that."

"Give it a try."

Hagop grudgingly took a deep breath and lay perfectly still.

"How do you feel?" asked Sarkis.

"Silly."

"Then you're not relaxing enough."

"I could relax a lot more if you went and got a knife."

"Shh—none of that. Now lie back and keep perfectly still."

Hagop took another deep breath and tried again. "Okay, I'm relaxing."

"Good. Now isn't that much better?"

"Yes, but ..."

"No 'buts.' Remember, you're relaxing, and 'buts' are not allowed. Also, no 'howevers' or 'ifs.' Those are the rules." Sarkis made a closer examination of the boy's predicament by tweaking at the rope here and there. "How does the rope feel now?" he asked. "I mean, does it feel as tight as before?"

"I guess not, if I don't move."

"Excellent. See what progress we're making already?"

"But Sarkis, we haven't done anything yet!"

"There you go again with your 'buts.' We'll never get anywhere this way. Now relax and stop worrying."

The boy braced himself. "Okay, I'm not worrying. What next?"

"Close your eyes and make your mind a blank." Hagop closed his eyes and tried to make his mind a blank. "Now here's the important part," continued Sarkis. "While your mind is a blank, I want you to touch your left ear with your right hand."

"Wha— ? How am I supposed to ... ?"

"Is your mind a blank?"

"How can my mind be a blank when you tell me to do something goofy like that?"

"Your mind must stay a blank. You must stop thinking about everything."

"Well, how do you do that?"

"You don't do it. You stop doing it. That's the whole point."

"You can't stop thinking when somebody tells you not to think."

"Try."

"Are you sure this is going to work?"

"No one said it would be easy."

"Okay, I won't think about anything."

"Which is not the same as thinking about not thinking. You do see the difference, of course."

"Oh, sure. Anybody knows that."

"Good. How's your right hand doing?"

"It's not doing anything."

"I see," muttered Sarkis. He leaned closer to the boy as if checking his vital signs. "If that doesn't work, try your left hand on your right ear. Or maybe both hands on both ears."

Hagop gave Sarkis a most dubious look. "I know you must be kidding now."

"I never kid when my friends are in trouble."

Hagop could no more bring either hand to either ear than do cartwheels across the lawn. His efforts, however, were not without tangential results. While failing to move his hands, he noticed one foot wagging at him like a welcome. Similarly, while bringing Sarkis's attention to the moving foot, he was able to point to said foot with his hand.

"Sarkis, I moved my foot and hand."

"Now we're getting somewhere."

"What's going on?"

"I don't know, but we shouldn't look a gift horse in the mouth."

Hagop now accelerated his efforts to free himself. Surely, he thought, only a few more knee jerks stood between himself and freedom. Unfortunately, in his haste to get free, he not only undid what progress he had made, but entangled himself deeper into a maze of intertwining loops and knots. By the end of his efforts he looked like someone ensnared in a net. "Oh, what's the use?" he groaned.

"Don't rush. Don't even think about getting free. It's a philosophical truth, Hagop. You'll never do what you want to do until you stop wanting to do it."

"So that means I should want to stay tied up in this rope for the rest of my life."

"Well, not exactly," hedged Sarkis. "We wouldn't have to go that far, either."

"So what now?"

"Try whistling."

"Whistling?"

"Whistling always helps."

"Sounds like more dumb stuff to me."

"What have you got to lose?"

True enough, thought Hagop. At this advanced stage of his predicament what did he have to lose? One might say (if given to shameless puns) that the boy was at the end of his rope. Accordingly, he lay back and closed his eyes. He took a deep breath, sucking in his cheeks, and began whistling a song his mother used to sing to him not so many years ago, "You Are My Sunshine." At first the music sputtered a bit, some notes trapped between his tongue and teeth, but once disengaged, it found its way into lilting strains that floated through the air like a barcarole. Who can say how the boy's left hand slipped free and started swinging like a baton in perfect 3/4 time, or how his right foot, formerly bound at the ankle, grazed his instep on its passage from bondage to unfettered space. At no time did Hagop question these developments. He accepted them as the impulse of something beyond his control, beyond his best sense of what made sense. He just kept whistling away without a care, serenading the treetops and filling the air with musical staffs and clef notes.

With his final reprise of the song Hagop charmed two whippoorwills out of a magnolia tree and sent them circling above the rooftop like grace notes.

With his freedom imminent now, the boy unraveled the few remaining loops and came to his feet. For the rest, he had only to shimmy like a dancer and let the rope collapse harmlessly around his feet. By way of celebration, he grabbed the rope with both hands and, with a heave-ho, tossed it into the air.

"I did it!" proclaimed the boy.

"Hagop, you're a genius."

"I wish I knew what I did, though," said the boy, with a slaphappy shake of the head.

Sarkis looked no less stumped as he sat cross-legged on the ground with his chin propped in the palm of one hand like a bemused sage. "I keep thinking there must be a moral in all this, but for the life of me I don't know what it could be."

"Sarkis, some kooky things have happened to us in Asbury Park, but this must be the kookiest yet."

"You may be right."

"Oh, well," sighed the boy, glad to have the incident behind him. "Can we go for our walk now?"

"I think we both could use one, don't you?"

Sarkis slapped his kneecaps as a cue to rise and get on with the day. Coming to his feet, he dismissed Hagop's odd predicament, or perhaps more accurately, removed it to an obscure corner of his mind reserved for life's little unsolved mysteries.

Sarkis swung an arm around the boy's shoulder and the two left Mrs. Lilly's yard and sauntered down the row of tree-lined streets to the boardwalk.

DOWN AND OUT IN ASBURY PARK

For someone other than Sarkis, being flat broke on a Tuesday morning in Asbury Park would be a depressing state of affairs. For Sarkis, however, poverty had a sanguine affect. Traipsing along the boardwalk with Hagop, he felt exhilarated, expansive in spirit, and diabolically alive in a way he had never felt before. Reduced to a worm's eye view of the world, he had an expansive view of the world's possibilities. Nothing could disadvantage him. He was like a pauper for whom a penny found or favor granted was a bonanza of good fortune. Being without money, Sarkis was free of those standards of taste and judgment that attach to material comfort. He could never have a bad meal when he was hungry or sleep on a poor mattress when he was tired. Being without money, he could never demean himself to an unworthy task, since he placed himself above nothing. Being without money, he could never be cheated or compromised. Having no vested interest in anything except his own survival, he could thrive on whatever contributed to that survival, as would a gull scavenging for refuse on the beach.

Of course being without money had its disadvantages, too, the most notable being hunger. By mid-afternoon, Sarkis and Hagop were feeling the pangs of such hunger, made all the more acute by the sight of so many food concessions along the boardwalk and of people munching on subs, French fries, and pizza slices.

Presently the man and boy came upon a small crowd gathered around a dais. The object of the crowd's attention was a salesman demonstrating the many uses of a kitchen slicer. He chopped up an assortment of foodstuffs: cheeses, cucumbers, radishes, tomatoes, hard boiled eggs, onions, and the like. All fell under the slicer's swift, razor-sharp blade, only to be swept aside as disposable leftovers. Sarkis was staring raptly at the remnants like a famished wayfarer who had just stumbled upon a banquet table.

"Hagop, I think we're in luck."

"What's going on? I can't see," said Hagop, his view obstructed by people in front of him. Sarkis hoisted the boy onto his shoulders saddle style. "Oh my!" sighed the boy, his eyes opening wide.

The salesman was a portly huckster, slouching toward middle age, who displayed all the attributes of a seasoned professional. His banter was brisk and nonstop, and not without a dash of humor to keep the audience entertained.

"... easy to operate, easy to clean. Why, folks, a child could dish up a jiffy salad with this miracle worker, and what a relief that should be to you mothers, hmm? Why now, you can have your son or daughter working right beside you in the kitchen where you can keep an eye on the little devil—oops!—I mean darling." A smattering of chuckles rippled through the audience.

"What's he going to do with all the food he cuts up?" asked Hagop.

"Throw it away," said Sarkis.

"... and when was the last time you ladies can remember slicing onions without crying in your lettuce?" the salesman said as he shredded an onion in a swift, guillotine stroke.

Hagop sighed as if he were watching the demise of a friend.

"There go the onions," he said.

"If we had some oil and vinegar," said Sarkis, "we could make a delicious salad on that table."

"For cheeses," said the salesman, "switch the Quick-O-Matic to extra fine and you'll have as smooth a slice of cheddar or Monterey Jack as ever sat on a dairy shelf."

"I could sure go for an onion and cheese sandwich," said Hagop.

Sarkis smacked his lips resolutely. "Hagop, as sure as my name is Sarkis Levonian, we're going to get our hands on some of that food."

"How?"

"I don't know. I'm thinking."

At the close of the demonstration, Sarkis and Hagop joined a line that had formed to purchase Quick-O-Matics. Both looked self-conscious and furtive, like a pair of thieves expecting to be apprehended at any moment.

"Sarkis, what are we doing on line? We can't buy anything."

"Shh. The first step in our plan is to get as close to the food as possible. We'll worry about the second step later."

As the line dwindled to one customer ahead of them, Hagop became increasingly nervous.

"Sarkis, what are we going to do?"

"I'm still thinking."

"We're next in line."

"I know."

A moment later they stood face to face with the salesman.

"And how many Quick-O-Matics can I get for you?" asked the salesman with a smile.

Sarkis cleared his throat and spoke up in a deep voice exuding confidence and authority.

"Levonian's the name, Sarkis Levonian. I want to tell you how much I enjoyed your presentation. I was impressed, genuinely impressed. I don't remember ever seeing a more versatile demonstration in the field of household appliances."

"Why, thank you. Thank you very much."

Sarkis edged toward the table. "I only wish we could have had a closer look at this slicer in action. My, my, this is quite an apparatus you have here." Sarkis picked up a radish and held it to his eye like a jeweler appraising a precious stone. "Fine cut. Fine cut, indeed. Mind if I have a taste?"

"Oh, no, help yourself," said the salesman, somewhat puzzled by the intense scrutiny.

"Thank you," said Sarkis, tossing the radish into his mouth and sampling it like a professional gourmet. "Good. Mm. Very good. Clean taste. Healthy aroma. No signs of metallic chromotosis. Here, Hagop, try one of these," and he handed a slice to the boy.

The salesman had begun squinting about six words back.

"Pardon me? Metallic what ... ?"

"Chromotosis," said Sarkis, savoring the radish as one might a succulent fruit, and daintily rubbing his thumb and index finger in lieu of a napkin to clean his hands. "Metallic chromotosis. It's a toxic bacterium that rubs off the cutting edge of inferior metals. Over a period of time, it can cause eye spasms and temporary aphasia."

The salesman frowned skeptically. "I never heard of it."

"Believe me, not many people have," said Sarkis. "We're keeping our findings on this little bugger under wraps until we can take some concrete preventative measures. No point inciting public alarm." He stepped to the table and sampled another radish. "To be perfectly honest, it's probably the most insidious form of viral transmission I've come across in all my years as a consumer disease specialist."

"Consumer disease specialist?" The salesman's eyes bulged for an instant.

Sarkis, upon noticing another customer behind him, stepped aside. "But forgive me, I didn't mean to interrupt your business. Please tend to your customer. I'll just stay out of your way and ... eh ... sniff around a bit, if it's all right with you."

"Hey mister, anything wrong here?" said the customer, an elderly, bandy-legged gentleman wearing a Hawaiian print shirt and Bermuda shorts. "You sound like somebody who knows what he's talking about."

"Wrong? Not that I can see." Sarkis crossed in front of the salesman. "Excuse me, would you mind if I tried one of those cucumbers?"

"Cucum— oh, no, go right ahead," said the distracted salesman. Both he and the customer now watched intently as Sarkis shared two slices of cucumber with the boy.

"Hagop, have you ever tasted a more delicious cucumber in your life? I can't believe this machine cuts as well as it does without a hint of metallic tartness, let alone any sign of chromotosis."

"Hold on," interrupted the customer. "That's the word you used before. Chromo ... what?"

"Oh, please, just ignore me," said Sarkis apologetically. "Sometimes I get carried away and start talking shop in public. It's a bad habit of mine."

The customer kept watching Sarkis as if awaiting some final

stamp of approval on the product. Sarkis deliberated over another slice of cucumber, then winked at the customer. "Excellent appliance. Don't see how you could possibly go wrong."

The salesman breathed easier.

"Well, okay, then," said the customer. "Wrap one up. The wife's gadget happy, and this'll give her a new toy to play with for a while."

Upon completing this final transaction, the salesman turned to see Sarkis snooping among the vegetables like a bloodhound sniffing for food scraps. He moved from one food group to another, hunched over the table with his nose almost nudging the vegetables.

"What are you doing now?" asked the salesman warily.

Sarkis remained silent until he completed what appeared to be an extensive olfactory examination. Standing upright, he sniffed at the air as if some mysterious bouquet lingered there, then concluded his study with a few smacks of the lip. "Personally I'm sold on the Quick-O-Matic. I only wish my wife were here to see for herself. She would be delighted as well." Sarkis's face took on a guilty, confessional look. "Listen, I realize what I'm about to say will sound ridiculous, and you would have every right to tell me to get lost and mind my own business, but might it be possible to take a few of these scraps home to show my wife?"

"You want to take food scraps home?"

"Believe me, I'm embarrassed to even make the suggestion. It's just that ... well ... you know how particular women can be. And my wife—well, to be honest, she's a little touchier than most when it comes to household appliances. You might say it's an occupational hazard." Sarkis gave a shrug of forbearance. "Being a little suspicious just comes with the job for her."

"Oh? Is she in the appliance business?"

"You might say that. Being an undercover agent for the Department of Health, she naturally comes across cases of fraud and misrepresentation in one area of product safety."

"Undercover agent?" The salesman shot a nervous glance around him. "By any chance, you and the wife ... I mean, you wouldn't be here on any kind of official business, would you?"

"Official business? You mean an investigation of some kind? I should say not. No, no, my friend. The little lady and I are here for a well-earned vacation. We've been working around the clock tracking down health code violators and appliance con artists. 'Boardwalk bandits,' we call them. Oh, no, we've come to the shore for a rest. Sun and surf, that's the ticket for us. I just thought if I took a few scraps home, she could put her mind at ease and be back here this afternoon to buy a Quick-O-Matic for herself and—who knows?—maybe one or two for friends."

"Well, it is a bit irregular ..."

"But I can see you have qualms. Believe me, I understand completely. Perhaps we should forget the whole idea. I'll simply tell the wife your company is not in the habit of letting customers inspect food cuttings, and that'll be the end of it."

"Well, no," stammered the salesman. "You don't have to put it that way. It's just that no one has ever asked before. I mean, I suppose it's all right. Food only gets thrown out anyway."

"Are you sure it's all right? I'll only need a few scraps of your leftovers to satisfy any suspicions my wife may have about the Quick-O-Matic."

"No problem. I'll even give you a hand," said the salesman, pulling out some plastic bags from under the counter. "How about some tomatoes for a start?"

"Tomatoes? A slice or two, no more," Sarkis's taste buds began salivating as he watched the salesman shovel a scoopful of juicy reds into a bag.

"Hard boiled eggs?"

"The same." Sarkis reconsidered. "Hold it. You'd better double up on the eggs. Dairy products have a complex enzyme structure. You can never be quite sure of what you're getting with dairy products." Sarkis hemmed momentarily. "They sometimes require multiple lab tests."

"Lab tests!"

Sarkis dropped his head in a show of embarrassment." Don't ask me why, but she brought her microscope and petri dish with her."

The salesman gawked. "Brought her mic ... her petri ... on vacation?"

"I think the job may be getting to her."

The salesman nervously bagged the eggs and scanned the table again. "Cheese?"

"Why not? In fact throw in a little extra in case we run into the enzyme problem again."

By the time the salesman finished bagging scraps from every food source on the table, Sarkis had his arms full. Even at that, the salesman kept looking around as if some final, culminating touch remained to be added to his offering. At length, he sidled up to Sarkis and whispered out of the side of his mouth. "Listen, what would you say to some real food?" The salesman's eyes took on a slightly diabolical look.

"Real food?"

"A little extra something for you and the wife, something to make your stay in Asbury Park—shall we say, a little tastier."

"Tastier?" Sarkis's face lit up.

The salesman edged closer, maintaining the strictest confidentiality. "As a matter of company policy I keep in the backroom a few select food items for special occasions— promotionals, giveaways, and events of that nature. At present I have in my possession a loaf of freshly shipped, imported Genoa salami. I'm not talking pizza topping here, my friend. I'm talking prime, top-of-the-line, deli cuisine. How about a few cuts? You and the wife will love it."

"Salami?" said Sarkis, his eyes rolling with anticipation. Just then he felt a prohibitive yank on the arm from Hagop who was eager to flee with what booty they had amassed. Sarkis reluctantly deferred to the yank. "But no, I couldn't accept such a kindness. You've done too much already." Sarkis started to leave, then stopped and turned around. He tilted his head thoughtfully. "Then again, there's no denying salami would make an ideal specimen for chromotosis study. The meat possesses unique properties not to be found in any other luncheon meat—oily base, recessed seed pockets, a topography that normally would be a haven for microbe infestation." Sarkis assumed an air of deliberation. "In fact, I would say that once a slicer passes the salami test, there's really nothing more to be done. Case closed. Any attempt to bring the matter before an administrative panel would be laughed out of court."

The salesman blanched. "What court?"

"Forget I even said that. The chances are so remote they're not even worth mentioning."

"Don't move!" yelped the salesman, throwing up his hands like a roadblock. "I'll be right back!"

He withdrew to a prefabricated curtained shed behind him and promptly reappeared with the salami loaf, a brickish red hunk of succulence. Upon adjusting the slicer for fine cuts, the salesman lopped off a dozen slices then wrapped them with the care one might give to the most fragile glassware. The pungent, appetizing aroma filled Sarkis's nostrils and almost sent him into a ravenous swoon. "Just a little something for you and the wife," said the salesman. With a wink he added, "You tell the little lady there's more where that came from if she runs short."

"You're much too kind," said Sarkis, adding the package to the others tucked into the crook of his arm. "We're most thankful. I daresay, you'll never know how much."

The salesman gave a self-effacing shrug. "I'm just a guy who likes doing for people. Sometimes I do for them and sometimes they do for me. Know what I mean? That's what life's all about, right? People doing for each other."

"A beautiful philosophy. I couldn't have put it better myself." Sarkis flashed a sly smile to let the salesman know certain veiled references had been grasped and taken into confidence. "But now we really must be on our way. I wouldn't want these scraps to go stale. Test results are always more reliable when the food is fresh." Sarkis nudged the boy to start walking. "If you don't hear from us in an hour, assume all test results were positive. Or is it negative? I never could get those terms straight."

Sarkis and Hagop headed down the boardwalk and out of sight. In their wake they left the salesman standing beside a table of food scraps and wearing a befuddled look. It was the look of a man who, under the least prodding, might not only confess to a crime he had never committed, but a crime the nature of which was still a mystery to him.

Sarkis and Hagop made for the first unoccupied bench they could find. They unwrapped their bounty of food scraps, spread out the delectables and feasted. The first item to go was the scrumptious salami, topped with tomato slices and onions. Cheese and hard boiled eggs were not far behind. At length, with an ample meal under his belt, Sarkis stretched his legs across the rail guard and smiled with a consummate sense of well-being. He patted his belly as if to congratulate all gastro-digestive functions for a job well done, and finished off this postprandial ceremony with a little belch. Having fortified the needs of his stomach, he was a man for whom life could afford no greater fulfillment.

"Hagop, I want to go on record as saying that food earned by honest labor can never match the taste of food earned by your wits. Food earned by honest labor has a blander, more tired taste—I guess because the food is taken for granted as the just desserts of your labors. But food earned by your wits? Ah, that's when eating is eating. Just imagine it, Hagop. You go from day to day never knowing where your next meal is coming from. Each meal may well be your last. And then out of the blue, like a gift from the gods, an opportunity arises to eat again. Can anything compare to the taste of such food? The senses heighten, the palate tingles. Each morsel becomes as precious as life itself. Eating becomes an act of homage, a cause for exultation." Sarkis burped as a final commemorative tribute. "That's the truth of the matter, Hagop, if the truth matters for anything."

"That must be the truth," said Hagop, gobbling up a mouthful of cheese and radishes.

With appetites satisfied, our two companions continued their walk along the boardwalk and past refreshment stands, souvenir shops fronted by postcard racks and T-shirt displays, and assorted food emporiums. Soon they came across another gathering, this one assembled outside an auction showroom. There, a young man, garbed in red suspenders and a matching bow tie, was soliciting customers for the auction soon to take place inside, and doing so with all the flair of a carnival showman. For openers he whetted the curiosity of the crowd by announcing he would perform a feat of magic; namely, that he would transform, right before his audience, a one dollar bill into a ten dollar bill. To this end he pulled out a dollar from his pocket and wagged it before the gathering. For the next ten minutes he diverted his audience with clever digressions and rapid fire patter, and, in short, deferred a trick that would never see the light of day. Not only did the young man sidestep any pretense to magic, but he wheedled a good faith deposit of a dollar from every person interested in attending the auction.

"Hagop, we're just in time for the auction," said Sarkis, his voice tingling with anticipation. For as long as he could remember auctions had always held a special fascination for him. He looked upon those who conducted these events as belonging to a breed apart, to a world of nomadic wanderers comparable to gypsies and circus folk. Auctioneers seemed to appear out of nowhere with their massive cargoes of furniture, housewares, and *objets d'art*, and then, a day or two later, to disappear as suddenly as they had arrived on the scene. Their comings and goings, like those of tent folders, seemed shrouded in mystery, and their fringe societies governed by secret laws.

"Sarkis, what's gonna happen?"

"You'll see," said Sarkis, leading Hagop to the entrance of the showroom.

Inside, they took seats near the front, the better to experience the full sweep and spectacle of the sale. On a stage, cartons of merchandise were stockpiled while other goods were already on display: lamps, chairs, picture frames, paintings, silverware, and items too numerous to mention.

"Where do they get everything to sell?" asked Hagop.

"From people who have to sell their belongings, or sell the belongings of a relative who has died. It's sad to think about, but auctions are often born out of people's misfortunes."

"Do you think we should sit so close to the front? Remember, we can't buy anything."

"Shh," muttered Sarkis, with a finger raised to his lips. "At an auction if you don't buy anything, you have to pretend you're not buying because you're not interested, not because you have no money."

"I feel like everybody can see us up front."

"They can."

Just before the auction began, one last patron appeared at the door and made her way down the aisle. She was an imperious looking woman with an upright carriage that was literally heightened by a silver-gray bouffant hairstyle. She wore a white chiffon dress with matching white gloves and high heeled shoes. She was bedecked in jewelry. Bracelets rustled from her wrists, rings glittered from her fingers, and a pearl necklace dangled from her neck. Her attire would seem more in keeping with a royal gala than an Asbury Park auction, and yet her deportment and grace were such that she did not appear overly dressed for the occasion. To the contrary, she gave the regal impression of being *de rigueur* while making everyone else in the shirt-sleeved crowd appear improperly attired.

The lady entered the row in which Sarkis and Hagop were seated.

"Excuse me," she said as she crossed in front of the man and boy and took a seat several chairs away from Hagop.

With the appearance of the auctioneer, the sale got underway. He was an attractively tanned, middle aged gentleman whose crop of wavy black hair was streaked with gray at the temples. Taking center stage, he promptly ordered one of his aides to close the doors in the back and thus seal off any distractions from the boardwalk. As the doors closed behind them, Sarkis and Hagop shared a humble but exhilarated feeling of being part of a select, secret society.

"The auctioneer's about to speak," said Sarkis.

"Ladies and gentlemen," came the resonant voice from the stage, "before we begin, I'd like those of you who gave my assistant a dollar outside to raise your hands. Now I don't know who among you gave money, and maybe I'll see more hands than I have dollars for, but that's the chance I'm going to take. Some of you showed your trust by putting your money on the line, and I intend to repay that trust." Reaching into a carton nearby, he pulled out a handful of ballpoint pens. "I'm giving out these Dynamo ballpoint pens to anyone who gave a dollar outside. So let's see those hands." He began hurling pens throughout the audience while people lurched and lunged to catch them. "These pens retail for two dollars apiece, but they're yours now for half the price. That's the way we do business around here. You not only get what you pay for, you get more than you pay for. If anybody loses, it's me."

"Isn't he brilliant?" whispered Sarkis. "A true master at his trade."

"Why don't you put your hand up?"

"That would be dishonest."

"Oh. I thought maybe you wanted a pen."

"The pens are no good anyway. They stop writing after two or three postcards."

From the outset of the bidding, the auctioneer proved himself to be a shrewd salesman, a wily psychologist, and, on occasion, a flamboyant showman. Starting with miscellaneous items such as embossed napkin holders and whatnot figurines, he covered a range of merchandise from cuckoo clocks to oil paintings, all of which were acclaimed as unique or superlative examples of their kind. Whenever the bidding stalled, the auctioneer never hesitated to chide the audience for its lack of appreciation. These reproaches, however, were so adroitly delivered they made the audience feel more guilty than resentful, and served to spark more active participation in the bidding. After a series of moderate successes, the auctioneer removed his jacket and loosened his tie as if to dispense with any formal barriers that might still exist between himself and his audience. By this time, his voice had developed a touch of hoarseness, but his enthusiasm and intensity never flagged.

About midway through the afternoon's activity, the auctioneer paused as though to signal the end of one phase of the day's business and the beginning of another. He smiled at his audience. Then, with an air of solemnity, he retreated to the stockpile of merchandise behind him. From the clutter of collectibles, he lifted a hefty silver serving tray. Holding it above his head with both hands like a trophy, he displayed it to his audience. The auctioneer did not utter a word, his silence commanding the kind of respect reserved for dignified, not to say reverential, occasions. The tray was a formidable if faintly tarnished piece of work. It featured bulky handles and detailed engravings around the edge. The richness of its ornamentation, the durability of its appearance, and the hand-tooled flavor of its workmanship gave it the earmarks of a collector's item.

"My friends," began the auctioneer, "I've saved the best for now because I wanted to be sure you were the kind of group that could appreciate the aesthetic as well as the practical. I believe you are such a group, and I'm prepared to put my trust in your hands. You see before you a serving tray of classic elegance. I wish I could pass it among you so that each of you could appreciate its craftsmanship and its delicate, filigreed design work, but, of course, time will not permit me to do so. Ladies and gentlemen, I offer you today a prime example of the tradesman's art. Here, in the tradition of the great silversmiths of Renaissance Italy is a treasure to be cherished the rest of your life. A little old? Yes. A little weathered in the crevices? Yes, that too; I won't deny it. But it is a work that resonates with a sense of history and pride of workmanship all but extinct in today's assembly line, cookie-cutter world. Notice, if you will, the solid, heavy-duty handles and the sculptured inlay work. And then, as a crowning jewel, we have engraved around the perimeter an inspiring pictorial essay, the story of Adam and Eve in tableau sequence. Imagine it, friends, the parable of Creation—from Man's awakening in the Garden of Eden to his Fall from Grace, all of it depicted in loving detail on this tray. My friends, at first I was reluctant to place this item on sale because I thought a public auction would be too demeaning a fate for such a work of art. For a time I considered offering it to a private collector, or even donating it to an archive society where it could find a home among other valued heirlooms. But then I thought of my duty to you. I made you a promise that I would withhold nothing from your appraisal, and I will not break that promise now. All I ask is that you show your most discriminating appreciation for this piece because, my friends, you and I will never see its likes again."

Sarkis was reduced to near tears by the auctioneer's presentation. "The man's an inspiration," he said to the boy.

The lady in white, sitting near Hagop, had not participated in the auction thus far, or shown any but a peripheral interest in the items offered. For the most part, she had been sitting with her legs crossed, browsing a fashion magazine with a bored, desultory air. With the presentation of the tray, however, her attention picked up.

"Forty dollars," she called out; after which, she resumed the browsing of her magazine.

"I have an opening bid of forty dollars," said the auctioneer.

A succession of bids followed:

"Forty-two dollars."

"Forty-three fifty."

Sarkis followed the bidding like a spectator viewing a six-way tennis match.

"Forty-five dollars," said the lady in white, looking up just long enough to post her bid.

"I hear forty-five dollars," said the auctioneer. "Forty-five dollars. Come now, ladies and gentlemen. The handles alone are worth forty-five dollars."

"He's right," whispered Sarkis. "Forty-five dollars is a crime for that tray."

"Forty-seven dollars," came a voice from the rear.

"Fifty dollars," said the lady in white.

Sarkis moved to the edge of the chair. "Now we're getting some action."

"Fifty-one dollars," said another voice.

"Fifty-five," added the lady in white.

Suddenly Sarkis bounced to his feet like a jack-in-a-box. "Fifty-seven fifty," he blurted; whereupon, Hagop gagged and pulled him down by the seat of his pants.

The boy squealed in a whisper, "What are you doing!"

"I couldn't help myself," said Sarkis. "All my life I've wanted to make a bid at an auction, and I couldn't hold out another second."

The lady in white smiled at Sarkis as though to acknowledge a rivalry in the making. Sarkis smiled back sheepishly, as though to apologize for having the temerity to even mount a challenge.

"Fifty-eight dollars," came a voice.

"Sixty dollars," said the lady, a bid that had the dual effect of reaching a milestone and of eliminating the early competition. A hush fell over the audience. "I hear sixty dollars," said the auctioneer. "Sixty dollars. Why ladies and gentlemen, if I sold you this tray for sixty dollars, I'd be guilty of giving it away."

"He's right again," said Sarkis, who had come to accept anything the auctioneer said as the unvarnished truth.

"Sixty-one dollars," came a voice from the rear.

Sarkis bolted to his feet. "Sixty-two fifty," he called out as Hagop lunged forward and pulled him down by the seat of the pants again. The boy curled up in his seat like someone trying to roll himself into a ball and hide.

"Seventy dollars," said the lady in white, who throughout the bidding had given the impression of merely toying with the competition.

Sarkis came to his feet again, this time with a confident mien, as in one having acquired a certain expertise in the protocol of auction bidding. Exuding an air of *savoir faire*, he said, "Seventy-five dollars. And, may I add, worth every penny of it." With a gracious nod to the lady in white he took his seat.

Hagop moaned like a sick pup.

"Eighty dollars," countered the lady.

Sarkis rose to the challenge. "Eighty-five dollars," he said with the aplomb of a seasoned veteran. "And may I take this opportunity to compliment the lady to my left for her impeccable taste in silverware and her high-minded sense of good sportsmanship."

Hagop slid deeper into his seat. "I wish I was dead."

"Ninety dollars," said the lady, a bid that marked another milestone and brought the audience to a tense, expectant hush.

"Hagop, sit up," urged Sarkis. "I don't want you to miss any of this."

"I can't watch," said the boy, and he nervously began munching on some leftover onions from lunch.

"Did you hear my last bid?"

"We're going to jail if you don't stop."

"I don't know if I can quit now. I've come too far."

The auctioneer reprised the last bid of ninety dollars. "Do I hear more? Ninety dollars going once. Ninety dollars going twice ..."

"Ninety-five!" came a voice from across the room.

"One hundred dollars," countered the lady in white. "And, may I add, my final bid." She closed the magazine and crossed her legs as she awaited the final disposition of the matter. Another silence fell over the room. The audience seemed to be waiting for a last, clinching bid from Sarkis.

"Hagop, I'm one bid away from taking it all."

"You're out of your head, that's what you are."

"You know I deserve that tray. No one has taken more chances than I have to get it."

"Keep your mouth shut—*puhleeze!*" begged Hagop. "Whatever you do, don't say a word."

"I hear one hundred dollars," announced the auctioneer surveying the audience for challengers. "One hundred dollars going once ..."

Sarkis bit his lip to restrain himself. "I'm letting my moment of victory slip by."

"One hundred dollars going twice ..."

Sarkis clenched his fists. "This is too painful."

"Last call," cried the auctioneer, his eyes sweeping the audience, but lingering momentarily on Sarkis, who moved to the edge of his seat. The moment proved to be insuppressible. Grabbing hold of the chair in front of him, he was starting to rise when Hagop, in a desperate flash, grabbed a fistful of onions and stuffed them into Sarkis's mouth before he could utter a sound. Sarkis's eyes popped. He gagged, and swallowed involuntarily.

"Sold for one hundred dollars to the lady in the third row," declared the auctioneer.

Sarkis rasped and fell back in his seat. Between a stinging sensation in his eyes and nostrils, and a gagging in his windpipe, he could barely see or speak. Tears began trickling down his reddened, glassy eyes. The lady in white, while unable to see precisely what was going on, could not help but notice Sarkis writhing in discomfort.

"Is anything wrong?" she asked.

Sarkis couldn't speak, and Hagop was too embarrassed to tell the truth.

"He feels bad because he couldn't have the tray," the boy said.

The lady was taken aback by what seemed a disproportionate amount of grief over a tray. "I had no idea the tray meant so much to him."

Sarkis was doubled over in his seat, his head between his knees, as he tried to recover from this blitz upon his senses. He was rubbing his stung eyes with both fists as the tears continued down his cheeks. "A family heirloom," he croaked in an effort to bolster the boy's explanation.

"A family heirloom? My goodness. Was there no way to keep it from being auctioned off?"

Sarkis raised his waterlogged eyes and looked haplessly at the lady.

"Creditors?" he peeped, afraid he might be taking his story too far, but still unable to check himself.

"Creditors? How unspeakably sad."

Sarkis embellished the moment with a few sniffles. "When mother passed, the creditors took everything. The boy and I rushed here in the hopes we might at least try to save the tray. It was mother's favorite." Sarkis lowered his head as though to pay silent homage to the memory.

"Why, the tray must be invaluable to you. Had I only known ..."

"Know? How could you know?" Sarkis heaved a sigh of relief as the sting of the onions abated. "But I'm sure the tray has found a good home now. If you don't mind my saying so, you look to be the kind of person who could provide it with the care and attention it needs."

The lady, who, as it happened, had a fierce respect for blood lines and things traditional, said, "I can do much more than that, my good man. The tray is yours! Had I known the circumstances, I never would have bid for it."

Sarkis gasped at this turnabout. "Oh, no, no. Please, the tray is yours."

"Nonsense, I won't hear of it. The tray is yours. To me it is no more than an interesting artifact to be added to an endless number of interesting artifacts I already own."

"But you don't understand ..."

"I understand only too well, my good man. You have been stripped of a precious family heirloom, and I am returning it to you, its rightful owner. It's really quite simple."

"No, no, you mustn't," said Sarkis. He took a deep breath, resolved now to end this charade. "You see ... everything I've been telling you ..."

"Has touched me deeply," concluded the lady. "My goodness, I would no more think of keeping this family memento from you than I would of robbing a person of his name."

"Miss ... please. Let me explain." Sarkis braced again for his confession. "Everything I've told you is a lie. I've never seen this tray before in my life."

"Tsk, tsk," said the lady, with a sly, knowing smile. "Your sense of honor is most admirable, but you needn't feel you have to lie to salvage your pride. You have nothing to be ashamed of, my good man. Life deals us all unfair blows. As far as I'm concerned the matter is closed and I'll entertain no more discussion on it."

"But miss, it's the truth ... You see, it was the onions. I really wasn't crying. I was choking on the onions."

"I haven't the slightest idea what you're talking about. Now that's quite enough," she added in an admonitory tone.

An abashed Sarkis dropped his head. "Yes, ma'am."

"The tray is yours by right and not mine by virtue of the fact that I could afford to purchase it. There are some things that money cannot buy, and pride in one's lineage happens to be one of them."

"Yes, ma'am."

"Good." The lady rose to leave. "I'll make the necessary arrangements, and you can pick up the tray at your convenience."

"You're much too kind," said Sarkis abjectly.

The lady waved off the compliment with the flick of the hand. "To tell the truth, I've never been a particularly kind or friendly person. If I possess any virtuous traits, it's probably that of honesty, but even that is often compromised by insensitivity to the feelings of others." The lady paused. Her expression softened into a self-deprecating smile. "Who knows? Perhaps I need to give you the tray more than you need to have it." Her smile lingered over the irony of these words. "Motives are such tricky devils, aren't they? One can never be quite sure why one does anything. But if you'll excuse me now, I'll take care of our business at the front desk and be on my way. I wish you both a pleasant afternoon."

Sarkis's eyes followed the lady from the time she made her way to the front of the room to make arrangements for the tray, to her exit up the aisle and out the door. Watching her leave, he wiped the last onion tear from his eye.

"Hagop, there goes an elegant lady."

"What'll we do now?" asked the boy.

"I'm not sure," puzzled Sarkis. "Unless we just leave the tray and sneak out the back door."

"But the lady just paid for it, didn't she?"

"Yes, she did. I could see from here she was writing a check at the desk." Sarkis's eyes lit up. "Wait a minute. The lady's name and address, and probably her phone number, would be on her check. If we leave the tray here, the auction people are bound to get in touch with her, and see that the tray goes to its rightful owner."

"Good, let's do it."

"We'll have to be careful here. When we head for the door, walk, don't run. We don't want to look like we're running away from anything."

The two sidled out to the aisle and headed toward the back door as unobtrusively as possible. They were just steps away from a successful escape when they were accosted by an employee, who as it happened was the young man in red suspenders who had solicited customers on the boardwalk earlier. "Excuse me," said the young man, "but you've forgotten your tray."

"My tray?" said Sarkis, feigning surprise, not to say umbrage. "There must be some mistake. I don't own a tray. I was outbid for it."

"There's no mistake, sir. The lady who bought the tray was quite explicit in her instructions. The item is to go to you."

"You're sure she meant me?"

"Oh, yes. In fact, she made a point of saying you might forget to pick it up. Which is why I've been keeping an eye on you to make sure you didn't leave without it."

"Oh," muttered Sarkis like a miscreant caught in the act.

"You can pick up the tray at the front desk. It's wrapped and ready to go."

"Tell me, young man, would it be possible to make a gift of the tray back to the lady? That's what I'd really like to do."

"That's something you and the lady will have to work out between yourselves. My instructions were to make sure you don't leave the showroom without the item. Whatever you do after that is entirely up to you, sir."

And so it came to pass that Sarkis and Hagop became the not-so-proud possessors of a hefty, silver-plated and somewhat tarnished serving tray, as cumbersome as it was distinctive.

When you're down and out in Asbury Park, practical considerations outweigh all other concerns. Accordingly, whatever aesthetic charms the tray may have possessed were secondary to whatever price it could bring in the marketplace. In this instance the marketplace was a local pawn shop in downtown Asbury Park. There, the shopkeeper gave the tray a cursory, disinterested inspection and concluded, "Ten dollars, take it or leave it." Sarkis was quick to accept the money, but Hagop appeared none too pleased. In fact, by the time they left the shop, the boy was quite miffed over the transaction.

"How come the lady paid so much for the tray and we got so little?"

"Because the shopkeeper is a businessman and he has to make a profit."

"But we got cheated good."

"I suppose so, but we needed the money, too."

"And you're not even a little mad?"

"Look at it this way, Hagop. We started out the day without any food in our stomachs or money in our pockets. We now have full bellies and ten dollars to spend. I'd say we were doing pretty well."

"The man in the shop will get lots more money for the tray when he sells it."

"Yes, he will, but look at what he has to do to earn his money. He has to sit in that musty shop all day and hardly ever get any fresh air. He has to worry about whether business is getting better or getting worse. He has to keep records on how much money comes in and how much goes out. At closing time he has to set his burglar alarm and hope he doesn't get robbed in the middle of the night. The next morning he has to come back to the shop and do the same thing all over again. Tell you the truth, I'm not sure who's the one getting cheated."

"I still think we are."

"Maybe so, but let me ask you this: How can you cheat two people who started out the day with nothing to lose?"

"I don't know."

"Neither do I. Let's go see what Mumfred's doing."

THE END OF SOMETHING

Nothing could have prepared Sarkis and Hagop for the shock they received upon arriving at the merry-go-round. In the presence of scattered onlookers standing around, three workmen in coveralls were dismantling sections of the platform, reconnecting struts and adjusting wires in the control box. Moreover, two policemen were on the scene to keep onlookers clear of the work area. Among those onlookers was a fuming Mumfred Lewis. With hands clasped behind his back and a scowl on his face, he was struggling to maintain his composure while witnessing what he considered to be nothing less than a wrecking crew operation. As for the workmen, shuffling here and there, they went about their task with a plodding, lugubrious air. Whether stacking boards, resetting clamps and bolts at the hub of the merry-go-round, or fiddling with the circuitry in the control box, they generated all the zeal of a team of grave diggers.

An atmosphere of foreboding permeated the room. There was a feeling here of things having gone awry, of unseen forces having been set into motion, forces fixed on a course that allowed for no appeal. The bystanders themselves seemed to sense as much. The scene was strangely quiet, notwithstanding the bang of a mallet or the thud of boards being dropped. People, if they spoke at all, did so in hushed, furtive tones as they might at the scene of an accident.

"Sarkis," cried Hagop, "what's happening?"

"I don't know."

They hurried to where Mumfred was standing, and one look at the proprietor's distraught face told them to expect the worst.

"They're altering the merry-go-round. They're making it go forward," said Mumfred.

"What!" exclaimed Hagop. "They can't do that."

"How did it happen?" asked Sarkis.

"Somebody formed a citizen's committee and filed a complaint. They sure didn't waste any time. The police showed me a signed court order not two hours ago, something to do with custom and practice of county recreational facilities."

Sarkis murmured to himself, "Jared's father," the words sounding like a refrain that he knew one day would haunt him.

"Sarkis, tell 'em to stop," implored Hagop. "Tell 'em they can't do this."

"Mumfred," said Sarkis, "isn't there anything we can do?"

"They've got two police officers here to see the job gets done. You tell me what you think we can do."

"I don't care," protested Hagop. "They have no right."

"There's even a newspaperman wandering around here somewhere," said Mumfred. "He caught me at a bad time, and what I told him you couldn't print in a family newspaper. He may come looking for you, too, Sarkis. Seems like the merry-go-round has made some news around here."

The three friends watched the workmen lumber to and fro, one of them occasionally giving orders to the others.

"Look at them," said Mumfred disdainfully. "They've been puttering around here as if they know what they are doing, but they don't."

"Are they the maintenance specialists?" asked Sarkis.

"I didn't stop to ask, but if they are, wouldn't you know they'd show up the one time you didn't need them."

Hagop looked on anxiously, fidgeting from side to side like someone handcuffed and unable to move freely. Suddenly he bolted toward the platform, but just before reaching it, ran into the arms of one police officer standing guard. The officer literally swept the boy off his feet and held him at bay.

"All right, young fella, just stand out of the way, now. These men have a job to do, so let them do it."

"They don't have a job to do, because there's nothing that has to be done."

Mumfred came up behind the boy and took him to one side. He put a protective arm around Hagop's shoulder as the boy's outrage and frustration gave way to sobs and tears. Mumfred held the boy closer. The owner bristled with a kind of public defiance toward anyone who might dare lay another hand on the boy.

* * *

In the course of the afternoon, the newspaper reporter had been circulating among bystanders and covering the story from a variety of "angles." From passersby he obtained the man-on-the-street angle; from the two policemen the law enforcement angle; from various children the human interest angle; and from the workmen themselves the repairman's angle, although this last group, being a phlegmatic crew, had the least to say. About the only angle still to be covered was that of someone directly connected with the merry-go-round. In this venture he had been the least successful. In light of his fractious encounter with Mumfred, the reporter now sought out Sarkis, who had been pointed out to him by a bystander in the gathering.

The reporter was a short, wiry young man with his pen and notebook at the ready. To be sure, his every mannerism, from a snoopy hunch in his shoulders, to the way his eyes scoped out a room at a single glance, seemed primed for the quintessential task of note taking.

"Good afternoon, sir," he said, finding Sarkis standing alone at the rear of the pavilion and removed from the busy work attending the merry-go-round. "Ron Fritzo—*Asbury Park Dispatch*. I understand you work here at the merry-go-round." Sarkis acknowledged as much by his silence. "I'm covering the story for our evening edition. Mind if I ask you a few questions?" Again, Sarkis's silence served as consent. "Won't take but a few minutes of your time." The reporter flipped open to a page in his notepad. "Your full name?"

Sarkis hesitated before giving it. "Levonian," he finally said. "Sarkis Levonian."

Fritzo double checked the spelling. "Armenian, right? The i-a-n—that's the giveaway. I know some Armenians. Good people."

He resumed his questioning. "And how long have you been working here at the merry-go-round, Mr. Levonian?"

"Three days."

"Oh, a newcomer. Just you and Mr. Lewis, the owner, run the business?"

"We just help Mr. Lewis."

"We?"

"The boy and I."

"Oh, I wasn't aware of a third person. There's a boy working here, too?"

"Hagop."

Fritzo checked this spelling, too, and recorded the boy's age. "Your son?"

"No. A close friend."

The reporter raised an eyebrow, then jotted down the information and went onto other business.

"Mr. Levonian, what our readers would really like to know is how this kooky business all got started. I mean, whose idea was it to make the merry-go-round go backward?"

"Whose idea?"

"Yes, who dreamt up the gimmick? If I say so myself, it was a terrific promotional stunt."

"No one dreamt up anything."

"What I meant is, it had to come about some way. We know for a fact that until a few days ago this was just a normal, everyday merry-go-round."

"That's right."

"And then?"

"The merry-go-round had stopped running. We tried to fix it."

"Oh, I get it! So you fixed it to go in reverse."

"Well, let's just say we did what we could to get it started again."

"And what exactly was that?"

"I couldn't tell you in any detail. We just jiggled with the controls and made sure we didn't leave any loose wiring in the control box."

"But you must have done something to reverse the power."

"Yes, I guess we did, but I couldn't tell you what."

The reporter frowned skeptically. "That's a little far-fetched, wouldn't you say, Mr. Levonian?"

"No doubt of that, but true all the same."

"If you'll pardon my saying, you almost make it sound as if this machine started going backward on its own."

Sarkis smiled thoughtfully. "Who knows? Maybe machines are like people. They both need a change of direction now and then."

"Hey, that's clever. I like that," said the reporter, animated by the quip and quick to jot it down. "Maybe we could give this story a fairy tale slant. What would you think of that?" Eliciting an impassive reaction, the reporter flipped a page in his notepad and went on to a different subject. "Perhaps, Mr. Levonian, you could share some of your feelings with our readers. After all, you couldn't have been pleased to see the merry-go-round—how shall I put it?—being altered."

"My feelings?"

"Yes. Were you angry? Were you outraged? Our readers are always interested in the human side of a story as well as the factual."

Sarkis deliberated on the question. "Anger? Yes, I'm sure I felt anger; but I felt scared, too."

The reporter furrowed his brow. "Scared? That's a little strong, isn't it, Mr. Levonian? I mean, no one's life is in danger here. No one's physical well-being has been threatened. Why scared?"

"I suppose because everything has happened so fast. A number of well-meaning, civic-minded people have come together in the furtherance of an act that makes absolutely no sense. That's a little scary, don't you think?"

"But you have to admit that rules and ordinances have been violated. There's no disputing that, is there?"

"No, there's no disputing that," conceded Sarkis, hoping to keep this interview as short as possible.

"Keep in mind you do have a right to appeal. Have you or Mr. Lewis given any thought to challenging the judge's decision?"

"It never crossed my mind. As for any appeals, you'd have to ask Mr. Lewis. He's the proprietor and sole owner."

"I've already tried talking to him and he wasn't very cooperative."

"You may have picked a bad time to ask him what his feelings were."

"Suppose you were in Mr. Lewis' place; what would you do?"

"What would I do?"

"If you were the owner and sole proprietor of this merry-go-round, what action would you take?"

"Probably none," said Sarkis with a deadpan expression.

"None?" said Fritzo, caught off guard by Sarkis's answer. "You wouldn't want to explore your legal options? You wouldn't want your grievances redressed?"

"I'm not sure I have any grievances."

The reporter balked. "I'm afraid I don't understand you, Mr. Levonian. You have the right of appeal, the right to have your day in court. Why would you not challenge the judge's decision?"

"Let me put it this way, Mr. Fritzo. I don't pretend to know why this merry-go-round began doing what it did, or what, if anything, it means. But I know this. If there's a story it's trying to tell us, it has nothing to do with making legal appeals or reversing court decisions."

"I was only trying to present your side of the story."

"I've told you what I know."

"Maybe you have, maybe you haven't," said the reporter. His expression lapsed into a smug smile as he closed his notebook with a flip of the finger. "We'll be following this story for the next few days. Who knows? Perhaps our paths will cross again."

Sarkis let his attention wander to the workmen disassembling the platform.

"It's a small world," he said.

Evening came and the workmen still had made no progress in altering the direction of the merry-go-round. They plodded away in a tenacious, humdrum fashion, without a complaint or even a trace of discouragement. Periodically, they tested the merry-go-round, but the animals either continued to go backward or not move at all. Following each unsuccessful test, the workmen huddled for a conference, then dispersed and resumed their efforts. Meanwhile, Sarkis, Hagop, and Mumfred kept an uneasy vigil in which they kept hoping for continued failure while fearing eventual success.

"I don't want to watch anymore," said Mumfred, turning away

from the unrelievedly persistent operations taking place on the platform.

"Maybe they won't be able to fix it," said Hagop.

"Oh, they'll fix it," said Mumfred, "even if they have to tear it down and start all over again." In disgust he turned aside. He took a moment to collect himself. "Sarkis, as a rule I'm not given to the imbibing of alcoholic spirits, but there come those times in a man's life when no other remedy seems appropriate. In short, how would you like to join me for a drink?"

"Mumfred, you read my mind. Hagop, how about something for you? You look like you could use some refreshment."

The boy shook his head. "I'm staying," he said. "Somebody's got to watch."

"Are you sure you want to stay?" said Sarkis. "There's really nothing we can do."

"Somebody's got to watch," repeated the boy, his words like an unwavering pronouncement. "I'll wait for you here."

"We shouldn't be long," said Mumfred. "In case we're not back before those workers finish, make sure they clean up their mess before they go."

Hagop nodded grimly, like an orderly invested with the gravest of responsibilities.

As Sarkis and Mumfred headed toward the door, the owner said, "I saw you talking to the newspaperman this afternoon. Did he get the story he wanted?"

"I think he's still working on it," said Sarkis. "But it's a cinch he doesn't know much about merry-go-rounds."

* * *

Sarkis and Mumfred repaired to The Wonder Bar, a food and drink emporium near the boardwalk. At the bar they took their seats and scanned their surroundings, a racetrack milieu with photos of derby champions, track luminaries, and Winners' Circle presentations hanging from the walls. The two men ordered jiggers of whiskey with water chasers. A brisk opening round led to a more leisurely second, and then to a salubrious third. At this juncture in their tippling Sarkis and Mumfred had crossed the line of mere conviviality and entered the domain of chummy fellowship. Feelings heretofore guarded were openly expressed, and moods subject to quixotic changes. On the spur of the moment the men might feel sad or they might feel happy; they might feel humble or they might feel cocky. At times they would be seized with an impulse to celebrate life, and a moment later, an irrepressible urge to lament it. In sum, Sarkis and Mumfred were fortified, not only by alcoholic spirits, but by a heightened sense of life's bittersweetness. Theirs was a brand of camaraderie known only to those who have shared a fellowship in the environs of a friendly neighborhood bar.

"I propose a toast," said Mumfred, raising his shot glass. "Here's to Hagop, you and me, and a once-in-a-lifetime merry-go-round."

"To Ferris wheels and penny arcades," added Sarkis.

"To maintenance specialists—whoever, whatever, and wherever they may be."

They quaffed their drinks, and with the next round raised their glasses again. "Sarkis, I propose a toast to the medicinal powers of alcoholic spirits. Every now and then a man needs to throw caution to the wind and boost his spirits with a little fire water. Otherwise he's liable to get too serious. Life doesn't reward too much seriousness." His face saddened and he lowered his glass. "I'm worried about Hagop. Sometimes I think he's too sensitive. He feels things too deeply. It's not good to be so sensitive, is it, Sarkis?"

"He's hurting right now, but he'll be all right. And when he is, he'll be better than ever."

"A beautiful boy," said Mumfred, wistfully remembering a moment that had become special to him. "The other night when he suddenly hugged me, and said to me, a complete stranger, 'I love you, Mr. Lewis' ... well, a man doesn't have too many moments like that in his life." He shook his head with a smile. "Quite a kid. And he did it out of happiness for you, Sarkis; did you know that? He did it because I hired you and gave you the job you always wanted."

"Here's to Hagop," said Sarkis, raising his jigger. "May he always be who he is." He frowned. "That didn't come out the way I meant it, but I think you know what I mean."

"To Hagop." They clinked glasses, downed their drinks, and

ordered yet another round. The two paused momentarily in thought. "What else can we drink to?"

"Anything we want," said Sarkis.

"We don't want to overlook anything."

"Absolutely."

"Tell you what. Let's drink to everything under the sun. That way we can't leave anything out."

"Good idea."

Mumfred raised his glass, then paused with a melancholy sigh. "I'm feeling a little blue tonight, but I'd still like to drink to everything under the sun."

"A generous gesture, Mumfred. Here's to everything under the sun."

"To life."

"The sacred absurdity."

They drank with brio, and set their glasses down with a sense of accomplishment, not to say triumph.

"I guess that covers everything," said Mumfred.

"I'd say we touched all the bases."

"The only trouble is once you drink to everything under the sun you don't leave much room for anything else, do you?"

Sarkis looked glumly at his glass. "You're right. We just may have drunk ourselves into a corner."

"We were doing so well, too."

"It's a shame. I don't know when I've taken part in a more eloquent display of toast making."

"Neither have I."

"You would think a testimonial of some kind to be in order, wouldn't you?"

"Absolutely," chimed Mumfred, "some modest token of appreciation." An impish gleam twinkled in his eyes. "A little toast, perhaps."

Sarkis twinkled back. "We deserve it."

They ordered another round of drinks and clinked their glasses.

"Mumfred, I would have to say that your idea of having a drink tonight was nothing less than inspired."

"I'm not much in the idea department, but every now and then I'll come up with a zinger."

"Here's to us," said Sarkis.

"Down the hatch," said Mumfred.

* * *

The workmen on the merry-go-round were ready to conduct another test. One of the men stationed himself at the controls while awaiting a go-ahead signal from the crew chief. The third member of the crew, having no part in the test, stood idly by, wearing the vacant, unemployed expression of one whose life somehow was devoid of meaning without an order to obey.

"Okay," said the crew chief. "Let's run 'er one more time and see what happens. Terminal wires grounded?"

"Check," said the workman at the controls.

"Cable ribs attached?"

"Tight as a drum," said the third workman.

The crew chief backed up a few steps to where Hagop was standing. "Step aside, son. We don't know what might happen. This could be dangerous."

"It wouldn't be dangerous if you went away and left it alone," snapped the boy.

"Now don't get your dander up, young fellow. I'm only doing my job."

"That's what everybody says."

The worker at the controls called out, "I'm ready, chief."

"Start 'er up, then. Nice and easy at first. Don't jam the throttle."

The worker at the controls eased the throttle forward. Nothing happened for several seconds. Then the merry-go-round moved and began to edge forward, to the approving nods of the crew chief.

"Looks good," said the crew chief. "Let 'er out some more."

The workman at the controls leaned more heavily on the throttle. The platform rotation began to accelerate. As it did, however, a disturbingly whiny sound began emanating from the merry-go-round. The noise grew more dissonant and louder until it pierced the air like a wail. By the time the animals hit full stride, the sound had reached the level of a cacophonous din.

The crew chief shouted, "What the devil is that?"

"I don't know," replied the confused worker at the controls.

The third worker finger-plugged his ears as the animals sped along.

Hagop was listening hard to the jangled sounds as if trying to decipher a code. Suddenly his eyes lit up. "It's the music!"

"What are you talking about, son?" said the crew chief, giving the boy a dour, quizzical look. "That's not music."

"Is so!" shouted Hagop. "It's playing backward!"

"Whaddya mean 'playing backward'?"

"Backward—upside down."

"There's no such thing."

"You made the merry-go-round go straight, but the music went the other way."

"That's crazy!" said the chief, although he couldn't deny a certain barrel organ timbre to the disturbance. His face contorted in utter bafflement as he barked at his subordinates, "How the devil did the recorded sound unit get hooked up with the rotator controls?"

"Don't ask me," cried the worker at the controls. "Benjy was the one who re-circuited the sound system."

The one called Benjy was still finger-plugging his ears. "I followed the manual step by step."

"Cut it off! Cut it off!" bellowed the crew chief, waving his arms in a plea of surrender. "It's driving me crazy!"

Hagop leaped about in circles as if the strident, discord of sound were sheer music to his ears. The crew chief, meanwhile, seeing the boy in such jubilant spirits, glowered suspiciously.

"All right, son, did you have anything to do with this?"

"You're mad because the merry-go-round won't do what you want it to do. It won't listen to you."

After the worker at the controls brought the animals to a stop, the crew chief scolded his men. "All right, you gerbil heads, get to work and find out what's wrong here!"

* * *

Back at The Wonder Bar, Sarkis and Mumfred had lapsed into the mellowest of moods. They had come to a stage in the evening's libations when both were feeling nostalgia for something lost, something ineffable and just beyond the reach of memory. So finely tuned was their rapport at this time that incomplete and barely intimated thoughts were fully grasped by the listener, and sentiments that normally would be considered confusing or obtuse were viewed as the essences of clarity. It was that stage of a fellowship when a perfectly innocuous remark might be praised for its wisdom, and a blank pause taken for the profoundest of deliberations.

"I used to have a favorite song," Mumfred was saying, "but I can't remember the name."

Sarkis mused, "That was my favorite song, too."

"How can your favorite song be one I can't remember?"

"Because I can't remember it, either."

Mumfred frowned. "I never thought of it that way."

"Strange, isn't it?"

"More than strange," said Mumfred. "Why, the odds against a coincidence like that must be astro ... astro ...Well, you know what I mean." Mumfred succumbed to the thrall of a memory he couldn't quite recapture. "You know, I would always sing that song whenever I felt sad or had a problem, and afterward, I always felt better."

"A lovely tune." Sarkis smiled wistfully.

They drank to their favorite song, after which, both fell silent, each with a comfortable smile on his face. Suddenly Mumfred's eyes widened. He snapped his fingers excitedly. "'You'll Never Walk Alone!'" he piped.

Sarkis nodded gratefully. "That's very kind of you. Thank you, Mumfred."

"No, the song, 'You'll Never Walk Alone.' Was that the song?"

"No, I don't think so."

Mumfred reprised some of the lyrics in a gravelly, baritone voice. 'When you walk through a storm keep your head up high ...'"

"No, I'm sure that wasn't the song."

Mumfred sighed disappointedly. "Too bad."

"Even if it were the song, the advice is patently absurd."

"How's that?"

"Silly thing for anybody to do in a storm."

Mumfred reassessed the lyrics to himself and nodded affirmatively. "You're right," he said.

"I should think a person would want to keep his head *down* in a storm, wouldn't you?"

"Absolutely."

"Can you imagine a crowd of people walking through a hurricane with their heads up high?"

"Sounds a little foolish."

"They have no business even being out in such weather."

"Obviously the song is not the one we can't remember."

The men nodded in agreement and gazed at their empty glasses.

"Mumfred, you know what I think? I think what we need is a breath of fresh air—time to clear our heads. Once we do, I'm sure we'll see this problem more clearly."

"Good idea."

Having imbibed their fill of alcoholic spirits, Sarkis and Mumfred took leave of The Wonder Bar, both a shade unsteady on their feet, but holding due course. They headed back to the pavilion by way of the boardwalk, where balmy, ocean breezes caressed them like an embrace. They let the fresh air be as a tonic to their dulled senses. Sarkis was smiling broadly and taking deep, chest-expanding breaths.

"Mumfred, in case I never get a chance to tell you, let me say here and now, it's been a pleasure and a privilege to know you."

"Likewise, Sarkis. It's been a pleasure and a privilege to know you, too."

The ensuing silence underscored the sincerity with which these compliments were exchanged. Then Mumfred added, "Do you know what's wrong with the world, Sarkis?—people taking too many privileges with each other and not enough pleasures."

"Mumfred, that's exactly what's wrong with the world."

"Take what happened today. Some people thought they had the privilege to change the merry-go-round, but if they knew how much pleasure the merry-go-round gave, they wouldn't worry so much about what their privileges were and they'd start enjoying their pleasures more."

"A perfect statement of the case, Mumfred. May I say it's always a pleasure and a privilege to watch you lock horns with an idea and bring it to its knees."

"Thank you, Sarkis."

They walked on, pleased with themselves as if having unraveled, with little ado, one of life's knottier conundrums.

"Now if we could only remember the name of that song we've forgotten," said Sarkis.

"My memory isn't what it used to be," confessed Mumfred.

"Or mine. You know, years ago, I used to have a favorite dance, too, but I can't remember what that was, either."

"I think I know the one you mean."

"How could you know?"

"It's on the tip of my tongue. I just can't get it out."

"Mumfred, are you saying we're both trying to think of the same dance?"

"I'm pretty sure of it."

"That's amazing."

Humbled into silence by what they considered a happenstance of the most extraordinary order, both men assumed a more introspective manner. They slowed their pace as though weighted down by the gravitas of the moment. Sarkis clasped his hands behind his back in the way philosophers and those with prestigious intellectual credentials are sometimes depicted when taking meditative strolls by the sea.

"Sarkis, I just thought of something. I might be barking up the wrong tree here, but is it possible—I mean is there the slightest chance that the dance we can't remember ..." Mumfred faltered.

"... was the one we did to our favorite song?" proffered Sarkis. Once completing the connection, he fell silent. "Does make you wonder, doesn't it?"

"You'll have to admit the idea has a certain ironclad logic to it."

"Not to mention perfect symmetry."

"Yes, the balance is certainly there."

"To be honest, Mumfred, the more I think about it, the more hard pressed I am to see it any other way."

Mumfred protruded his jaw as if balancing a thought on the tip of his chin. "I'd have to agree," he said. He smacked his lips like someone confirming the validity of a proposition that had withstood the strictest intellectual scrutiny.

"I knew it was only a matter of time before we cracked this mystery," said Sarkis.

With the matter resolved to their satisfaction, the two men experienced that supreme sense of well-being that comes from having fitted together the last elusive pieces of some intricate, cosmic puzzle. For the present, theirs was the consoling belief that behind all the disparate, contradictory, and inexplicable forces of life, a certain purpose and benign order were at work.

"You know what?" mused Sarkis as they approached the amusement park. "Sometimes the truth is so simple, people can't see it when it's right under their noses."

"True, very true," agreed Mumfred. "Just a matter of opening your eyes."

* * *

The merry-go-round house lay in semi-darkness. Only the refracted lights of the amusement park filtered through the windows and created broken shadows across the floor. In this eerie light the animals assumed a ghostly aspect. Their lacquered bodies resembled specters haunting a playroom. Sarkis and Mumfred came to the door and took a minute to accustom their eyes to the gloom.

"Hagop, you there?" called Sarkis squinting around the room. Soon, though, he made out the boy on the far side of the merry-go-round. He was slouched in the saddle of a golden-maned horse, his cheek nuzzled against the back of the head, his hand stroking the side of the horse's face. "Hagop, are you all right?" Receiving no answer, Sarkis and Mumfred hastened to the boy's side. Hagop never looked up or acknowledged the arrival of his friends. He kept stroking the horse as though administering to a wounded animal.

"They almost couldn't do it," said the boy. "They tried everything and once even the music went backward and they all started yelling at each other."

Sarkis and Mumfred did not have to ask about the final outcome of the workmen's efforts. Aside from the boy's despondent appearance, the physical surroundings attested to a thorough overhaul, a mission accomplished. The platform had been reassembled and swept clean, the animals buffed to a glossy finish, and the glass panels of the control booth washed and wiped to a luster. The entire entourage had about it the spanking-new look of a showpiece. If appearances were all, the merry-go-round had never looked better.

"Well, at least they had the decency to clean up after themselves," said Mumfred.

The owner cast a dispirited eye about the premises and stepped onto the platform. He weaved his way among the animals like a mindful caretaker looking after his flock. Occasionally he would brush his hand across their lacquered bodies as if extending condolences for the treatment received. Coming full circle, he rejoined his friends and smiled plaintively to no one in particular.

"Well, that's that," he concluded. "Nothing more to be done here." He turned to the others. "No need for you guys to stay. Go on home and get some rest."

"We'll help you close up," said Sarkis.

"Nothing to help with," said Mumfred, indicating the impeccable condition in which the room had been left. "I'll leave soon. You two go on."

Hagop, still slumped on the horse, looked up to the others. "All the fun is over now, isn't it, Sarkis?

Sarkis hemmed, at a loss for words. "Hagop ..." he started. He stopped and started again. "Things change," he offered feebly. "I mean they're always changing. Isn't that right, Mumfred?" Sarkis eyed Mumfred in hopes the owner could help him over this impasse, but Mumfred looked no less at a loss. "Why, if things always stayed the same," said Sarkis, "the merry-go-round never would have gone backward in the first place now, would it?"

"Is it still a symbol like you said it was?" asked the boy.

"Why, of course it is," said Sarkis. "Do you think Jared's father and a court order can change that?" But Hagop, unswayed by Sarkis's insistence, lowered his gaze despondently.

A silence fell over the three companions as each relived memories of the past three days and of events that had vaulted his life from the commonplace to the rare. For each, the merry-go-round held special meanings that lay beyond the province of words and verbal expression. Perhaps time and reflection would yield more clarity, but for now it was enough to know that something had come into each life and graced it with a touch more wonder than it had before.

"Ready to go, Hagop?"

The boy was slow to respond. At length he eased off his horse with a listless rollover motion and landed on his feet. As he dismounted, a secret part of him seemed to know he would never set eyes on this merry-go-round again. Similarly, Sarkis and Mumfred had like premonitions. Each had a foreboding sense that this leave-taking was not just a casual goodnight but a final farewell, and that whatever reasons fate had decreed their paths to cross were no longer extant. Their parting words were mundane and had a hollow ring, as though spoken by actors lacking conviction in the parts they had been asked to play.

"Tomorrow, then?" said Mumfred.

"Tomorrow, of course," said Sarkis as he and the boy turned to leave.

"Usual time?"

"Usual time."

"We still have the merry-go-round and it's still running. That's the main thing, isn't it?"

"Yes, that's the main thing," said Sarkis, unconvincingly.

Sarkis and Hagop started for the door. Mumfred watched them leave and the door behind them close. Suddenly, he started after them, then hesitated midway across the floor. He wanted to bring back his friends but couldn't give himself a reason for asking them to stay. He stood motionless in the center of the room. He appeared unsure of himself and of his bearings, a solitary figure lost in space. Mumfred looked to his right and then to his left as if uncertain how he had come to be standing here alone in the half light of an empty merry-go-round house.

The owner retreated to the merry-go-round and seated himself on the hem of the platform. He remained there long after the amusement park lights had turned off, long after the lampposts along the boardwalk had ceded their light to the first glimmers of dawn. Occasionally he glanced about the room, his eyes panning the various ornaments on the walls: crinkly clowns and papier-mâché harlequins, jesters in foolscap, a theatrical mask of comedy. He never noticed the passing of night into day. He just sat there on the platform, amid the colorful decorations, like the last guest at a party that ended hours ago.

AND THEY LIVED…EVER AFTER

Sarkis was restless. Already he had awoken several times throughout the night, and now did so again. For a time he paced about the room, then came to the window and gazed outside. The first glimmer of daylight was breaking, but he did not watch the burgeoning day for long. Turning aside, and for want of knowing how to occupy himself, he decided to work on his book. So as not to disturb Hagop, he moved the typewriter into the outer cellar, where he sat himself on a hassock and propped the machine on a spare table. He began typing, but quickly lost his concentration. The book was too removed from his thoughts, or perhaps the opposite—too close to his thoughts—since he now had a strong premonition as to how his story would end. He rose and began pacing to and fro across the length of the cellar. Eventually he returned to the typewriter and tried working again. He had not typed more than three or four sentences when he heard Hagop rustling in the next room. The boy called out:

"Sarkis, is that you?"

"Yes, it's me."

"Are you working?"

Sarkis came to the door of their room. "I couldn't sleep."

"Neither could I."

Sarkis moved to the boy's side, and Hagop made room for him on the bed.

"Then I guess we'll just have to keep each other company for a while," said Sarkis as he propped himself beside the boy. After fidgeting and shifting a bit, they made themselves comfortable.

"What do people do when they can't sleep?" asked the boy.

"Lots of things. They smoke cigarettes, or they see what's to eat in the refrigerator, or if they have someone to talk to, they do what we're doing now."

For a silent minute their eyes wandered about the room and eventually settled upon the crooked limb of driftwood standing in the corner. Their attention lingered on the wood, which was dry and ravaged. In many spots, the bark had peeled, giving the limb a splotchy, mottled texture.

"I like the wood more and more," said Hagop. "Sometimes I think wood knows things and has secrets."

"Sometimes I think people who collect junk know more secrets than anybody else. Junk is very mysterious."

"Like cracked flower pots?"

"And broken picture frames."

"And old, beat-up suitcases?"

"Anything that people throw away and can't use."

Exhausting their list, they fell into another comfortable silence. Suddenly, though, a sharp pounding was heard at the back door. The man and the boy gave a frightened start.

"What's that?" yelped the boy.

"Someone in the yard."

Following a pause, the pounding was heard again, the sound insistent, querulous.

Hagop huddled close to Sarkis. "Sarkis, what's happening?"

"I don't know."

"Somebody's trying to break in."

"I'm not sure."

The man and the boy held on to each other and waited.

Standing in the back yard were two policemen, patrolmen Bottomflat and Rooker. Bottomflat, the taller of the two, had his revolver drawn and aimed at the door as if he might have been placing the doorknob under arrest. He was a gangling, lantern-jawed peace officer whose uniform was at least a full size too short for him. His pinched shoulders were complemented by sleeves that never reached his wrist bones, and pants that barely reached his ankles. By contrast, his partner Rooker was short and stocky with thickset shoulders that obliterated any sign of a neck. Standing at the door, the two officers kept exchanging glances as if looking to each other for a cue to action. Both appeared grimly serious about the business at hand. And yet, notwithstanding the earnestness with which they approached their assignments, or, perhaps, because of it, and because of their striking physical contrast, they emitted the distinct air of two vaudevillians about to perform a skit.

"Open up!" hollered Bottomflat. "We know you're in there. This is the law speaking."

"Maybe they slipped out the back way."

"This is the back way, stupid! They were trailed to this address, and no one has left the house." Bottomflat rapped on the door again. "The jig's up, Lavoonian, or whatever your name is. Come out peacefully or we'll smoke you out."

"We don't have any smoke bombs."

Bottomflat winced in dismay. "What do you mean we don't have any smoke bombs? This guy could be armed and dangerous."

"Try the door. Maybe it's open."

"Use your head," said Bottomflat. "A kidnapper fleeing from justice is not about to leave the door of his hideaway open." He tried the doorknob and it turned. "Hmm," he muttered. "This guy may not be as smart as we thought." He edged the door open an inch or two and called into the cellar. "All right, Lavoonian. Surrender the boy and no harm will come to you."

"Maybe we should bust in."

"Guess we have no choice. All right then, when I kick open the door, we make our move and take cover right away. Ready?"

"Ready."

Bottomflat cocked his revolver and began counting, "1 ... 2 ... 3 ..." And with a sidelong nod to his partner, gave the word, "Okay, let's go!"

He banged open the door with his foot. Both men charged into the house, but in their eagerness to stake out the premises collided in the doorway. Rooker cried, "Dammit!" and lunged for cover in the laundry room. Meanwhile, Bottomflat dashed toward the sitting room, but unable to see in the dark, tripped over a gasoline can and sprawled on his belly. His gun slammed to the floor and went off. "Keep your cover," yelled Bottomflat. "Looks like we're in for a shootout."

"That was your gun, blubber head!" shouted Rooker from the

laundry room.

"No matter. They still could be armed."

Bottomflat came to his feet and raced the length of the basement to the closed bedroom door, under which shone a light from inside. No sound emanated from within. The officer stood to the side and mustered his courage. Then he pushed open the door and leaped into the room. Dropping to a crouch and steadying his gun hand in training manual style, he aimed the revolver at the two occupants who, startled out of their wits, were clutching to each other in desperation. Sarkis was shielding the boy with his arm.

"All right, Lavoonian, on your feet, hands up, belly to the wall. Let's move it." Sarkis complied without a word. "It is my duty to warn you that anything you say ..." And with these words Bottomflat initiated a reading of Sarkis's rights. Upon completion, he nodded toward Rooker, who had arrived behind him. "Rooker, search the room."

"Right."

"What's this all about?" said Sarkis, while standing at the wall and feeling his pockets being searched.

"No more out of you, Lavoonian," said Bottomflat. "You'll have your day in court to make whatever defense you think you can make."

Hagop protested. "We didn't do anything wrong!" Saying as much, the boy began to quiver as if chilled with fever.

"Easy there, son. It's obvious you've been through hell. You're trembling like a leaf."

Into the room rushed Mrs. Lilly, who had been shocked out of her sleep by the gun going off in the basement. She was even more shocked now by the presence of two police officers and the sight of Sarkis standing with outstretched arms against the wall like a prisoner.

"Sarkis, what's the matter? What's going on here?"

"Do you know these two?" Bottomflat asked as he held the gun to Sarkis's back.

"Of course I know them. That's Sarkis and Hagop. They rent this room."

"Correction," said Bottomflat, tipping the barrel of his revolver toward the boy. "That's Jack Silveri, son of Mr. and Mrs. Anthony Silveri of Washington Heights, New York. He's been missing for three days. He was apparently kidnapped by this man."

"Kidnapped?" Mrs. Lilly grew faint and leaned against the wardrobe locker to keep her balance. "I don't understand."

Bottomflat turned Sarkis around and pushed him back toward the bed beside Hagop.

"A very nifty caper, Lavoonian. Organized right down to the last detail, I'm sure. But you made one mistake when you gave that newspaper man your real name yesterday afternoon. We've had a missing person's tracer on you and the boy for two days now."

Hagop said, "Why don't you go away and leave us alone?"

Bottomflat came to the boy's side. "Did this man harm you in any way, son? You don't have to be afraid to tell us now. He can't hurt you anymore."

"Sarkis, what's he talking about?"

"He's only doing his job," said Sarkis.

Hagop blurted out a complaint directed to the world at large: "I'm sick of people who are only doing their job!"

"Easy, son," said Bottomflat.

"Go do your job someplace else!" cried the boy.

Bottomflat grimaced at Sarkis. "You've really twisted this boy's mind, haven't you? You're not only a kidnapper; you're probably a pervert to boot."

Meanwhile, Patrolman Rooker, who had been searching the room, came forward holding the warped limb of driftwood in his hand.

"I'm not sure what to make of this," he said to Bottomflat. "It was standing there in the corner."

Bottomflat took the wood, examined it and smacked his lips conclusively. He held it before Hagop like an attorney offering a prime exhibit to his star witness. "Did he ever hit you with this, son? You can tell us the truth. If you stepped out of line or maybe tried to run away, he'd give you a few whacks with this peacemaker, wouldn't he?"

Hagop stared down the officer. "Somebody ought to give you a few whacks over the head with it."

Bottomflat handed the wood back to Rooker. "Keep it for evidence. It might be important, especially if they uncover any bruises on the boy."

Sarkis explained, "We kept the wood as a souvenir, a

memento."

Bottomflat snickered. "Come, come, Lavoonian. An old pro like you can come up with a better story than that. People don't keep a dirty, rotting piece of wood around the house for a memento."

Mrs. Lilly irately stepped between the two officers. "Now that's quite enough! I don't know what you two men are trying to do, but this much I can tell you. No one has been beating up anyone in this house or perverting anyone's mind."

Rooker took Bottomflat aside and whispered in his ear. "The old lady may be in cahoots with the guy."

"Could be," murmured Bottomflat. "Keep an eye on her. We may have stumbled into an underworld ring here."

At that moment sounds were heard in the basement, the rush of footsteps accompanied by muted voices. At the door appeared Ron Fritzo, the newspaperman, and with him a photographer weighted down with camera attachments and assorted paraphernalia hanging from his shoulders. Fritzo's eyes beamed with excitement upon discovering everyone in the room.

"I see you've found them," said Fritzo, making his way center stage. "I was afraid they may have left town."

"How did you know where we were?" asked Bottomflat, somewhat put off by the intrusion.

"I'm a newspaperman. It's my business to know what's going on and where."

The photographer sidestepped his way into the now crowded room. He immediately sized up who was who, and prepared to start snapping pictures.

"Hold off," ordered Bottomflat. "No pictures while an official investigation is in process."

"What do you mean no pictures?" objected Fritzo. "This is the biggest story to hit Asbury Park since the boardwalk burned down."

Bottomflat relented. "Well, make it quick, then. But don't forget to mention the arresting officers. I'm Waldo Bottomflat, and this is my assistant Horace Rooker."

"What do you mean assistant?" said Rooker. "We're partners, remember?"

"Oh, don't start quibbling," said Bottomflat. "Partner,

assistant. It's only a technicality, for God's sake."

The photographer dropped to one knee and snapped a picture of Sarkis and Hagop. The explosive flash from the camera blinded the man and the boy, who shielded their eyes from the light.

Fritzo smirked toward Sarkis. "I'm a hunch player, Mr. Levonian, and yesterday you just had the look of a man who had something to hide. Damned if you didn't." Sarkis was still wincing from the after effects of the flash. Fritzo went on to instruct the photographer, "Get a shot of the room, too. We'll run a full-page spread tomorrow." The reporter visualized the headline by spreading his hands at eye level. "'Kidnapper's Underground Lair Raided by Police.'"

After the photographer's second flash, Patrolman Bottomflat took the limb of driftwood from Rooker and sidled up to the cameraman. "Listen," said the officer confidentially, "I have a great idea. How about a picture of Lavoonian here about to pelt the boy with this hunk of wood, and me stepping between them and grabbing his wrist just before I backflip him? Your readers will love it."

"I don't think that'll work," demurred the photographer.

With the snapping of more pictures around the room, Hagop, besieged by the blinding flashes, cowered in the bed and tried to keep from shaking again.

"Sarkis, I'm scared."

Rooker, seeing the boy huddled in fear, drew Bottomflat aside for a conference. "Listen, don't you think it's time we got the kid away from that guy? He's done enough harm to the boy already."

"You're right, but it won't be easy. The kid's confused right now."

"Maybe I can coax him away."

"I'll take care of it," said Bottomflat, as if the task required skills for which only he was qualified. "I've worked with kids before in the Catholic Junior League."

Keeping a respectful distance from the bed, Bottomflat took a step toward Hagop. Clearly, the officer was approaching this matter with utmost tact.

Having elicited no disruptive reaction with his first move, Bottomflat took another step and stopped. Without a word, he beckoned to the boy with open arms as one might to a frightened puppy cornered in a room.

"Son? Why don't you come with me now and stand on the other side of the room? You'll be safe there, and with friends."

Hagop glowered at Bottomflat. The policeman took another step toward the bed. The boy braced his back against the headboard as a way of girding himself for the approaching officer. Hagop maintained a steely-eyed demeanor. Bottomflat paused as though to reconsider his strategy, but then took yet another step. The boy drew up his knees to his chest. He was ready to kick up a furor should the officer make any attempt to displace him.

"If you touch me," warned the boy, "I'll tell everybody you beat me up, and that you wanted money to let us go, and that you fired your gun when you didn't have to … and also what a lousy policeman you really are. So you'd better just get away from me."

Bottomflat toed the line. He eyed the boy with a kind of perplexed wonderment. Meanwhile Hagop kept his legs drawn and ready for action should the need arise. Bottomflat backed off and turned to the others. He threw up his hands in exasperation. "Geezuz, I'm beginning to wonder if this kid is worth saving!"

From outside the house came the sound of more voices. Someone began knocking at the back door.

"I'd better answer that," said Mrs. Lilly.

Bottomflat looked harried. "This place is turning into a circus."

Presently, three new faces appeared at the door, that is, new to everyone but Sarkis and Hagop. The faces belonged to Hagop's mother, Sandra; his father, Anthony; and Sarkis's wife, Annahid.

Hagop's mother was first to break through the logjam of people in the room. Quickly spotting her son, she rushed to him and hugged the boy tightly. She was sobbing with relief and rocking Hagop in the fold of her arms as if to keep telling herself he was alive and safe.

"Thank heavens! Thank heavens!" was all she could say.

"I'm all right, Mom. I'm all right." Hagop was uncomfortable being the focus of such excessive attention.

Mrs. Silveri did not release her son until her excitement abated, and she was able to exercise a measure of self-control. Wiping her eyes dry, she turned toward Sarkis. If her eyes had not the look of daggers, the gaze still had an almost palpable cutting edge to it.

"Sarkis Levonian, you're a fool, and that's only the kindest word I can think to call you right now. If I really told you what I felt ..." But she restrained herself and said no more for the time being.

Sarkis respectfully acknowledged Mrs. Silveri with a muted, barely audible hello.

Officer Bottomflat, backed to the wall by the influx of people, erupted in frustration, "Everybody out! We can't even breathe in here."

Into the room now pressed Mr. Silveri. He was a man of about Sarkis's age, though shorter and considerably trimmer. He appeared haggard, although his movements were quick and decisive as he shouldered and sidestepped his way into view. His black hair was rumpled, and his eyes drawn and baggy from an obvious lack of sleep. His unbuttoned topcoat sagged upon his frame as if he might have slept in the garment. To top off his disheveled appearance, he was wearing neither a belt nor socks, a result of having dressed in a mindless haste earlier that morning after receiving word of his son's whereabouts.

"I'm Anthony Silveri," he said to Patrolman Bottomflat. "That's my son over there. Mrs. Levonian is here, too."

"Feels like the whole neighborhood's in here," complained Bottomflat. "Rooker, clear these newspaper people out of here— and take the landlady, too. But don't let her go too far. We're still not sure where she fits into all this."

The room partially cleared, allowing for the last of the new arrivals to step inside. Without a glance toward Sarkis, Annahid Levonian crossed the room and took a seat on the cot opposite the bed. She was a woman of distinctive Middle Eastern features—an olive complexion and shoulder-length black hair that tonight had a careless, untended look to it. Her most compelling features were her eyes—large, melancholy eyes that seemed in their depths to house secrets of which she, herself, was unaware. Her face possessed that arresting quality of being revealing and mysterious at the same time.

As Annahid Levonian took a seat opposite Sarkis, her eyes still had not engaged his, while his seemed to have followed her every move from the time she arrived. She sat with her hands folded upon her lap as one who had perfected the art of forbearance. She appeared neither angry nor hurt, only drained from the ordeal of recent events. When she spoke, her voice was dry and lacking emotion.

"Were you coming back?" she asked, her eyes still avoiding his. Sarkis said he was. Her expression remained stoic, unmoved. "Today? Tomorrow? Next year?"

"I don't know."

Annahid Levonian finally looked up at her husband. She searched his face for a clue to what he was thinking or feeling.

"And you weren't going to tell us where you were? No message? No letter? No phone call?" Sarkis said nothing, not because he wished to skirt an answer but because he had none.

In the outer room, a heated discussion was taking place among Mr. Silveri and officers Bottomflat and Rooker. The policemen were upset by an unexpected turn of events.

"What do you mean you're not pressing charges?" said Bottomflat. "This man's a kidnapper, a felon."

"He may be soft in the head," said Mr. Silveri, "but he's no felon."

"I risked my life saving that boy!" said Bottomflat indignantly.

"Listen," said Mr. Silveri. "I've already discussed this matter with your captain at the precinct. If you have any questions, you can call him now, and he'll explain everything to you himself."

Rooker looked dismayingly at his notepad in which he had been writing almost from the time he had entered the house. "You mean I took all these notes for nothing?"

"I really appreciate all you've done, but the truth is we have no further need of you."

"You may be letting a very dangerous man off the hook here."

"I'll take that chance."

A disappointed Bottomflat directed his partner, "Rooker, call the precinct and have the captain verify this man's story."

Meanwhile, back in the room, Hagop's mother anxiously paced the floor while awaiting her husband's return. Between puffs on a cigarette, she darted looks out the door to see what could be taking him and the officers so long. At other times, she cast sidelong glances at Sarkis as if resisting the urge to give him a stinging piece of her mind. With each glance, though, she seemed to be losing the struggle. Upon finishing her cigarette, she squashed it underfoot on the bare, cinder block floor. Seeing her husband was still in conference, she took aim on Sarkis, her prosecutorial urge finally getting the best of her.

"Sarkis Levonian, I'm at a loss." She took a deep, anxious breath. "What is wrong with you? Could you please tell me that?" Neither expecting nor receiving an answer, she resumed her pacing. She stopped and renewed the interrogation. "Could you please tell me what on earth possessed you to do what you did? Running away on a lark is your own business, but why in God's name with my son?"

Sarkis's eyes were downcast. "I have no explanation."

"You have no explanation?" said Hagop's mother in amazement. What scant patience she had for this confrontation was quickly dissipating. "After disappearing with my son for three days, you mean to sit there and tell me you don't know why you did it? You damned well better have an explanation. Did it ever occur to you, in that dimwitted head of yours, what you were doing to us, the boy's parents, not to mention your own wife and children?"

"No, not really."

Hagop's mother was agape. "I don't believe what I'm hearing." She stared at Sarkis as she might at an unidentified alien species. "You walked off with my son, deserted your wife and family, and never once felt any concern or remorse for the pain and suffering you were causing everyone involved? Are you a freak of some kind? Do you have any feelings at all?" Sarkis said nothing and did not look up to engage his questioner. "Sarkis Levonian, I'm talking to you," she persisted. "I asked if you had any feelings. Do you care about anybody in this world except yourself?"

Sarkis glanced toward his wife who, if listening, gave no sign of it.

"I love my wife and children very much," he said.

"Love?" blurted Hagop's mother, and she threw back her head with a kind of disparaging grunt. "You can't possibly know the meaning of the word. You don't inflict this kind of emotional pain on people and talk about love!"

"If I could have gone away without hurting anyone, I would

have."

"You could have gone away without taking my son. Did you ever think of that?"

Sarkis hemmed. "If I had thought about what I should or shouldn't have done, I never would have done anything."

Hagop's mother turned away in a fit of annoyance. "I won't even pretend to understand what that gibberish is supposed to mean." She pulled out another cigarette from the pack in her snatch purse and lit it. At first she seemed done with this discussion, but after several anxious puffs, she again turned her attention to Sarkis. "And what, may I ask, did you do for three days? Can you at least tell me that?"

"We didn't do much of anything," said Sarkis with the barest hint of a shrug. "You didn't do much of anything? And my son? He spent three days not doing much of anything with you?"

"We were almost always together."

Hagop's mother could feel her anger surfacing. "Then just for the sake of argument, what in God's name was the point of running away? To do nothing?" She took a few moments to bring herself under control. "Sarkis Levonian, people do not disappear for days at a time to do nothing. If they did, they'd be put away in little padded cells somewhere—which on second thought may be just the place for you."

Sarkis formulated his next words carefully, as much for his own benefit as his interrogator's. "Good things always seemed to happen to us. I don't think good things could have happened unless we were prepared to do nothing."

Mrs. Silveri squinted with puzzlement. "That's double-talk," she decided. "That's pure, unadulterated double-talk!" And with that she gave up any further attempt to communicate with her son's abductor.

Anthony Silveri entered the room alone, the policemen having departed and Mrs. Lilly given leave to calm her nerves with a cup of tea. Hagop's father looked physically and emotionally drained.

"The charges have been dropped. We're all free to go." And then with an exhausted sigh he turned to Sarkis. "But I'll be damned if I can make heads or tails out of this stunt of yours, Sarkis. If it weren't for Annahid and your kids, I'd let them drag you off to jail. Maybe a little time in the slammer would knock some sense into you."

"If Sarkis goes to jail I'm going with him!" piped Hagop.

"That's enough out of you!" snapped Anthony Silveri. "If this moron doesn't have a lick of sense in his head, I expect you to have some. Is this what we brought you up to do? To leave your mother and me going crazy with fear and worry while you run off with the neighborhood tailor?"

"Tony," said Sarkis, "don't blame the boy. I'm the one responsible for everything that's happened."

"I'm blaming him because I happen to think he has more sense than you. I'm convinced you'll never grow up, but I still have good reason to think my son will." Anthony Silveri glared at Sarkis. "What in the world did you think you were doing? What is this all this about, Sarkis? Is this some mid-life crisis? Are you going through the change or something? Is that what we have here— some need to turn back the clock and be a kid again? I mean, tell me, is that it?"

"I don't know. Maybe it is. I don't know."

"Sarkis, wake up." Anthony Silveri stepped back as a means to restrain himself and, perhaps, clarify his own thoughts. "Sarkis, there's a world out there. It's a real world, and it makes demands and creates obligations. We can't walk away from it whenever we feel like it."

"Tony, I'm sorry I put you through all this, I really am. I won't try to justify what I've done, but I can't apologize for it, either."

"I'm not looking for your damn apology! I'm trying to knock some sense into that thick skull of yours. What did you think you were doing by acting like an overgrown juvenile?" Mr. Silveri stopped to collect himself, lest he explode in a rage. "Sarkis, listen to me, will you?" he said, keeping his emotions under control. "I'd like to be a kid all my life, too. Who wouldn't? Those years were some of the best of my life. I wouldn't trade them for anything. But there's a time to be a kid, and there's a time to stop being a kid. In case you haven't been keeping track, you're way past that time. Grow up, for chrissakes."

Sarkis looked up with earnest, inquiring eyes. "Grow up to what, Tony?"

"Grow up to what?" Anthony Silveri grimaced. "Don't play

games with me, Sarkis. I don't have the patience right now. Grow up to at least know that you don't disappear and leave your family going crazy trying to figure out where you've gone."

"I wasn't playing games with you. I'm serious. Grow up to what?" Sarkis kept searching his friend's eyes as if an answer might be forthcoming. "You know, Tony, all our lives we've either been told to act like grown-ups, or we've been telling our kids to act like grown-ups. But I'm not sure I've ever met a grown-up. I mean I look around and see us all getting older, grayer, and balder, but that's all I see, and to be honest, not many of us handle that in a grown-up way. So tell me, where are these grown-ups we're all supposed to be like? Are they in politics? Are they the ones making speeches that even my 12-year-old son can see through as a lot of double-talk and hogwash? Are they in the world of sports and entertainment—celebrities who live each day as an exercise in self-glorification? Are they in science, Tony? Are those the grown-ups who keep finding new toys and gadgets for us to play with when they're not drumming up more ingenious ways for people to annihilate each other? So I am being serious. Grow up to what?" Sarkis smiled sardonically. "You know, Tony, as a kid, I used to believe that no matter what went wrong in the world there were grown-ups around who would meet in this secret room somewhere and put everything right again. You know what? A part of me still believes that, or wants to believe it so badly it amounts to the same thing. But lo and behold, I came to discover there was no secret room, and nobody was making these grown-up decisions. Everybody was just a kid playing at grown-up games, and this world, which we want so much to believe has some order and design to it, just stumbles along from day to day like someone who can't help tripping over his own feet in the dark. We survive, not because we know any better, but in spite of the fact that we don't. So I'm all for growing up, Tony, if you can tell me where the grown-ups are and what I'm supposed to grow up to."

"You're talking a lot of high-sounding foolishness, Sarkis. There's such a thing as responsibility, and that's where growing up starts. No one said the world was perfect, buddy, and maybe a lot of fools out there keep messing up the works, but you acting like one more fool isn't making the world any better."

"You know what I think? I think maybe we're all growing up

backward. Tell me something, Tony. Why is it that people as they grow older become less tolerant, less kind, less understanding? Why do their lives become more selfish and petty when the very opposite should be happening? I mean if people were really growing up, they should be growing, more expansive, more loving in nature. Life is supposed to get better the longer we live because we've had more time to learn how to live it. But you don't see that happening very much. So maybe we're doing something wrong. Maybe we've got the process turned around somehow. And as for this responsibility you talk about, what is it that people are being so responsible to? Certainly not each other. Why there's never been more distrust, dishonesty, and outright cruelty in the world than there is among so called grown-ups. So where's this responsibility people of a certain age are supposed to be attaining? Most people would say they're responsible to their jobs, which is to say, to show up for work every morning and earn a living. But the people I know go to work because they have to go to work. So how responsible is that? If someone has no choice, what does the word responsibility even mean? It's a fairy tale, a word we've made up to take credit for something we never did. I've seen more responsibility in your son these last three days than I have in a lifetime of so-called grown-ups."

"If you can't see the stupidity of your own actions," said Anthony Silveri, "then I feel sorry for you, Sarkis. But I didn't come here to argue. I came to take my son home. If you and Annahid want to drive back with us, you're welcome. Otherwise you can do what you want."

Sarkis looked to his wife for an indication of her wishes, but she remained silent, implacable.

"If my wife will stay," said Sarkis, "I thought we might take a bus back in the morning. We may want to talk."

Annahid Levonian rose and crossed over to the head of the bed. Her eyes turned to Sarkis. "Talk about what?" she said. "Sarkis, what is there to talk about? You're fifty years old. You have a wife and family. Your children need you and depend on you. What is there to talk about?"

Anthony Silveri hurried his son. "Get dressed, Jack. Let's get started."

"I don't want to go without Sarkis!" Hagop did not move from the bed.

Anthony Silveri reacted sharply. "Don't give me any of your lip!" He shook an intimidating finger at the boy. "Listen, buster, and listen good. I do a million things every day that I don't want to do, but I do them. And do you know why I do them? To keep my family together the only way I know how. If I didn't do them, you wouldn't have the damned luxury of sitting there and telling me you don't want to go without Sarkis. You'd be worrying about where your next meal is coming from, or whether you'll have a bed to sleep in at night. So don't tell me what you want or don't want to do. I'm not interested. Get dressed and hurry up about it."

Hagop felt confused and frightened as he drew closer to Sarkis on the bed.

"Sarkis, you said we could stay as long as we wanted. So why do we have to go?"

Sarkis cradled the boy in one arm and rocked him gently as if they were keeping time to a lullaby that no one else could hear. As they did, Sarkis looked to the boy's parents by way of asking permission to have a private moment with Hagop. The Silveris reluctantly consented by standing off to one side. In the interlude that followed, Sarkis and Hagop were alone again. The world belonged to them as it had from that moment three days ago when they met at the newsstand and headed up St. Nicholas Avenue—a childish man and a not-so-childish boy.

"Remember what I told you when we started?" said Sarkis. "I said we'd know when to come home when the time came, and not a moment before. Well, this is the time, Hagop. Even if we could stay, we wouldn't feel the same. We'd feel sadder about leaving everybody."

Across the room, Anthony Silveri puzzled aloud, "What's this 'Hagop' business?"

Annahid Levonian smiled wryly. "Sarkis has a habit of christening his friends with their Armenian names."

"Do you want to go home?" asked Hagop.

"I think so," said Sarkis.

"Why?"

"Because a part of my happiness is at home, just as a part of my happiness has been here in Asbury Park."

"I don't want to go home because nothing ever happens at

home. It's boring."

"It won't be boring now. You'll have wonderful stories to tell your friends."

"I don't have any friends, I told you already. Except Georgie and my cousin Dewey and you."

"You'll make other friends now. Everybody will want to know about the adventures you had on the merry-go-round and on the Ferris wheel, and how you met Ellie, and the fun you had together."

"Nobody will believe those stories."

"If people don't believe you, Hagop, send them to me, and I'll make sure they believe everything that happened."

"I had more fun than I ever had in my life."

"So did I. But listen—this is the important part. I'm not going to leave any of my happiness behind me. Do you know what I'm going to do with it?"

"What?"

"I'm going to take it with me and give it all away."

"You're going to give it away?"

"That's right."

"What'll you do when you don't have any left?"

"Impossible," said Sarkis. He took the boy's hand and held it in the palm of his own. "Happiness is a crazy thing, Hagop. It works backward like the merry-go-round. The more you give away, the more you have."

"Suppose you're not happy when you go home?"

"Then I have no one to blame but myself."

Hagop's mother came forward with the boy's clothes. "You have to get dressed, Jack. Your father is waiting for us."

Hagop rose from the bed and began dressing. He did so in a slow, lethargic manner as he did most days when getting dressed was prefatory to doing things he never cared much about doing, such as going to school or to church or to the homes of relatives. Sometimes, it seemed, that's all there was to life—going places he didn't want to go.

"Hagop!"

At the sound of Sarkis's voice, the boy looked up from dressing to see that his friend had strayed to the window and with a wag of his head was beckoning the boy to come there. "Come see," said Sarkis,

Hagop finished belting his pants and came to the window. One look outside and his eyes began filling with wonder and excitement. There, beyond the poplar trees in Mrs. Lilly's back yard, he could see the great, fireball sun edging above the horizon. The sun was a radiant burst set against a sky of pastel yellows and reds. Hagop was mesmerized by the spectacle. Never in his life had he seen anything so beautiful, so majestic, and so full of being born.

"The colors are like magic," he sighed.

Sarkis stood behind the boy, and they watched the luminous globe of light gradually emerge into full view.

"A sunrise is magic," said Sarkis.

Anthony Silveri called from the door, "Come on, Jack. We have a long drive ahead of us."

Hagop reluctantly backed away while keeping his eye on the sun as long as possible. He turned to leave but then a thought came to him. He stopped. The thought was important to Hagop because it had come to him without anyone's help. No one had prompted it. No one had spoken of it elsewhere, or, like his schoolteachers, written it on a blackboard to be copied down and memorized. This thought was his and his alone.

"Sarkis, the sunrise loves to happen, doesn't it?"

Sarkis turned from the window and looked to the boy one last time. "Oh, it does," he said in a soft, exultant voice. "It certainly does."

"I thought so," said the boy, nodding as though to acknowledge a truth that had evaded him until now. Turning away, he followed his parents out the door.

At the window Sarkis viewed the awakening dawn with his elbow propped on the sill and chin resting in the palm of his hand. Presently his wife, Annahid, came to his side. Sensing her presence, Sarkis pressed her hand into his own, then gently let go. They did not speak. They were together but they were not together.

Sarkis gazed out the window dreaming daybreak dreams.

ABOUT THE AUTHOR

Born and bred in New York City, Mr. Vartoukian has spent the greater part of his working life as a writing educator at the Howard University School of Law. His work has appeared in various literary reviews such as The Ararat and The Armenian Review. "The Adventures of Sarkis and Hagop" is his first novel. Mr. Vartoukian currently resides in Maryland with his wife and daughter.

www.ingramcontent.com/pod-product-compliance
Lightning Source LLC
Chambersburg PA
CBHW070302120726
47910CB00007B/2346